Final Moments

Emma Page first began writing as a hobby, and after a number of her poems had been accepted by the BBC and her short stories began appearing in weekly magazines, she took to writing radio plays and crime novels. She was first published in the Crime Club, which later became Collins Crime.

An English graduate from Oxford, Emma Page taught in every kind of educational establishment both in the UK and abroad before she started writing full-time.

By Emma Page

Kelsey and Lambert series

Say it with Murder
Intent to Kill
Hard Evidence
Murder Comes Calling
In the Event of My Death
Mortal Remains
Deadlock
A Violent End
Final Moments
Scent of Death
Cold Light of Day
Last Walk Home
Every Second Thursday
Missing Woman

Standalone novels

A Fortnight by the Sea (also known as
Add a Pinch of Cyanide)
Element of Chance
In Loving Memory
Family and Friends

Final Moments

Emma Page

HARPER

Harper
An imprint of HarperCollins*Publishers*
1 London Bridge Street
London SE1 9GF

www.harpercollins.co.uk

This paperback edition 2016
1

First published in Great Britain in 1987 by Collins Crime

A catalogue record for this book is
available from the British Library

ISBN: 978-0-00-817582-5

For the homesteaders
(and the tramps' kitchen)
Long may they flourish

CHAPTER 1

In Northwick Road, a humdrum shopping area in a workaday suburb of Cannonbridge, the shopkeepers were closing the tills and putting up the shutters. An overcast evening, unseasonably cool for the second week in May, the last stages of a wet, blustery spell that had interrupted a fine, early spring.

No. 47, Franklin's, occupied premises somewhat larger than the chemist and draper on either side; it was housed in what had originally been two small shops, now knocked into one. Franklin's dealt in the sale and rental, service and repair of television sets, radios, washing-machines, fridges and other items of domestic electrical machinery.

One of the service engineers drew up in his van and went briefly inside to cash up, hand over his lists and jobsheets, check if there were any evening calls for him. There were four repairmen, as well as a young male assistant in the shop. Roy Franklin, the owner, worked harder than any of his employees, putting in long hours behind the counter as well as going out on emergency calls in the evenings and at weekends.

'You can get off now for your bus,' he told the young assistant when the last of the repairmen had made his call and left. Franklin went upstairs to the living quarters, and into the kitchen. The flat was scrupulously clean, very plainly and economically furnished. Everything severely practical, involving no unnecessary work.

He didn't switch on the radio but stood for a moment in the middle of the room with his eyes closed and his head thrown back. The place was silent; only the muted sound of traffic and the shift and stir of the fridge. He opened his eyes and blew out a long, noisy breath. 'Tea,' he said aloud. He crossed to the sink and filled the kettle. He was a lean, sinewy man of medium height, in his middle thirties. Dark hair and dark blue eyes. A bony face, good-looking enough ten or fifteen years ago, but the skin stretched tight now over the cheekbones, his hairline already beginning to recede, the lines scoring his forehead deepening day by day. He had a quick, intent gaze, the look of a man who saw life as an arduous battle he was determined to win.

He made himself a sandwich while he waited for the kettle to boil; he began to eat the sandwich with an abstracted air. Every couple of minutes as he drank his tea he glanced up at the clock, crossed to the window and stooped to look up the road. The third time he did this he was rewarded by the sight of his wife Jane—his second wife, married to him for more than two years now—turning into the road on her scooter.

His air of abstraction vanished. He left the window and switched on the radio. He finished his sandwich and poured himself another mug of tea. He was listening to a current affairs programme when his wife entered the flat.

Jane didn't speak when she came into the kitchen. She flashed him an assessing look as she put down her things and poured herself some tea. Her face was set and unsmiling, her posture rigid and controlled. Her coming filled the kitchen with a sense of tension and conflict; the silence between them seemed like the stubborn silence in the middle of some fierce disagreement rather than the expression of chronic hostility.

She was a year or so younger than her husband, a well-built, athletic-looking woman with strong, rounded arms; she was dressed in neat, inexpensive, no-nonsense clothes. Her gleaming chestnut hair, thick and straight, was cut in a trim helmet shape. She wore no make-up; she had an aseptic, scrubbed look.

She went over to the kitchen cabinet and selected a small glass bottle from among several standing on a shelf. She tipped a couple of tablets out on to her palm and swallowed them with her tea. Roy stood watching her without comment.

'I had a sandwich,' he said at last. 'I've got to go out on a call. I shouldn't be long, about half an hour, I should think.'

She moved her shoulders. 'I'll have supper ready when you get back.' Her manner was tired and irritable. She took a pan from a cupboard and made a start on preparations for a simple meal. 'I won't be able to do the books this evening,' she told him over her shoulder. 'I'm doing the night shift at the nursing-home. One of the staff is away ill.' She was an assistant nurse, working full-time for a local agency. In what little spare time she had she helped her husband in his business; they usually worked on the books on Tuesday evenings.

'We'll do the books tomorrow instead,' Roy said easily. He had inherited the business from his father. It had originally been a small family grocery store but his father had always had an interest in radio and television and had begun to carry out small repairs for his customers on an amateur basis. Later he had branched out into selling sets and later still into renting them out. When Roy left school he went into the business and soon took charge of the electrical side. He spent a good deal of time trying to persuade his father to expand that part of the business and forget the groceries, but his father had continued cautiously and stubbornly to cling to what he saw as the enduring, reliable, bread-and-butter trade. On his father's death Roy had lost no time in closing down the grocery side. As soon as the opportunity arose he bought the shop next door in order to enlarge the service and repair side of his trade. He was anxious now to expand yet again, into stereos and videos, home computers.

Jane crossed to the sink and pulled on a pair of rubber gloves. She began scrubbing vegetables. Roy stood in silence, looking at the back of her head, then he said in an expressionless tone, 'Venetia phoned this afternoon.' Jane stiffened at his words, her hands fell idle in the water. 'To arrange about the weekend,' Roy added. 'What time I'm to pick up the children.' Venetia was his first wife. There were two children of their marriage: Simon, aged eight, and Katie, six, both living with their mother. The children often stayed with Roy for a weekend. He was very fond of his children, and Jane, busy as she was, was always happy to see them.

She stood waiting for him to continue but he said nothing more. She turned abruptly from the sink and burst out at him with vehemence, 'Didn't she say anything about the money? Isn't she going to answer your letter?'

He gave a long, weary sigh. 'I've already had a reply to my letter.' He raised a hand to silence her. 'It came on Saturday morning. I didn't tell you about it, I didn't want to upset you.'

She tore off her rubber gloves and thrust out a hand. He took a letter from his pocket and handed it to her. 'It's from her solicitor,' he said.

She ran her eye over the brief, formal communication: Far from wishing to consider any reduction in the amounts regularly paid over to her, Mrs Franklin was currently contemplating an application to the court to increase the maintenance award for the two children; there were additional expenses as they got older and inflation continued to present a problem.

Jane uttered an angry sound and flung the letter down on the table. She burst into tears and then, even angrier because of this show of weakness, uttered another sound, of intense irritation, and dashed the tears from her cheek.

Roy went over and put an arm round her shoulders. 'Don't get so upset about it,' he urged. 'It'll sort itself out one day.'

She pulled away from him. 'I'll be thirty-five next month. It'll soon be too late to start a family of our own.' She flung round to face him. 'You must go and see her. Writing letters is no good. You've got to talk to her, make her see reason.'

He shook his head with finality. 'She wouldn't listen. She'd simply tell me to talk to her solicitor. I knew it was a waste of time writing to her but you would have me do it.'

She went back to her vegetables and resumed her task with unnecessary force. 'Then if you won't go, I will,' she threw at him, defiantly resolute. 'I'll make very sure she listens to me. She won't push me off to her solicitor.'

He seized her shoulders and swung her round. 'Oh no you won't!' His tone was sharp and imperious. 'You'll do nothing of the sort.'

She tried to jerk herself free but his grip was too fierce. 'You can't stop me,' she told him.

'I want your solemn word that you won't go.' He gave her shoulders a brisk shake. 'Promise me.'

She glared back at him for several seconds, then all at once she abandoned the struggle. 'Oh, very well,' she said, suddenly deflated. 'I promise.'

He let her go. He drew a deep breath, then put an arm round her in a gentle embrace. 'It'll be all right one of these days,' he assured her. 'You mustn't get so worked up about it.' He drew her to him and they exchanged a long, lingering kiss.

Thursday dawned brilliantly clear. At midday the sun rode high in a cloudless sky, by late afternoon the swifts were beginning to dip and soar over Foxwell Common, a mile or two out of Cannonbridge. On the paved terrace at the rear of her cottage on the edge of the common, Venetia Franklin reclined at ease on a sunlounger of gaily striped canvas. She lay with her eyes closed, her hands linked behind her head, a faint smile on her lips.

Beside her, on a wooden table, a radio played light music. The scent of honeysuckle drifted over the garden; from the top of an apple tree dense with pink and white blossom a greenfinch poured out his silvery runs and trills. A delicious emanation of heat rose up from the old grey flagstones. I do believe the fine weather's come back to stay, Venetia thought with pleasure. She revelled like a cat in warmth and sunshine. Her skin took on a delicate honey tan in the summer, the soft curls of her barley-blonde hair grew even paler.

From the shrubbery the voices of the children, Simon and Katie, floated out as they darted about in one of their complicated games. The sound of sheep bleating strayed across from the common.

She yawned and stretched, opened her eyes and glanced idly round the garden. Her eyes were large and luminous, a deep sea-blue, with long, dark, curling lashes. At twenty-nine she was a good-looking woman; she had been a ravishingly pretty girl. Not very tall, slightly built and fine-boned, with narrow wrists and ankles.

The phone rang from inside the cottage. Her face broke into a smile. She sprang to her feet and ran in through the back door, along a passage into the sitting-room. She snatched up the receiver.

'Venetia?' At the sound of Philip Colborn's voice her smile vanished.

'Oh, it's you.' Her tone was easy and amiable. She remained standing, turning her head this way and that as she listened, glancing about the room. From time to time she interjected a word or two, giving him no more than surface attention.

On the wall nearby hung a long mirror. She considered her image with a critical eye, studying her new dark blue cotton sundress with its bold white patterning, pondering the effect against the silky skin of her shoulders.

A note of remonstrance appeared in Colborn's voice. In the garden the children laughed and called. She half turned to scrutinize her rear view in the glass. With her free hand she raised the skirt of her sundress. She stood with her head inclined, the gaze of her sea-blue eyes detached and assessing, contemplating the reflection of her slender, shapely legs.

Springfield House, the home of the Colborn family for over two hundred years, occupied a prime position in Cannonbridge, close to the town centre but retaining, with its large grounds, a good deal of quiet and privacy, a sense of the spacious, leisured Georgian days in which it had been built.

The Colborn who had chosen the site and built the house had been a successful lawyer, the son of a country parson. In early middle age he had gone into politics, representing the borough of Cannonbridge for the next thirty years; he had achieved minor office. He took for his wife the daughter of an earl, a high-principled, handsome, energetic young woman. Lady Wilhelmina made a lasting name for herself in Cannonbridge by her devotion to good works. There was still a Lady Wilhelmina Crescent in the town, a Lady

Wilhelmina Memorial Hall, a Lady Wilhelmina tavern.

After this splendid start the fortunes of the Colborns suffered a long, slow decline. Succeeding generations were less talented, less enthusiastic, less energetic. The family remained prosperous, well esteemed locally, until the early part of the twentieth century, when the gentle decline began to accelerate. A son was killed in the Boer War, another in the Great War. A third Colborn was killed in the Second World War and a fourth, Philip Colborn's father, died five years after the war of wounds received at Alamein.

At the time of his father's death Philip, his only child, was seven years old. Philip's mother felt the loss of her husband as a savage blow. Always a dependent, clinging woman, she sank rapidly into isolated, grieving widowhood, withdrawing from all social life and before long retreating even further, into outright invalidism. She lived on until Philip was a grown man but never again made the slightest effort to bestir herself to go out into the world.

The house slipped into neglect and from neglect into decay. The magnificent gardens became a wilderness. Several rooms were shrouded in dust sheets and closed up. It wasn't money that was in short supply but energy and resolution, interest and motivation. Little by little the name of Colborn slid from the consciousness of the town.

At half past seven on Friday morning Philip Colborn woke in his bedroom on the first floor of Springfield House. His eyes ached, his head throbbed. His sleep, as often of late, had been uneasy and broken. He and his wife Ruth had occupied separate bedrooms since the time three years ago when he had been struck down by influenza.

He got slowly out of bed and went over to the window. He was forty-one, with a tall, rangy figure. He had been handsome as a young man and was still good-looking enough, with his fair hair and grey eyes, to attract a female glance. He drew back the curtains and gazed bleakly out at the day. A sparkling May morning, sunlight glittering the dewy lawns. From downstairs he could hear a radio playing, something from Bizet, hauntingly beautiful.

The gardens were once more a superb sight, thanks to

the determination and dedication of his wife Ruth. They had married nine years ago, eighteen months after the death of Philip's mother. He had wanted to sell Springfield House which he saw only as the gloomy, secluded, dilapidated dwelling in which he had grown up. He had thought of buying a much smaller house on one of the new developments on the edge of Cannonbridge; he believed the move would provide a sense of release, of a fresh, hopeful start.

But Ruth had been horrified at the notion. She was certain the house could be restored to its old glory within a few years, the gardens even sooner. The fabric of the dwelling was still essentially sound. All the furnishings and pictures, all the objets d'art were still there; nothing had been disposed of. And there was more than sufficient money. Philip had inherited the whole of his mother's estate and in addition he had his salary from the bank where he worked. He had allowed himself to be persuaded.

'Are you awake, darling?' Ruth called up to him now from the foot of the stairs. He crossed the room and opened the bedroom door. The music rose up at him, imploring, yearning. An alluring odour of coffee drifted over the threshold. 'I won't be long,' he called down.

When he came into the kitchen a little later Ruth had already finished eating. 'I have a particularly busy day ahead of me,' she reminded him. She was a year or two older than her husband. Not very tall, delicately made, with a calm, pale, oval face and small regular features. Her thick, heavy brown hair, the colour of beechnuts, was wound carefully and becomingly round her head in shining braids and loops that gave her a look of a Brontë or Jane Austen heroine.

She moved swiftly and efficiently about the kitchen, attending to half a dozen tasks. From the radio a pair of voices soared in harmony. Philip went over and switched the radio off. Ruth halted for an instant and glanced at him in surprise.

'I'm sorry.' He sat down at the table. 'I have a headache. I slept badly.'

She gave him a look of tender concern. 'Shall I get you an aspirin?'

'No, thanks. Just some coffee.' She tried to persuade him to eat but he shook his head. While he drank his coffee she went along to the front hall to look for the post and came back with a handful of mail, mostly for herself. She always had a good deal of mail; since her marriage she had assiduously followed the example of Lady Wilhelmina and worked tirelessly for a dozen charitable causes. She slit open the envelopes, swiftly sorted out what must be dealt with promptly, what might safely wait a little. She sat down opposite Philip and poured herself some coffee.

Philip glanced through his letters without enthusiasm. He was employed by the bank where the Colborns had always kept their accounts; he had been manager of the Cannonbridge branch for four years now. Ruth had worked for the same bank herself. She wasn't a native of Cannonbridge; she had been transferred to the Cannonbridge branch a year or so before she and Philip were married—that was how they had met.

She glanced up from her correspondence and saw his dejected air. 'Cheer up,' she said in a tone of bracing optimism. 'It's a beautiful day.'

He was jerked out of his thoughts. He gave her a long look as if he hadn't really seen her for some time, then he leaned across the table and laid a hand on hers. 'I do appreciate all you've done for me,' he said with feeling. 'I may not say so very often but that doesn't mean I'm not deeply grateful.'

A flush rose in her cheeks, a tear shone in her eye. She looked at him without speaking, giving him a tremulous smile, surprised and pleased.

He gave her hand a squeeze before releasing it. He made an effort to take an interest in her day. 'I know you told me what you're doing,' he said apologetically, 'but I'm afraid I've forgotten.' He knew it was some big occasion but he couldn't for the life of him remember what.

She gave him a quick rundown of the morning ahead: a committee meeting, some essential calls, a look-in at a fund-raising coffee morning. 'But it's this afternoon I'm really looking forward to,' she said with a smile of profound

15

pleasure. 'It's the presentation of the purses at Polesworth.'
Polesworth was a stately home, the seat of a viscount. It
stood in a magnificent park ten miles out of Cannonbridge;
the presentation was in aid of the county branch of a national
charity for underprivileged children. Two hundred years
ago, in the days of Lady Wilhelmina Colborn, there had
been occasional trafficking between Springfield House and
Polesworth; in the decades after Lady Wilhelmina's death
the trafficking had dwindled and eventually ceased. Now,
nine years after Ruth had come to Springfield House as a
bride, her feet were about to take her in for the first time
though the noble portals of the mansion.

'I hope it all goes well,' Philip said warmly. 'I'll ring
you tomorrow evening.' He was spending the weekend at
Danehill Manor, some sixty miles away. The manor belonged to the bank who used it for conferences, staff courses,
seminars. Philip was being picked up at the bank at three
o'clock by the manager of a neighbouring branch who was
also going to Danehill; they wouldn't be back till Sunday
night.

He frowned anxiously. 'I'm not at all happy about my
paper,' he said. He had to read a paper on the role of banks
in the expansion of small businesses. He had revised the
paper yesterday evening, had asked Ruth to glance over it
once again before going to bed.

'It's fine,' she assured him now, as she had already assured
him half a dozen times. 'You've nothing to worry about. I
know it'll go down well.'

She stood up, leaving the breakfast things to be dealt with
shortly by her daily woman, an efficient and competent
worker, much superior to the ordinary run of dailies, an
invaluable assistant to Ruth in her busy life.

In the hall Philip picked up his briefcase and overnight
bag. He rarely came home to lunch, either taking out a
client or going to his club. He gave Ruth an affectionate
kiss. 'Look after yourself,' he told her. 'Don't go overdoing
things.'

She smiled up at him. 'Make your mark at Danehill. It's
a good speech. It'll be a great success.' She stood watching

in the doorway as he got into his car and set off down the drive. As he approached the elegant wrought-iron gates, already standing open, a woman turned in at the entrance. She was pushing a wheelchair that held a vacant-looking, lolling boy; she stood aside to let the car go past.

Philip raised a hand in greeting and she waved back. The boy gave a vague grin and flapped a hand. Dorothy Pickard and her brother Terry, familiar figures about the streets of Cannonbridge and the lanes of the neighbouring country-side, regular callers at Springfield House. Dorothy was forty but looked older. Her naturally pleasant, lively expression was overlaid with an air of chronic anxiety.

Terry was seventeen but appeared much younger. He was small and slightly built; he had been the unexpected child of his mother's middle age and had suffered from birth from severe multiple handicaps. His mother had done her best to weather the difficult years that followed. Her husband, a building labourer, took himself off when Terry was four, unable or unwilling to share the burden any longer. Mrs Pickard continued stoically to soldier on until herself struck down by ill-health. Dorothy was at that time unmarried, living at home, doing what she could to help her mother in the evenings and at weekends. She worked full-time as an assistant at a garden centre on the outskirts of Cannon-bridge; she had always been fond of an outdoor life. When Mrs Pickard's health failed Dorothy gave up her job to look after her mother and brother, taking any casual work she could find for a few hours here and there: fruit-picking, serving in a local greengrocer's, putting in half a day at a garden stall in the market.

Mrs Pickard grew steadily worse and Dorothy was forced to give up even these small jobs. Twelve months ago Mrs Pickard died and the entire responsibility for the boy fell on Dorothy. She accepted the duty without resentment or complaint, one of the hazards of existence, to be borne as cheerfully as possible.

Now, as she pushed the wheelchair along the drive of Springfield House, Ruth Colborn came out to meet her, smiling and waving at Terry. The Colborns had no children.

As soon as Terry became aware of Ruth's approach he gave his vacuous grin and flung his hands about. Ruth crouched down beside the wheelchair and spoke to him, as she always did. He made incoherent, grunting sounds in reply.

'I've put out the leaflets for you,' Ruth told Dorothy as she straightened up. In the course of her daily perambulations Dorothy delivered notices, brochures, electoral handouts. Ruth's leaflets were to advertise the annual charity garden day at Springfield House, to be held this year on the first Saturday in June.

To the left of the drive lay a large secluded shrub rose garden. Dorothy halted by the entrance and glanced in. Springfield House had always been noted for its magnificent shrub rose garden, devoted to the old varieties. After her marriage Ruth had resolutely set about rescuing the shrubs from the wilderness of neglect.

'They'll be a wonderful sight in another three weeks,' Dorothy said, eyeing with lively appreciation, and a certain amount of knowledge from her garden-centre days, the graceful forms of Rosa Alba, Rosa Gallica, the Musk, China and Moss Roses, the Noisette and Rugosa. The branching sprays were tightly packed with clusters of buds beginning to show colour, snowy white, delicate cream, pale shell pink, lilac, purple, velvety crimson.

Airy wafts of fragrance floated after them as they moved off again towards the house. 'I won't be a moment,' Ruth said as she went inside for the leaflets. While she was gone Dorothy wheeled Terry along the gravelled walk surrounding the house, pausing to peer in through the windows at the many splendours. When she reached the drawing-room she pressed her face against the glass, gazing up at the full-length portrait of Lady Wilhelmina occupying the place of honour to one side of the fireplace.

The portrait had been painted in London by an artist of note, shortly after Lady Wilhelmina's marriage. It showed a young woman of erect carriage and slender figure with a handsome, serious face, a wide brow and fine eyes. She had a fresh complexion, thick, shining brown hair arranged in heavy loops and bands. There was some slight natural resemblance between Lady Wilhelmina and Ruth Colborn. It had taken Ruth some years after her marriage to grow her hair to a length where she could arrange it in the same style as Lady Wilhelmina's gleaming tresses; she had accomplished the feat at about the same time as she had completed the restoration of the house and gardens. Another, later, portrait of Lady Wilhelmina hung in the Mayor's parlour at the Town Hall and the resemblance between the two women, considerably heightened by Ruth's new hairstyle, was often remarked on. The similarity in the charitable activities of the two women was mentioned with increasing frequency in the local press. Ruth never failed to note these references with an inward glow of pleasure.

'Oh—this is where you've got to,' Ruth said as she came hurrying up with the leaflets. Dorothy stepped back from the window and took the bundle from her, stowing it away in a basket fixed to the wheelchair. Her expression now was hesitant and uncertain, she was visibly bracing herself to say something to Mrs Colborn. She plunged in at last before she lost her nerve.

'I don't know if you've had time to think over what I asked you about the other day,' she said in a rush. 'About getting Terry admitted to Lyndale.' This was a home for the handicapped and disabled, standing in an outlying suburb of Cannonbridge; it was run by a charitable trust and provided for roughly a score of residents. Ruth was a member of the managing committee, a frequent visitor to the home.

'I wouldn't dream of asking you,' Dorothy continued urgently, 'if there was anything else I could think of. You're the only person I know that could possibly help me.' A man Dorothy had known for years, a man who worked the local markets, selling seeds and plants, flowers and shrubs, had recently made her a proposition. He had been a widower for eighteen months; his wife had always worked the markets at his side. He had one daughter who had helped in the business since leaving school but she was shortly getting married and going to London to live.

The man—Ken by name—had recently told Dorothy that if she could make some suitable arrangement for Terry, he would like to marry her. He would expect her to work the markets with him as his wife and daughter had done; he was confident she would pull her weight. It wasn't that he had anything against Terry but there could be no place in such a life for a severely handicapped lad whose problems must increase as he grew older.

'Ken isn't selfish or hard-hearted,' Dorothy had explained to Ruth. 'He's a decent, kind, hard-working man.' But he was also a practical, realistic man; he had seen more than one marriage broken by the presence of a handicapped youngster. Nor had Dorothy forgotten the example of her own father.

'Lyndale would be just the place for Terry,' Dorothy had assured Ruth. On a scale closer to the domestic than the institutional, where he could more easily settle in, and near enough for her to be able to visit him regularly. The place wasn't strange to him. She often called there with Terry in the course of her errands. Everyone was kind to the boy, he would probably scarcely notice the transition from his own home.

'I'm very sorry,' Ruth said gently. 'I'm afraid I can't have made myself clear the other day. It wouldn't be kind to let you entertain false hopes. There really is no possibility, none at all. Lyndale simply will not take anyone of Terry's age. Twenty-one is the absolute minimum. But there are places that might take him. I could—'

'Not round here,' Dorothy broke in, like a terrier pouncing on a bone. 'Not in Cannonbridge.'

'There's a very good place only fifteen miles away,' Ruth said patiently but Dorothy burst in again. 'They'd listen to you at Lyndale. If you spoke up for Terry, they'd take him for sure.'

Ruth smiled slightly. 'I'm afraid I can't attempt to turn their policies upside down. They don't make these rules without a lot of thought.'

'But they did have one or two youngsters there at one time,' Dorothy persisted. 'I'm sure I can remember.'

'Well, yes, that is so,' Ruth conceded. 'They did make an occasional exception—'

'There you are then!' Dorothy cried in triumph. 'That's what I've been saying all along. It isn't a hard and fast rule. If they could make those exceptions then, they can make one for Terry.'

Ruth sighed. 'It's a hard and fast rule now, I'm afraid. It's just because of those earlier exceptions that the committee decided to be very strict in future. The truth is, those particular admissions didn't work out very well.' She glanced at her watch. 'But in any case, quite apart from Terry's age, there's a much stronger reason for not admitting him. He really wouldn't fit in very well at Lyndale.'

Dorothy's frown returned. 'He's not a troublesome boy. You know that.'

'Yes, I do know that, but the committee have decided that in future they will only admit applicants who are capable of making some kind of personal, social contribution to the life of Lyndale, who are able to help themselves and each other to some extent. It's far better for the residents, makes them more independent, more sociable, gives them a sense of purpose. It produces a much healthier atmosphere, and of course on a practical level it means the home can be run with fewer staff—and that's no small consideration these days.' She paused and then asked gently, 'Can you honestly see Terry being able to fit into that pattern of life? I'm afraid he'll never be capable of any more than he is at present.' She looked down at Terry who grinned amiably up at the pale blue sky.

'I can't lose this chance,' Dorothy said with fierce determination, darting at Ruth from another angle. She knew Ken wouldn't wait for ever, or even for very long. He needed a wife now; if not her, then he would find someone else. She pressed her hands together. 'I know we could make a go of it. We've always got on well, and I'd love the life. I'll never get another chance like this.'

Ruth turned towards the house. 'You mustn't give up hope,' she said in a tone of great kindness. 'I'm sure we can find somewhere suitable for Terry. I'll make some more inquiries.'

But Dorothy shook her head stubbornly. 'It's got to be Lyndale,' she said, totally unmoved by everything Ruth had said, still confident of the final outcome. 'Lyndale or nothing.'

Over the weekend the weather continued fair, showing signs of becoming settled again. Along the avenues the laurels raised their creamy candles; on the hills above the town the rowans were in bloom. By two o'clock on Friday afternoon the first fair of the season was in full swing on a stretch of open ground beside the railway station.

Shortly before half past four on Monday afternoon the phone rang in the Franklins' flat in Northwick Road. Downstairs in the shop Roy heard it ring. He had just finished serving a customer and was busy returning a selection of food processors to their places on the shelves. He paused for a moment and stood listening. Along the counter his assistant explained to a woman the terms on which they offered credit sales.

The phone stopped ringing and Roy resumed his task. A minute or two later there came the sound of someone running down the stairs from the flat. The door at the end of the shop burst open and Jane Franklin darted in. She ran up to Roy.

'Sunnycroft School's just rung,' she said breathlessly. 'Venetia hasn't turned up to collect the children. They rang the cottage twice but there's no answer. They wanted to know if you'd pick the children up. I said we'd be over right away.'

'There's no need for you to come,' Roy said brusquely. 'You can give a hand in here while I'm gone.'

She shook her head with determination. 'I'm coming with you.'

He looked as if he might argue but then thought better of it; he gave a little jerk of his shoulders. He spoke to the assistant and then went rapidly out with Jane behind him.

Sunnycroft School, a small private establishment, was

situated in a residential suburb at the other side of town. The traffic was building up towards the rush hour and it was a good fifteen minutes before Roy drove up to the front entrance. He jumped out and pressed the bell.

The door was opened by one of the teachers. 'I've just rung Foxwell Cottage again,' she told Roy. 'There's still no answer. The children tell me their mother went away for the weekend, they've been staying with you.'

Roy nodded. 'I expect something cropped up to make her late setting off for home.'

The teacher frowned. 'I would have thought she'd have rung to let us know. She's never missed picking them up before, she's always very punctual.'

'If her car broke down on the road,' Jane put in, 'she might not have been able to get to a phone.'

'Yes, I suppose that could be it.' The teacher led the way into the hall where Simon and Katie sat waiting. They had a subdued, anxious air, only partly dispelled by the sight of their father and stepmother. They got to their feet and stood glancing from one face to the other.

'Isn't Mummy coming?' Katie asked. She went up to Jane and slipped a hand into hers.

'I expect she's been delayed,' Roy said easily.

In the car Jane chatted to the children about their day at school. They answered briefly and flatly. Roy scarcely spoke and after a few minutes all four lapsed into silence.

They reached the edge of town and Roy headed the car towards Foxwell Common. It was a fine, sunny afternoon with a little thin, high cloud. The landscape looked serene and peaceful. Along the hedgerows the hawthorns were in full snowy blossom, the common was bright with yellow gorse, the grass thickly studded with golden dandelions.

The hamlet consisted of half a dozen dwellings. Roy drove past a black and white thatched cottage owned by a widow who used the parlour as a little general store, past a farmhouse, a pair of old dwellings modernized for letting out to holidaymakers but empty now, so early in the season. He turned the car in through the open gates of Foxwell Cottage.

'It's all right! Mummy's back!' Katie cried out on a note

of relief. She had caught sight of her mother's car over on the right, on the far side of the house.

Simon frowned. 'Why didn't she drive straight to school to pick us up?' No one answered.

Roy came to a halt and switched off the engine. He opened his door and got out. Jane and the children made to follow but he stooped and put his head in at the rear window. 'Stay where you are,' he commanded the children. Jane's head came sharply round and he flashed her a look. 'You stay with them.' She said nothing. All three sat upright and alert, looking out at him in silence.

He walked over the gravel to the front door and pressed the bell; it rang sharp and clear. There was no response. He glanced about. The cottage windows were open, upstairs and down. He tried the front door. It yielded to his touch and he went inside. On the floor of the hall lay a couple of envelopes, a picture postcard, a scatter of leaflets. He went in and out of the ground-floor rooms, calling out Venetia's name. There was no stir of movement, no whisper of sound. Nothing out of order in the sitting-room or dining-room.

He went upstairs, glanced in at the children's rooms, the bathroom. In Venetia's bedroom an overnight bag and vanity case stood packed at the foot of the bed. A summer dress, crisply laundered, had been carefully laid out on the coverlet. A shoulder-bag lay on top of the chest of drawers.

By now he had given up calling out. He went down to the kitchen. On the table in the centre of the room was a tray holding used tea-things, an open biscuit tin beside it.

The back door was propped open with an old firedog. He went out on to the paved terrace. A garden table stood beside a canvas sunlounger; on the table a couple of beakers and a jug that had held lemonade. A folded newspaper bearing Friday's date stuck out from behind the cushions of the lounger.

He stood for a moment with his head back and his eyes closed. The only sounds were the twittering of birds and the distant hum of a mechanical saw. He went round the cottage to where Venetia's car stood with its back to him, its front windows wound down. The boot wasn't locked. He glanced inside; it was empty except for the spare tyre and a bag of tools.

He went round to the nearside front door of the car, opened it and stooped inside; the keys were in the ignition. On the rear window ledge lay some children's comics and a rag doll. He knelt on the front seat, leaned over and glanced down—and there she was. Jammed into the space between the front and rear seats, facing him, her eyes closed. She lay on her back, in shirt and jeans, her knees drawn up. Her hair fell in disordered curls over her forehead. Her face was contused and contorted, with livid bruises, her lips swollen, her mouth wide open. Something had been rammed down her throat, some patterned stuff, brown and silky.

He remained staring down at her for several seconds, then he reached over and laid the back of his hand against her puffy, discoloured cheek. He drew a long quavering breath and got out of the car. He staggered over to the side of the cottage and stood leaning against the wall, his head in his hands. After a minute or two he roused himself and walked round to where Jane and the children still sat silent in the car.

They saw his face as he approached, white and shaken, his trembling, uncertain gait. They gazed dumbly out at him. He didn't glance at the children but put his head in at the front window and without looking at Jane said in a low, unsteady voice, 'You must take the children home at once and stay there with them.' He put a hand up to his eyes. 'There's been an accident. I must ring the police.'

Jane said nothing but gave a single answering nod. She slid into the driver's seat and switched on the engine. In the back the children had caught something of what he'd said. They sat in tremulous silence, their faces puzzled and uneasy.

Roy stepped back and watched as Jane turned the car and drove out through the gates, then he went slowly back to the cottage. All at once he began to shake violently. He couldn't control the fierce tremors, he could scarcely discipline his fingers sufficiently to open the front door.

The phone stood on a small table in the sitting-room. As

he approached it the tremors increased. The receiver rattled against its rest as he tried to pick it up. Suddenly he began to cry. It was some minutes before he managed to dial the number and all the time the tears ran down his face.

CHAPTER 2

Evening sunlight slanted in through the window of the kitchen at Foxwell Cottage. Detective Chief Inspector Kelsey stood leaning against the dresser. A big, solidly built man with a large face and craggy features; a freckled skin and shrewd green eyes, a head of thickly-springing carroty hair. At the table in the middle of the room Roy Franklin sat leaning forward, his arms crossed on the table top, his head resting on his arms.

Venetia's body had gone off to the mortuary. Inside the cottage, upstairs and down, in the garden and on the common, men were busy searching, sifting, probing, examining.

Inquiries had been made at the neighbouring dwellings but no one had seen or heard anything unusual over the weekend, no one had noticed any car turning in through the cottage gates, no one had been seen hanging about the cottage or the common, behaving in any way suspiciously. The common was of no great size and was full of gorse bushes. As a consequence it was not in favour as a picnic spot or playground. Venetia had never been on close terms with any of the neighbours. Her acquaintance with them had always been pleasant enough but had never progressed beyond an exchange of minor civilities when their paths crossed.

Among the leaflets lying in the front hall of the cottage was one advertising a bazaar at a Cannonbridge church hall. A phone call to the organizers of the bazaar supplied the information that the leaflets had been delivered by Dorothy Pickard. A constable had been despatched to talk to Dorothy.

26

He had returned to say that she had pushed the leaflets in through the door of Foxwell Cottage at about ten o'clock on Saturday morning. She had seen no one about the place, had heard no sound from inside the dwelling. The cottage gates were standing open, fastened back, and she had left them as she had found them. She remembered noticing Mrs Franklin's car parked at the far side of the cottage but she hadn't gone near it.

In addition to delivering leaflets on Saturday Dorothy was also selling raffle tickets in aid of a charity. Mrs Franklin had often bought tickets from her so she rang the bell in order to speak to her. When there was no reply she walked round to the back door which stood propped open. She saw the sunlounger on the terrace, the table with the used jug and beakers. From this and from the fact that all the windows were open she judged that Mrs Franklin must be somewhere on the premises. She knocked loudly at the back door and when there was no answer she put her head in and called out, again without success. She looked down the garden but saw no one. She concluded that Mrs Franklin might have gone up to the little shop or walked across the fields to the farm for some eggs.

By the time the police arrived at the cottage Roy Franklin had drunk a couple of stiff whiskies from the sideboard and had managed to get some kind of grip on himself. He had immediately suggested to the police that the murder was clearly the work of a criminal psychopath, possibly someone from a local psychiatric institution—there were two in the area. The circumstances of the crime had at once prompted the same thought in the Chief Inspector. Both institutions were contacted by phone and officers were sent to begin inquiries.

Venetia had been wearing a certain amount of jewellery: a gold wristwatch, gold stud earrings, a gold chain round her neck. She also wore three rings, a diamond engagement ring, a wedding ring and the sapphire and diamond ring Franklin had given her after the birth of Simon. No attempt appeared to have been made to remove any of these items.

Nor, apparently, had there been any attempt to enter the

cottage. There was no sign of disturbance nor, as far as Franklin could tell them, did anything appear to be missing. The cottage was well furnished and there were several ornaments and other items of value that could easily have been snatched up and thrust into a pocket. On the dressing-table in Venetia's bedroom was a jewel box containing several pieces of fair value. Inside the shoulder-bag on the chest of drawers was a wallet holding a sizeable sum of money, a cheque book and credit cards. Nothing apparently touched, nothing taken.

One of the buttons was missing from the shirt Venetia wore. The shirt was of fine cotton, striped in blue and white; the buttons were fancy, dark blue buttons of good quality, many-faceted. The missing button had been ripped from the shirt, tearing out a small piece of material. The search had so far failed to turn up the button.

According to Franklin he had called for the children, as arranged, at five o'clock on Friday afternoon. Venetia had given the children their tea on the terrace, as she often did in fine weather. He had exchanged a few words with her but they hadn't stood about chatting; he knew that she was going away for the weekend. She hadn't mentioned at what time she intended setting off but he had the impression that it would be as soon as she had tidied up and changed out of her shirt and jeans.

It had been agreed that he would take the children to school on Monday morning; Venetia would be back from her trip in time to pick them up at the school on Monday afternoon. This wasn't the first time they had made such an arrangement.

When the children finished their tea they ran into the cottage to wash their hands and faces. He went inside and brought out their cases. Venetia fetched a tray from the kitchen and began to clear the tea-things. When the children came out they said goodbye to her and got into the car. He immediately drove off, leaving the gates open, fastened back, as they had been when he arrived. That was the last time he had seen Venetia alive. He had had no further contact of any kind with her.

28

He didn't take the children straight to his flat. His wife Jane was at work and wouldn't be in till around six. Jane had never met Venetia; she had never wanted to and the necessity had never arisen. It had always been he who had picked up the children. It had been settled between himself and Jane that he was to take the children to the fair on the common by the railway, bringing them home at about seven, by which time Jane would have prepared supper. At the fairground he had seen various people he knew and there were other children from Sunnycroft School there with their mothers. He had spoken briefly to one of the mothers who was a customer at his shop.

At seven o'clock he had duly taken the children back to the flat. Jane was there and they all had supper and then watched television. The children went to bed at about nine and he spent the next hour or so in his workshop. He and Jane went to bed around half past ten. On Saturday morning he busied himself as usual in the shop and workshop. Simon spent the morning with him. Katie went out shopping with Jane and afterwards stayed with her while she attended to the housework and cooking.

On Saturday afternoon he left his assistant and one of the repairmen in charge while he and Jane took the children to a nearby safari park. Again they saw and spoke to other children and parents known to them from school. They returned to the flat at about eight. On Sunday they all four spent the day in a riverside town fifteen miles away. They took a boat out on the river, ate a picnic lunch and tea on the river bank, returning home around half past seven.

It seemed highly probable that Venetia had died very shortly after Roy drove away from the cottage with the children on Friday afternoon and the preliminary medical examination tended to support this impression. A short distance from the cottage, on the common, they had found a spot on a small rise, beneath the overhanging branches of a hawthorn, where the grass had recently been flattened. Someone standing under the branches could look down unobserved on the cottage and garden.

Chief Inspector Kelsey had asked Franklin if he had ever

before seen the silky brown scarf that had been stuffed down Venetia's throat but Franklin had shaken his head.

The Chief Inspector stood now looking down at Franklin as he sat at the table with his head on his arms. 'Have you no idea where your wife—your ex-wife—might have been intending to spend the weekend?' he asked suddenly.

Franklin raised his head and sat slowly up. His face was flushed, he had an air of immense fatigue. 'No idea at all. She never used to say where she was going when I went to collect the children. She never even used to tell the children where she was going.' Making sure they would be in no position to reveal information about her private life, Kelsey reflected, however skilfully Roy or Jane might try to pump them.

'Can you tell me about any men friends she may have had?' he asked. 'Do you know if she was thinking of marrying again?'

Again Franklin shook his head. 'I'm sure she did have men friends but she never mentioned them to me. I wouldn't have expected her to. She certainly never said anything about marrying again.'

'Did you ever make any attempt to find out about men friends?'

He frowned. 'I certainly did not. It was none of my business.' The divorce had come about because of his own infidelity, not that of his wife. He had never been jealous of her, had never been given cause to be jealous during their marriage, he didn't consider himself a jealous man.

'Would you have objected to her marrying again?'

He began to look angry. 'No, of course I would not. Why on earth should I object? I married again myself, I'm very happily married.'

'Did Venetia bear you any resentment over the divorce?'

'She did not,' Franklin said brusquely. 'We were on good terms. She was never a trouble-maker, she was always easy-going, never aggressive, never the sort to make unnecessary difficulties.'

The Chief asked if Venetia had had any kind of job.

'No,' Franklin told him. 'She never worked after we were

30

married. She wasn't the type to want a career.'

'Do you know of any close women friends?'

'I'm afraid not.' He supplied the Chief with patchy details of various women Venetia had been friendly with during their marriage but the friendships had never been close. 'I've no idea if she still saw any of them,' he added. He had been able to identify the picture postcard in the hall at the cottage—sent from Italy on holiday—as being from a married couple they had both known slightly during their marriage; he hadn't seen anything of them since the divorce.

'What about her family?'

Franklin looked thunderstruck. 'Her mother! I'd forgotten about her. I'll have to tell her.' He looked appalled at the notion. 'She's a widow,' he told Kelsey. 'Venetia's father died some years ago, not long after we were married. Her mother sold the house and went back to Wychford, that was where she'd lived as a girl.' Wychford was a small town ten miles to the west of Cannonbridge. 'She can't get about much, she suffers badly from arthritis. She moved into sheltered accommodation a few years ago, one of those places with a warden. I haven't seen her since the divorce.' He grimaced. 'She was pretty upset about all that—even though she'd never thought me good enough for her daughter.' Venetia had been an only child and he knew of no other relatives.

He looked uneasily up at Kelsey. 'I'll have to go over to see Mrs Stacey—Venetia's mother. I can't very well tell her over the phone.' He pushed back his chair. 'I'd better get cracking.'

'We can tell her if you like,' Kelsey offered. 'We'll have to see her anyway.'

Detective-Sergeant Lambert drove the chief over to Wychford. When they reached the apartment block Kelsey sought out the warden and explained his errand. She took them along to Mrs Stacey's flat, going in first to prepare the ground, and staying in the room while the Chief broke the news.

Mrs Stacey was a small, slight woman in her late sixties,

31

looking several years older. Her habitual manner appeared withdrawn and self-absorbed; she had a faded, desiccated air, a resigned and melancholy expression.

It seemed to Sergeant Lambert that she bore the news with a good deal more fortitude and self-control than might have been expected. As if she were walled off in her little flat from the happenings of the larger life outside and what filtered through to her restricted world could have no very profound or lasting effect on the small routines of her daily existence.

The warden brought in a tray of tea and waited till Mrs Stacey felt able to answer questions. When the door had finally closed behind the warden Kelsey began by asking Mrs Stacey if she had any idea where her daughter had intended going for the weekend.

'No idea at all,' she told him. 'But then I wouldn't expect to know.' She spoke without any sign of emotion, she might have been talking of some chance acquaintance.

She hadn't seen much of Venetia since she'd moved back to Wychford, she had seen even less of her after the divorce. 'She brought the children over to see me once in a way. For my birthday or at Christmastime.' She gestured with a knobby hand. 'She had her own life. We were never close, I was almost forty when she was born. She was always a lot closer to her father.'

Kelsey asked when she had last seen her daughter. 'The best part of two months ago,' she said. 'It was a Sunday, early in March, a beautiful sunny day. She just put the children in the car and brought them over. She could be like that sometimes, acted on impulse.' She looked at Kelsey with no expression on her lined, withered face. 'She didn't let me know they were coming. I don't have my own phone here but people can ring the warden.' Her hands drooped in her lap. 'I was having a nap after lunch when they came . . .' Her voice trailed away. It's beginning to get to her, Sergeant Lambert thought.

'Did you notice anything in particular about her state of mind?' Kelsey asked. 'Did she appear worried in any way? Did she mention any difficulties?'

'Do you mean difficulties about money? As far as I knew, she was all right for money. She never complained of being short and she always seemed able to afford what she wanted. She never discussed her financial affairs with me.'

'Did she mention any other kind of worries? Of a personal kind, perhaps?'

She shook her head slowly. 'She seemed perfectly all right, just as usual.'

'Do you know of any men friends?'

'She had men friends, of course. She was never short of boyfriends, right from when she was at school.' She glanced across at a photograph of Venetia as a girl of sixteen or seventeen. It stood with a dozen others on a Victorian whatnot in the corner. She gave a long trembling sigh and fell silent.

'Can you tell me the names of any of her men friends?' Kelsey prompted when she showed no sign of continuing.

She shook her head again. 'I'm sorry, I don't know any names. She'd just say something in passing, she'd been to a show or out to dinner, but she never mentioned any names.'

'Do you know if she had any intention of marrying again?'

'She did say once or twice that she'd never marry again, once was more than enough. She said it as if she meant it —but then another time she'd say something half-joking, as if she did think of marrying again.' She paused and then added, 'One day last year she said: "Do you remember how you always wanted me to marry someone respectable? A professional man of standing in the community?" She glanced up at Kelsey. 'She was teasing me when she said that, of course. Years ago, when she was a girl, I used to say that sort of thing to her sometimes, that she mustn't throw herself away on the first man that asked her, she ought to marry someone of substance.' She drew a little sighing breath. 'She laughed—this was that day last year —and said: "You never know, I might surprise you after all one of these days and do just that."'

'Do you think she had some particular man in mind when she said that?'

'I've no idea. You never knew when to take her seriously.' She closed her eyes and lowered her head. After a moment she fumbled in her pocket with her twisted fingers and took out a handkerchief; she dabbed clumsily at her eyes.

'She was only eighteen when she got married,' she said as she put the handkerchief away again. 'Roy was five or six years older. I was against it, I thought she was much too young. But her father never could stand out against her for long. And he thought Roy had a lot of go about him, he thought he'd do well in life.' She sighed again and shook her head. 'So I hoped for the best, I hoped it would work out all right.' She moved a hand. 'I can't say I was very surprised when it ended in divorce, I never thought they were really suited.'

'Were you surprised at the way the divorce came about?'

'You mean that it was Roy who found someone else and not Venetia? No, not really. After a year or two, when the honeymoon days were over, Roy started going on at Venetia, finding fault with her. He thought she was extravagant, she should help in the business. He wanted her to serve in the shop—she used to work in a shop before she was married but it was a very different place from Franklin's, very high-class. Youngjohn's, the china and gift shop, I expect you know it. They have such lovely things there and of course Venetia always liked beautiful things, she had very good taste.' Tears threatened again but she made a determined effort to blink them away. 'She never paid much attention to Roy's grumbles, she just went on in her own way. She used to laugh at him, say he took things too seriously, there was more to life than working every hour God sends.'

'What kind of terms was she on with Roy and his second wife?'

'Very good,' she said at once. 'There was never anything spiteful about Venetia.'

'Do you know of any particular woman friend? Someone she might have confided in?'

'She wasn't the kind to have close women friends.' She pondered. 'There's Megan, Megan Brewster, I suppose she

34

might have talked to her, though she hadn't seen her for years until about six months ago. Megan was the nearest she ever had to a sister when they were young.' The Brewsters had lived next door to them in Cannonbridge. The two girls were the same age, went to school together, sat next to each other in class. 'They were really very different,' Mrs Stacey said. 'I suppose it was the attraction of opposites.' She nodded over at the whatnot. 'Megan's in one of those photographs, with Venetia. On the second shelf.'

Kelsey went over and picked up the photograph. Venetia, eleven or twelve years old, very pretty in a short-sleeved cotton frock, her long curly fair hair tied up in a pony tail; she was smiling, posing theatrically for the camera. And Megan beside her, taller and thinner, with short, straight, black hair cut in a fringe. She stood erect and poised, her hands at her sides, her dark eyes looking squarely and unself-consciously out at the camera, her expression serious and thoughtful.

'The Brewsters left Cannonbridge when Megan was fourteen,' Mrs Stacey said as Kelsey sat down again. 'Mr Brewster was transferred to the West Country. The girls wrote to each other at first but after a while they stopped. And then one day just before Christmas last year, when Venetia came over here with the children to see me, she told me she'd had a phone call from Megan. She was really pleased to hear from her again. Megan's still single, she's a real career girl. She works for a department store.' She mentioned the name of a nationwide chain. 'She'd been moved to the Martleigh branch.' Martleigh was a good deal smaller than Cannonbridge and lay some twenty-two miles to the north-east of that town.

'I know Venetia went over to Martleigh more than once to see Megan.' Mrs Stacey broke off and put a hand up to her face. 'Of course—Megan won't know about Venetia. How dreadful—she'll probably hear it on the radio or see it in the papers.' All at once she began to cry, terribly and painfully, her head bent, her misshapen hands covering her face.

Kelsey waited in silence until she was again in command

35

of herself. She sat up and gave him a level look from her faded blue eyes. 'If you've any more questions to ask,' she said, 'don't worry about me. Go right ahead and ask. I'll be all right.'

'Just two more points,' Kelsey said gently. 'Do you feel you can shed any kind of light on what's happened?'

'Living in that cottage,' she said at once, with certainty. 'It's far too isolated. I never liked her living there alone, just with the children, after the divorce. I suggested to her more than once that she might think of moving into town but she said she liked it out at Foxwell, it was quiet and private. But I never thought it wise. So many unbalanced people about these days, people who'll stop at nothing. A young woman on her own like that, unprotected, it seemed to me to be asking for trouble.'

'I'm afraid this is going to be an ordeal for you,' Kelsey said as he took out the brown scarf folded into its plastic wrapping. He did his best to prepare Mrs Stacey, to lessen the shock before he asked her if she would look at the scarf to see if she could recognize it. She braced herself and looked down with careful concentration at the silky material with its subdued, paisley-type pattern. The scarf was not of good quality and was far from new. She studied it for several moments before she shook her head decisively. She was quite certain she had never seen the scarf before. 'I would be very surprised indeed if it had belonged to Venetia,' she said with conviction. 'It's not at all the kind of thing she would wear.'

CHAPTER 3

The results of the post mortem were expected around the middle of Tuesday morning. Before that there was the Press to deal with, the local radio station, a conference, briefings.

Shortly after eleven Chief Inspector Kelsey came down the hospital steps. There had been no sign of any sexual assault on Venetia Franklin. She had been struck a savage blow on the chin, powerful enough to break her jaw. The back of her skull had also been fractured, probably as the result of a fall caused by the blow to the chin. Death had followed swiftly upon the ramming of the scarf down her throat. The stomach contents revealed that she had died very soon after a light meal of tea and cake, such as she had eaten with the children just before Franklin arrived.

Sergeant Lambert followed the Chief across the hospital car park. Kelsey looked at his watch. 'We've time to call in at Venetia's bank before we go over to see Megan Brewster,' he told Lambert. He had spoken to Megan on the phone, had arranged to see her at twelve-thirty. And he had fixed an appointment with Venetia's solicitor for tomorrow afternoon. The solicitor couldn't see him before then, he would be in court the whole of today and tomorrow morning.

Venetia's account was with the Allied Bank, the oldest established bank in Cannonbridge. It was housed in a handsome period building in Broad Street, close to the town centre; it had an atmosphere of great calm and substance.

The assistant manager was at the counter when the two policemen crossed the marble floor of the spacious hall. 'I'm afraid Mr Colborn's not in,' he told the Chief. 'You've just missed him. He has an appointment with a business customer, he'll probably be with him for the rest of the morning.' But the assistant would be happy to furnish the Chief with any information he might require.

He took the two men into an office. 'Mrs Franklin opened an account with us after her divorce,' he told them. Before that she had had a joint account with her husband at another bank in the town. The last contact Allied had had with her was last Friday afternoon when she had looked in for a moment to say she had decided after all not to sell some shares she held. She had spoken to the assistant; she had seemed much as usual, in good spirits.

He went through the records of her account with the Chief. All very straightforward and unremarkable. Her income came from three sources, two of them deriving from her ex-husband. The first was a fixed monthly payment of a size which seemed to the Chief of the order of what might be expected in the way of alimony from a man in Franklin's position. In addition Franklin paid into her account every quarter a sum which varied up or down but was always fairly substantial. Venetia had lived comfortably within her income and from time to time she had, on the bank's advice, invested the surplus that arose. The dividends from these investments provided her third source of income, very small in relation to the other two. She had never paid in any money, cash or cheques, from any other source.

When the two men left the bank they went straight over to Martleigh, to the store where Megan Brewster worked as knitwear buyer. They took a lift to her office on the top floor.

She was a tall, very slim, very elegant young woman with dark, shrewdly intelligent eyes, shining black hair fashionably cut. She was still recognizably the girl in Mrs Stacey's photograph; she had the same direct look, the same disciplined air.

She answered the Chief Inspector's questions readily, in a straightforward manner. She had been appalled at the news of the crime, at the brutality of the killing, but after the initial shock she couldn't, in all honesty, say that she was totally surprised. Venetia had talked to her about visiting singles clubs and bars and Megan had thought this very unwise, had tried to warn her against it. She made a face of distaste as she spoke. She had told Venetia she believed such places acted as a magnet for every kind of undesirable. But Venetia had laughed, brushing her objections aside as prudish and old-fashioned. She was sure many of these clubs were highly respectable, providing relaxed, comfortable meeting-places for ordinary decent citizens on their own for perfectly valid reasons.

No, Megan couldn't supply the name of any particular bar or club Venetia had visited. She couldn't even say for certain that Venetia had actually visited any at all. She hadn't seen Venetia for five or six weeks. 'I've been in Europe on a buying trip,' she explained. She had been away for a month, had returned a few days ago. She had last seen Venetia ten days before she left for Europe. Venetia had driven over to the store, had spent the morning shopping there, had lunched with Megan, as she had done three or four times since Megan had got in touch with her again. On this last occasion she had asked Megan to help her pick out a couple of dresses. 'She wanted them to be high-fashion, youthful,' Megan said. She had heard nothing from Venetia since that day. Nor had she any idea where Venetia might have intended going last weekend.

Venetia hadn't discussed her personal affairs with her in any detail. She had given Megan a brief, sketchy account of her marriage and divorce but had shown little inclination to dwell on the past. 'She seemed to be just beginning to realize she was free,' Megan said. 'That she could live her life to suit herself. She felt all kinds of exciting possibilities were opening up.'

Megan didn't know of any close woman friend Venetia might have had. 'She didn't seem to have many friends of any kind,' she told them. 'It can be difficult after a divorce.'

Kelsey asked if Venetia had appeared to have any problems, if she had spoken of any worries, but Megan shook her head. 'Far from it. She seemed very pleased at the way her life was opening out. And she certainly didn't seem short of money, she seemed able to buy what she wanted when she came over here. That last time, when I helped her to pick out the dresses, she never even looked at the price tag till she'd decided what she was having. Pretty expensive dresses they were too, but she didn't turn a hair.'

The Chief showed her the scarf but she didn't recognize it. She said at once that she couldn't imagine Venetia owning or wearing it.

Venetia hadn't discussed her relationship with her ex-husband and his second wife but from passing references Megan had gathered that the relationship was amicable enough. Venetia did once mention the way in which her marriage had ended. 'She said Roy had grown more and more critical and pernickety but she didn't let it bother her.' Then one day, purely by chance, she had caught him out in a lie about where he'd been the evening before when he was supposed to be on a business call. She challenged him about it half-jokingly. He hesitated and then to her astonishment suddenly told her there was someone else and he wanted a divorce. As soon as Venetia got her breath back she told him that provided he could make acceptable arrangements for herself and the children she would offer no objection. 'She burst out laughing when she was telling me about it,' Megan added. 'She said she couldn't get the divorce fast enough—though she didn't go out of her way to make that plain to Roy.'

'Do you know if she thought of remarrying?'

Megan shook her head. 'I'm certain it was the last thing in her mind.'

'Do you know of any particular man friend?'

'I'm sure she wasn't in love with anyone. She did once mention someone, one day over lunch, some man who was keen to marry her. I gathered she'd been having an affair with him, it had started soon after the divorce. She wasn't serious about him, she'd plunged into the affair without much thought, a reaction from the divorce. She was cooling off by the time she spoke to me about it. He was getting too possessive. She said she hadn't cut herself free from one set of chains to let herself be tied up in another. She wanted fun and a good time, not dog-like devotion.'

'Did she mention his name? Or anything else about him?'

'She certainly never mentioned his name.' She pondered. 'The only thing I can remember her saying—and I don't really think it meant anything—was when she stood up at the end of lunch to go over and get her coat. She pulled a face and said: "Could you really imagine me being married to a bank manager?" I didn't get the impression he actually was a bank manager, I think she said that to give me an idea of the kind of person he was, the sort of life he led, conventional and respectable.'

'She didn't enlarge?'

'No. She came back with her coat, said goodbye and went off home. She never talked about him again.'

'Did you get the impression that she'd finished with him?'

Again she pondered. 'No, I don't believe she had. I think

she saw him from time to time. I remember her saying he still had his uses.'

It was two-fifteen when the two men again walked in through the massive mahogany doors of the Allied Bank. Mr Colborn had still not returned. 'He probably stayed late with the client,' the assistant manager told them, 'and then went out to lunch with him. If I can be of any further assistance . . .'

Kelsey asked if the bank had records of any payments Mrs Franklin might have made in recent weeks to clubs, bars, dating agencies, singles organizations and the like. A few minutes later the assistant told him that the account showed a payment made about a month ago to a singles club, and another payment a day or two later to a travel agent. Both these concerns were in Strettisham, a small town five miles away. As if, Kelsey reflected, Venetia had chosen to begin her forays at some little distance from her own doorstep.

When they left the bank the Chief told Lambert to drive to Springfield House on the chance that Colborn might have nipped off home after leaving his client, might have seized the chance to put his feet up for half an hour.

The Chief had never set foot inside Springfield House but he had been aware of its existence since his childhood. On his way to the library on Saturday mornings as a schoolboy he used to pass the house with its tall gates firmly closed, the drive rank with weeds, grass thrusting up through the circle of gravel before the house. The place had always seemed to him to have an air of mystery and romance, past grandeurs and faded splendours.

They reached the tree-lined road and Lambert turned the car in through the gates, standing open now, splendidly refurbished, the elegant black spears tipped with gold, glittering in the afternoon sun. A car was drawn up before the house, a blue Ford Orion.

Lambert's third ring at the bell was answered by Colborn. He wore a dark business suit, he looked pale and weary. He didn't appear surprised to see them—as if, Lambert thought, he was too tired to feel surprise about anything. Kelsey had come across him briefly at functions in the town but Colborn showed no sign of recognition. He stood in silence, looking at them.

The Chief introduced himself and explained that they had called in connection with the death of a customer of the bank, Mrs Venetia Franklin. Colborn listened with no expression on his face other than that of deep fatigue as Kelsey told him they had been to the bank and had been given details of Mrs Franklin's account. 'One or two questions arise,' Kelsey added. 'You might be able to help. We were passing the house, we took a chance you might be at home.'

'I dropped in for a bite of lunch,' Colborn said flatly. 'I spent the morning at Holloway's—Holloway's Heating and Plumbing. He kept me later than I expected.' He stepped aside for them to enter. 'This is a terrible business about Mrs Franklin,' he said as he closed the door. 'Utterly beyond belief.' He took them into his study and offered them drinks which they refused. He took a glass of whisky himself and sat cradling it. He seemed totally exhausted; his speech, movements and gestures were all profoundly lethargic. He displayed no impatience as he sat waiting for Kelsey to ask his questions, he stared down into his glass, his face drained, tinged with grey.

'How long have you known Mrs Franklin?' Kelsey began.

'About two years.' Still he sat gazing into his glass. 'She came to us after her divorce. She wanted a different bank from her ex-husband.' He glanced briefly at the Chief. 'That's very common.'

'Had you known her before that?'

He moved his head. 'Very vaguely. I'd come across her at some charity function in the town. I just knew her to stop and speak a word to.'

'No more than that?' Colborn shook his head in silence. He raised his glass and took a long drink.

'After she began banking with you,' Kelsey went on, 'did you extend your acquaintance with her?'

He turned his glass in his hands. 'As a customer, yes,

naturally. She asked my advice about investments, credit cards, and so on.'

'Did you become friendly with her on a personal level?'

'No, I can't say I did.' He passed a hand across his forehead. 'I'm afraid you've caught me at a bad time. I've had a pretty strenuous time at the bank lately. So many firms in difficulties these days, so much that can go wrong, one has to walk a perpetual tightrope when it comes to making decisions.'

'We won't keep you much longer,' Kelsey promised. 'I wondered if you knew Mrs Franklin from way back, before she was married?'

Colborn shook his head.

'Did you at any time form a close friendship with her?' Again he shook his head. He showed neither impatience nor resentment at the line of questioning, he didn't ask what the Chief was driving at. He said nothing at all beyond answering what he was asked, sitting there grey and fatigued, drinking his whisky.

'When did you last see Mrs Franklin?' the Chief continued.

'About ten days ago, in the bank.'

'In the way of business?'

'Not even that. She was standing at the counter when I happened to cross the hall. I just said good morning as I passed.'

'Have you any idea where she might have intended going this last weekend?'

'No idea at all.' He looked across at Kelsey. 'I'm afraid I've got rather a bad migraine. It tends to come on if I get over-tired. I had a fairly hectic weekend. I was at a seminar at the bank's place in the country. I went straight there from work on Friday afternoon, I didn't get back till Sunday night. I haven't had a chance to relax properly for days.' He glanced at his watch and uttered an exclamation. 'I must go, I have appointments.'

Kelsey stood up. 'We'll be off, then. Don't trouble yourself, we'll find our own way out.' He paused on the study threshold and glanced back. Colborn hadn't moved but still sat in his chair, looking as if all effort was utterly beyond him.

Outside in the car Sergeant Lambert said, 'He looked pretty rough. I hadn't credited banking with being such a wearing business.' As he switched on the engine he suddenly added, 'Youngjohn's—the shop where Venetia worked as a girl. It's in Broad Street, a few doors from the Allied Bank.'

Kelsey's head came sharply round, he sat for a moment in silence, staring at Lambert, then he said, 'That customer, the one Colborn spent the morning with—'

'Holloway's Heating and Plumbing.' Lambert knew where the business was situated, out on the industrial estate. A small, thriving business, bent on expansion.

'We'll nip along there now,' Kelsey said. 'We'll have a word with Holloway.'

Ten minutes later they were in Holloway's office. 'We've been trying to get a word with Mr Colborn,' the Chief told him. 'We understood he was here with you.

'He was here,' Holloway said with an edge of impatience. He was a short, thickset bull of a man with a jutting jaw. 'For all the good he did he might as well never have come. He left here some time ago, before twelve.' He flung out a hand. 'Total waste of time, he was in no state to make head or tail of my books. He looked half dead when he got here, as if he'd been up all night. I asked him if he was all right and he said he was. But when he started asking me the same questions twice over I put it to him fair and square that he hadn't got his mind on what he was supposed to be doing.

'Then he came out with it and said he had one hell of a migraine, he could hardly see straight. I said to him: "Why on earth didn't you say so right out, instead of carrying on with this pantomime? You could have cancelled the appointment, fixed another day."' He thrust out his jaw. 'I told him, "The last thing I need is my commercial future judged by a guy with migraine."' He walked with Kelsey to the door. 'So he gave in and took himself off. I don't know where you'll find him now. He may be back at the bank or he may have gone home to bed. That's where I'd be in his condition, he looked absolutely knackered to me.'

CHAPTER 4

'Back to Springfield House,' Kelsey directed as he got into the car. 'I'll lay you two to one Colborn's still there.'

And the blue Orion was still drawn up by the front door when they again turned in through the gates. This time it took four rings before Colborn came to the door. The grey had left his face, his cheeks were flushed, he looked as if he had just been wakened from a doze. Again he said nothing but stood looking at them without impatience or irritation.

'A couple of points we overlooked when we were here,' Kelsey said in a tone of apology. 'If we might step inside again. It won't take a minute.'

Colborn drew back the door in silence and they stepped inside. He closed the door and turned to face them. In the same moment the Chief produced the brown scarf in its plastic wrapping and thrust it out under Colborn's nose.

'Have you ever seen that before?' he asked abruptly.

Colborn jerked his head back in surprise. He stared down at the packet. 'It's a scarf,' Kelsey told him.

A look of appalled horror crossed Colborn's face. He glanced up at Kelsey. 'You mean it's the scarf—?'

Kelsey didn't answer that. He repeated, 'Have you ever seen it before?'

The colour had drained from Colborn's face, he looked on the point of collapse. He put out a hand and steadied himself against the wall. 'Do you recognize it?' Kelsey pressed him. Colborn drew a long trembling breath and shook his head. He looked poleaxed, utterly grief-stricken.

'You loved her,' Kelsey said. 'That's the truth, isn't it?'

Colborn dropped his head into his hands and began to weep, with great shuddering sobs. 'You'd better tell us about it,' Kelsey invited. Colborn made no response. The shuddering and sobbing continued. 'We can't stand here,' Kelsey said brusquely. 'We'll go along to your study.'

Colborn made a strong effort to take a grip on himself

and the shudders began to die away. He took a handkerchief from his pocket and dabbed at his eyes. After a minute or two he seemed to have regained some measure of control. He followed the Chief along to the study.

The moment Sergeant Lambert closed the study door behind them Colborn began to speak, in a rush, with an air of relief. 'It was a terrible shock when I heard about Mrs Franklin,' he said in a rapid, uneven tone, his face contorted at the recollection. All three of them were still standing. 'I was told of it when I got to the bank this morning. One of the girls had heard it on the local radio. I couldn't believe it.' He looked earnestly at the Chief. 'It was all over between us months ago. It was never anything very . . . intense, for either of us, it was—' He drew another trembling breath. 'Just folly, really. She was at a loose end after the divorce and I—' He moved his shoulders. 'I was restless, overworked. It seemed some kind of answer, a distraction from pressure and strain. She was always light-hearted, she took my mind off my worries.' He pressed his hands together. 'But it was an appalling shock, all the same. I was still fond of her. It didn't end in a quarrel, nothing like that, it was all very amicable.'

'How did it end?' Kelsey asked.

Colborn spread a hand. 'I simply came to my senses, saw the risks I was taking. I put it to her and she understood. I have a very good marriage, I value it highly, it was madness to risk losing my wife.' He broke off suddenly with a look of consternation. 'My wife—she won't have to know any of this?'

'She won't hear it from me,' Kelsey assured him. Colborn closed his eyes for an instant. 'But there's no telling in a case of this kind,' Kelsey warned him. 'These things have a way of coming out. It might be better to tell her yourself, right away. She'll probably be a lot more understanding than you think.'

'I couldn't do that,' Colborn said on a note of dismay. 'She'd be horrified. She doesn't know anything about Venetia, she doesn't even know she existed.'

'She'll know she existed by now all right,' Kelsey said.

'Everyone in the town will know about Mrs Franklin by now. Your wife's bound to discover she was a customer at the bank. You'll have to be prepared to talk about her. Your wife's bound to be interested, to ask you questions, it's only natural.'

'I can cope with that,' Colborn said. 'But I couldn't tell her the rest of it.'

'It's entirely up to you.' Kelsey made a dismissive gesture. He glanced about. 'We might as well sit down. Now—you told us earlier that you didn't know Mrs Franklin before she was married.'

'I did know her very slightly,' Colborn said. 'She was a good deal younger than me.'

'Were you in love with her at that time?'

He shook his head. 'She was just a pretty girl who worked in a shop near the bank. She used to come in for change. I talked to her sometimes.'

'Did you want to marry her at that time?'

'Good heavens, no! I was in no position to think about marrying anyone. My mother was alive then, I was living here with her. She'd been an invalid for years. I had enough to contend with without looking for new responsibilities.'

'And recently, when you took up with Mrs Franklin again, did you want to marry her then?'

Colborn was beginning to look immensely fatigued again. 'No, there was never any question of that, for either of us. It was never that serious.'

'Perhaps you wanted to marry her but she was unwilling?' Kelsey persisted.

Colborn shook his head.

'Did she perhaps agree to marry you and then later change her mind?'

Colborn pressed the fingers of both hands against his temples. 'No, that was never the situation.'

'Is there anything else you want to change in what you told us earlier? When you last saw her, if you knew where she was going for the weekend, and so on?'

Again he shook his head.

'She made no objection when you told her you wanted to end the association?'

'She would have liked to go on with it. She always took it lightly—she wasn't running any risks, it was just an amusement for her. But she understood when I pointed out that it could ruin everything for me, my marriage, my career. We didn't part on bad terms. If I saw her in the bank or if she wanted my advice about some business matter, it was always perfectly friendly, no hard feelings on either side.'

'There was never any awkwardness?'

'Never. She was a very pleasant woman, she had a very nice nature.' He suddenly dropped his head into his hands again. After a few moments he looked up and said with an attempt at composure, 'I can't deny I'm pretty shattered by her death.' His eyes were full of pain. 'It's caught me at a low ebb. It's the shock, coming on top of all the pressure I've been under lately.'

'Do you know of any new men friends she may have had in the last month or two?' Kelsey asked.

'No. I wouldn't expect to know.'

'You made no attempt to find out?'

'Certainly not.'

'Perhaps she told you she'd met someone else, that she wanted to break it off with you? Perhaps that was how you came to part?'

'No, that wasn't the way it ended. I've told you how it was.'

'Did you know she had joined a singles club?'

'No, not exactly, but it doesn't surprise me. She told me she intended going out more, making new friends.'

There was a brief silence, then Kelsey said, 'Jealousy can be a terrible emotion.'

'I was never jealous of her,' Colborn protested. 'It was never on that level, never that strong. The truth is, I was relieved when it was over. I didn't enjoy telling lies to Ruth, it's not in my nature.'

'Were you in touch with Mrs Franklin last Thursday or Friday? In any way at all?'

He shook his head.

'Where were you last Friday afternoon?'

'I told you, I spent the weekend at the bank's place in the country, Danehill Manor. I left the bank at three o'clock. I was given a lift by one of the other managers.'

'We'll have his name,' Kelsey said. 'You realize we have to check everything of this nature.'

There was an appreciable silence.

'If we could have his name,' Kelsey repeated. 'It's a matter of routine.'

There was another silence, then Colborn said, 'I'm afraid this is rather awkward.'

'In what way awkward?'

Colborn made no reply. His face wore a look of great unease.

'You did leave the bank at three and drive to Danehill Manor with your colleague?' Kelsey asked sharply.

'Well, actually, no, it wasn't quite like that,' Colborn said at last. He stared at the wall. 'My colleague rang me at the bank shortly after two to say something had cropped up and he wouldn't be able to get away as early as he'd planned.' He looked at Kelsey. 'I'd prepared a paper to read at the seminar, we all had to do that. I was nervous about it, I hadn't been able to give my mind to it properly. During the morning I kept thinking of other points I might have made but I had no time to do anything about it. I jumped at the chance to do some more work on the paper. I asked my colleague if he'd pick me up at home instead of at the bank. At three o'clock I left the bank and came over here. I worked on the paper till my colleague came to collect me.'

'Did you say anything about this alteration in your plans to any member of your staff? Did you tell your assistant you were going home?'

'No. When I left the bank they took it for granted I was being picked up outside by my colleague. I saw no reason to tell them otherwise.'

'You saw no reason to tell us either.'

He moved his shoulders. 'I didn't actually tell you my colleague picked me up at three outside the bank.'

'You knew that was what we believed. You allowed it to stand.'

'It didn't seem very important.'

'If something similar should crop up in the course of this interview, or any other interview we might have,' Kelsey said crisply, 'perhaps you'd be good enough at the time to correct any misapprehension under which you see me labouring, however unimportant it might appear to you.' Colborn gave a jerky nod.

'Can your wife confirm that you arrived here soon after three and worked on your paper?' Kelsey asked.

'I'm afraid not. She wasn't here at the time, she was at Polesworth all afternoon, for the presentation of purses.' Kelsey knew about the ceremonies at Polesworth. 'She went on afterwards to supper and a musical evening at the house of some friends.'

'At precisely what time did your colleague call for you here?'

'I can be very precise about that.' Colborn's tone began to show animation. 'It was half past five. I looked at the clock when he rang the bell and he commented on the time himself when I opened the door. He was concerned about being late getting to the Manor, he was full of apologies.'

'Right, then,' Kelsey said briskly. 'I hope we've got a proper tale at last. Now, if we might have your colleague's name and where we can get hold of him, we'll be able to confirm what you've told us.'

'For God's sake, don't do that!' Colborn said in alarm. 'It'll be all round head office, they'll wonder what on earth's going on, it'll do my career no good at all.'

'I see your point,' Kelsey said in the tone of a reasonable man. 'But you must see mine. We can't simply take at face value everything anyone cares to tell us. It's all got to be checked.'

'Yes, I see that,' Colborn said. 'But there must be some other way you can check it.' He struck his hands together. 'The garage—you can check there, he'll remember. It's just round the corner from here, the Silver Star. I always go there, the owner's a customer at the bank. When we left here my colleague said he had to get some petrol. We went to the Silver Star and while he was filling up I stood chatting to the owner. I told him where we were off to, that we were late, and he commented on the traffic.' He paused. 'I remember he looked up at the clock and said we'd be right in the thick of the rush hour. You ask him, he'll confirm what I've told you.'

'OK, we'll do that,' Kelsey told him and Colborn exhaled a long breath of relief.

'You remained here, working on your paper, the entire time between returning here shortly after three until your colleague collected you at five-thirty?

'Yes, that's right.'

'You have no reservations about this? No second thoughts? No little excursion from the house you may have overlooked?'

'No,' Colborn answered in a firm, positive tone. 'I was here the entire time.'

Kelsey regarded him reflectively. 'Do you consider yourself an impulsive man?'

Colborn frowned. 'No, I don't think so. I have my impulsive moments, like anyone else, but on the whole I tend to work things out before I take action.'

'Perhaps you were seized by an impulse last Friday afternoon. Perhaps you had some time to spare after you'd worked on your paper. You picked up the phone to have a little chat with Mrs Franklin. Maybe she told you she was going off for the weekend with some new boyfriend. So you went straight out and jumped in your car and drove over to Foxwell Cottage.'

Colborn lowered his head and closed his eyes. His face twitched with fatigue. He shook his head in silence.

'Maybe there was an argument,' Kelsey said. 'A quarrel. Did you strike her?'

'Good God, no!' He raised his stricken face. 'I worshipped the ground she walked on.'

There was a brief, electric silence. 'You worshipped the ground she walked on?' Kelsey echoed. 'I thought it was never very serious, never very intense.'

Colborn sat up. The fatigue had vanished, he looked alert and sharp. 'I don't know why I said that just now, about worshipping her.' He attempted a laugh. 'That's grossly exaggerating it. 'One's over-tired, one gets into a state and says these things—'

There was the sound of the front door opening and closing, footsteps in the hall. Alarm, fierce and naked, flashed across Colborn's face. He sprang to his feet. 'My wife! For God's sake don't let her know any of this!' Kelsey gazed up at him without speaking and Colborn dropped back into his chair. When the study door opened a moment later he was staring straight ahead with a face wiped clear of expression.

Ruth Colborn stood in the doorway. She glanced from her husband to the two policemen, back again at her husband. She wore an elegant summer suit; the shining bands of her beechnut hair were wound smoothly round her well-shaped head.

Colborn got to his feet. He didn't look at his wife. 'This is Chief Inspector Kelsey,' he said. 'And Sergeant Lambert. They're asking about Mrs Franklin. She was a customer at the bank. I expect you've heard what happened.'

'Yes, I did.' She looked at Kelsey. 'Absolutely horrific.' She gave her head a little shake. 'Terrifying.' She suddenly bethought herself. 'May I get you something? Tea? Or a drink?'

'Very good of you, but no, thanks,' Kelsey said. 'We're more or less finished.' He suddenly produced the scarf in its plastic wrapping and thrust it out in front of her. He heard Colborn give a startled gasp. 'Have you ever seen that before?' Kelsey asked Ruth.

She had jerked her head back at his unexpected action. Now she recovered herself and looked down at what he was holding out. 'It's a scarf,' he told her. 'Made of some synthetic material. Have you seen it before?'

She glanced up at him in astonishment and horror, then she stared down again at the scarf with open curiosity, fascinated repulsion.

'Is it the scarf Mrs Franklin—' she began and then stopped.

'Have you seen it before?' Kelsey repeated.

She shook her head. 'No, of course not.' She frowned up at him. 'Where would I have seen it?' Kelsey made no reply. She looked slowly from the Chief to her husband's ravaged face, back again at the scarf. 'What's all this about?' she asked sharply.

There was a brief silence, then Colborn said, 'It's just routine.' His voice was barely steady. 'They have to do it.'

She looked again from face to face. She saw that they were all waiting for her to go. She turned reluctantly. On the threshold she paused and looked back with another slow, searching look, then she went, closing the door behind her.

Colborn dropped into his chair. He looked white and shaken. He stared up at Kelsey with fierce reproach.

Kelsey looked down at him. 'Take my advice,' he said. 'Tell your wife the truth.'

By way of reply Colborn gave a stubborn shake of his head.

'We'll want a full statement from you,' Kelsey told him. 'And we'll need your fingerprints.' Colborn's expression slipped into stupefied dismay. 'All routine,' Kelsey said wearily. 'It's got to be done. I expect you'll be wanting to get back to the bank now. You can call in at the station this evening. Don't leave it too late.'

Colborn made no attempt to move. They left the room and went out of the house. There was no sign of Mrs Colborn.

CHAPTER 5

The two psychiatric institutions in the area were very different from each other: a large old Victorian mental hospital on the outskirts of the village of Chelmswood, some three miles to the north-east of Cannonbridge, currently in the process of being run down, and a much smaller and more modern unit attached to the general hospital in Wychford, now in the full surge of expansion.

It had been Chief Inspector Kelsey's intention to visit both institutions early on Wednesday morning but in the event he was compelled to spend the first couple of hours in briefings and a news conference. It was well after ten before he got away.

It was a warm, sunny day as Sergeant Lambert drove the Chief first to Chelmwood. Where once the hospital had sheltered several hundred patients there were now fewer than sixty, most of them in the eighth or ninth decades of their lives, nearly all either barely mobile or actually bedridden.

Lambert drove up the long winding drive through vast park-like grounds to a massive front entrance. An orderly took them along interminable corridors to the office of the Medical Superintendent, a man within sight of retirement who had been brought in a couple of years ago to oversee the death throes of the establishment.

He agreed unreservedly that the circumstances of the crime definitely suggested a severely disturbed personality and without doubt some of his patients had histories that might have prompted the notion that they could have been connected with the murder, had it not been for their advanced years and general frailty. Of the very few—half-a-dozen at most—still capable of slipping out of hospital to catch a bus or thumb a lift to Foxwell Common, all could be satisfactorily accounted for.

'We can forget Chelmwood,' Kelsey told Lambert as they got back into the car. He sat gazing out at the glittering morning as they drove over to Wychford.

The psychiatric department of the general hospital consisted of a central unit with half-a-dozen bungalows, occupied by patients, standing in the grounds. The bungalows were largely run by the residents, the gardens neat and carefully tended. Such patients as were in view displayed a degree of purpose and stability. They were as a group very much younger than those at Chelmwood, the average age being around thirty-five. They appeared in considerably better health, a good deal fitter and more active.

Here again there were several whose temperaments and

histories might suggest a link with what had happened at Foxwell Cottage. A patient might reach the common without difficulty; there were regular bus and train services to Cannonbridge.

But here again the final conclusion was the same as at Chelmwood: there was no patient even remotely likely to be a candidate for consideration who could not clearly be accounted for last Friday afternoon, in classes of various kinds, therapy groups, treatment sessions, supervised sports and hobbies.

It was turned twelve by the time they set off again for Cannonbridge. Kelsey's appointment with Mrs Franklin's solicitor was for three o'clock. As they approached the outskirts of the town Lambert suddenly said, 'Yesterday morning, at the bank, the assistant manager said Mrs Franklin called in on Friday afternoon about some shares she held. She told him she'd decided to hang on to the shares.'

'What of it?'

'It would seem to suggest that someone at the bank had been discussing the shares with her very recently.'

'You're right,' the Chief said with energy. He glanced at his watch. 'We'll nip along to the bank now.'

The assistant manager was standing by the counter chatting to a customer. He brought his conversation to a swift conclusion and came over to them. 'Just a minor point from our conversation yesterday morning,' Kelsey told him. He explained about the shares.

'Yes, I remember,' the assistant said. 'A customer phoned on the Thursday with instructions to sell some shares, they'd risen rather sharply over the last few days. After I'd rung the broker I remembered that Mrs Franklin held some of the same shares, she'd been wondering a couple of months back about selling them. I spoke to Mr Colborn and suggested I should phone her and tell her it might be a good time to sell. He said he'd phone her himself, there was something else he had to speak to her about. Next day, Friday, she called in here. I was on the counter. She said she'd decided to hang on to the shares.'

Kelsey asked if Mr Colborn could spare him a few

minutes. The assistant went off and came back to say yes, Mr Colborn was free at the moment.

'Chief Inspector,' Colborn said cordially as they came into his office. He stood up and held out a hand. 'Do sit down.' He offered them coffee, which the Chief refused. He had clearly got a grip on himself again. He had lost his exhausted air, his colour was good. His manner was friendly —and armoured, Kelsey noted, as if he would not again so easily be taken by surprise.

The Chief came straight to the point. 'You told us yesterday, in answer to a specific question, that you were not in touch with Mrs Franklin on Thursday or Friday.' Colborn sat looking at the Chief with a watchful, alert look. 'I understand now,' the Chief went on, 'that you did in fact speak to her about some shares.'

'That's right,' Colborn said at once. His manner didn't relax. 'I phoned her on Thursday afternoon.'

'Why didn't you tell us that?'

He made a dismissive gesture. 'It didn't occur to me that you meant anything as brief and trivial as that. I thought you were talking about contacts on a personal level. That was purely a business matter, the call didn't last more than a minute or two. I explained about the shares. She said she'd think about it and let us know.'

'That was all?'

'That was all.'

'Did she mention she was going away for the weekend?'

'She did not.' His control showed no sign of slipping. 'We didn't discuss any kind of personal matter.'

'You had been on intimate terms with her until quite recently. You went out of your way to make a phone call your assistant was on the point of making. But all that passed between you was a brief business conversation.'

'That's right.'

'Why did you go out of your way to make the call? Why not let your assistant handle it?'

He moved his shoulders. 'When things ended between us I made a deliberate decision not to avoid business contacts with her. I could easily have let my assistant handle anything that arose but I thought that would be a mistake. I decided to carry on as if nothing had ever happened between us—as much for her sake as for mine. I wanted her to see she needn't fear any awkwardness, an ordinary professional relationship was perfectly possible.'

'It did cross my mind,' Kelsey said, 'that you might have rung her to suggest going over to discuss the shares in person.'

'No, that never even occurred to me,' Colborn said easily. 'That would have been the last thing I wanted.' He gave the Chief a calm, level glance. 'It wasn't an easy decision, breaking off with her, and she didn't accept it right away. It would have been folly to go back on what we'd decided.'

'You'd been guilty of folly before, as far as she was concerned.'

His look didn't waver. 'All the more reason not to be guilty of it again. It is possible to learn from one's mistakes.'

'It also crossed my mind,' Kelsey said, 'that during the phone conversation she might have mentioned her plans for the weekend, that she was going off with some new boyfriend. Later, on Friday afternoon, when you found yourself at home with some unexpected free time, you could have decided to drive over to Foxwell, try to talk her out of going.'

'That's exactly what you suggested yesterday,' Colborn said in a tone of resigned protest. 'I told you then I didn't drive over to Foxwell.'

'You also told me you had no contact with Mrs Franklin on Thursday or Friday. Today you tell me you phoned her. I wondered if you'd had second thoughts about driving over to the cottage.'

He refused to be riled. 'I've had no second thoughts about that. I most emphatically did not drive over there on Friday afternoon.'

'I ask you now to consider very carefully your answer to this question: Was there any further contact of any kind, however trivial or fleeting, between you and Mrs Franklin after your phone call on Thursday afternoon?'

'There was not.'

'You would swear to that in court?'

'I would.'

The Chief regarded him for some moments and he returned the gaze steadily. Kelsey pushed back his chair and got to his feet.

Colborn also stood up. His manner suddenly lightened. 'I'm sure you'd like to know,' he said with animation, 'that I took your advice yesterday evening and told my wife about Venetia. I told her everything.' He walked with them to the door. 'You were absolutely right, Chief Inspector. I never could have credited it, she took it far better than I could ever have imagined. I'm most grateful, I would never have dreamed of telling her but for what you said. She was upset of course, she was very upset at first, she shed some tears. Then we had a long talk.' He drew a deep breath. 'It's a tremendous load off my mind. I slept properly last night, the first time in days.'

As they walked to the car Kelsey observed sourly to Lambert, 'That must have been an affecting scene at Springfield House yesterday evening, between Colborn and his devoted wife.'

'I can't see how he could possibly have had time to commit the murder,' Lambert felt impelled to point out. 'Roy Franklin drove away from the cottage with the children around five-ten or five-fifteen. At five-forty Colborn was standing on the forecourt of the Silver Star garage on his way to Danehill Manor.' They'd checked with the garage owner who clearly recalled the incident; he had positively and unhesitatingly confirmed Colborn's account of their conversation. Kelsey had pressed him closely about the time but hadn't been able to shake him. 'Colborn had twenty minutes at the outside,' Lambert said. 'To engage Venetia in some kind of exchange, kill her, put her in the car and then drive back to Springfield House in time to appear on his doorstep neat and tidy, composed and calm, ready for the off, when his colleague rang the bell at five-thirty.'

Kelsey gave a grunt. 'Maybe he couldn't have done it if Franklin's timing is right. But Franklin's as capable of a mistake—or deception—as the next man.'

The offices of Beaumont and Maddox, Venetia Franklin's solicitors, were near the centre of Cannonbridge. A secretary showed the two policemen into Beaumont's office, a cool, hushed sanctum furnished in leather and mahogany.

Beaumont was an urbane man of fifty or so with a keen eye and a quiet manner. 'An appalling business,' he said as they took their seats. 'I was speaking to Mrs Franklin only a couple of weeks ago. She seemed happy, full of life, looking forward to the future.'

Kelsey asked if she had made a will.

'She made one about two years ago, after the divorce,' Beaumont told them. A straightforward document, everything left in trust for the two children. It was no large fortune: her car, the furnishings of Foxwell Cottage, her personal possessions, some stocks and shares, money in the bank. 'And of course,' Beaumont added, 'the repayment to her estate of the sum invested by Mrs Franklin in her husband's business.'

Kelsey pricked up his ears. 'What sum was that?'

Beaumont put the tips of his fingers together. 'When Mrs Franklin's father died, a year or two after her marriage, he left her fifteen thousand pounds. Franklin was anxious at that time to buy the property next door to his shop, he wanted to expand his business. He asked his wife to put her legacy towards the purchase price. She consulted me about it—that was when I first had dealings with her. She wanted a proper legal partnership drawn up, a sleeping partnership, of course. Franklin wasn't at all keen on the idea. What he had in mind was an outright gift of the money or, failing that, an interest-free loan to be repaid on his death out of his estate. As far as Mrs Franklin was concerned, I need hardly tell you that a loan of that kind would have amounted to the same thing as an outright gift.'

He inclined his head. 'But Mrs Franklin wasn't to be persuaded and the deed of partnership was drawn up. In the event of her death the partnership would of course be dissolved and her husband would be called on to repay the fifteen thousand pounds to her estate. To cover that eventuality Franklin took out an insurance policy on her life

59

for that amount—a standard procedure in such circumstances.

'In return for her investment Mrs Franklin was to receive a percentage of the annual profits of the business.' He pursed his lips. 'In actual fact she had very little benefit from the partnership while the marriage lasted. The profits were fairly lean for some years and her share, such as it was, was paid into their joint bank account and used for ordinary domestic outgoings.'

He sat back in his chair. 'About three years ago Franklin asked her for a divorce. This came as a surprise to her. She asked me how she would stand with regard to the partnership—and of course with regard to all the other financial aspects, maintenance, ownership of the marital home, and so on—if she were to agree to the divorce. I told her that Franklin would be obliged to pay over to her her share of the business profits. This would be entirely apart from any other payments to her that he might be liable for, and would not, in fact, form any part of the divorce settlement, it was a totally separate matter. By that time, of course, the business was doing a great deal better.' He permitted himself a faint smile. 'As it was Franklin who wanted the divorce, we were able to drive a satisfactory bargain on all points.'

'What is the position now with regard to Foxwell Cottage?' Kelsey wanted to know.

'Franklin bought the cottage on mortgage when they got married; it was always the marital home. At that time he took out a mortgage protection policy so that if he died the outstanding portion of the mortgage would be paid off and the property would pass unencumbered to his widow. Under the divorce settlement Franklin agreed to continue paying the mortgage instalments and the rates and insurance on the cottage, together with any repairs and maintenance that arose. He retained ownership of the property but Mrs Franklin would have the right to live there until her children had grown up and left home. The cottage would then be sold and the proceeds split down the middle. Franklin told us at the time the divorce settlement was being drawn up that he intended—with our agreement—to vary the terms of the mortgage protection policy, so that it would pay out on the death of either of them and the cottage would become the sole property of the survivor. This is by no means uncommon and we offered no objection. So the policy now pays out and the cottage passes absolutely to Franklin.'

Kelsey asked him what relations were like between Franklin and Venetia after the divorce. 'Quite amicable, as these things go,' Beaumont said. 'There was never any argument over access to the children and Franklin paid over promptly all the monies due.' He paused. 'He did write to her recently to ask if she would agree to some reduction in the total annual amount he paid over. He and his second wife wanted to start a family of their own—which would mean not only extra expense but also that his wife would have to give up her job.'

'What reply did Mrs Franklin make to the letter?'

'She didn't answer it herself, she came to see me about it. This was a couple of weeks ago, the last time I had dealings with her. She told me that under no circumstances would she agree to any reduction; on the contrary, she felt that the maintenance for herself and the children must be due for an increase in keeping with inflation. I sent off a letter to Franklin along those lines. I also reminded him that the partnership monies could never be the subject of negotiation, they were Mrs Franklin's by right.' He spread a hand. 'We heard nothing more—nor did we expect to. I considered it a try-on, almost standard practice nowadays a year or two after divorce.'

Kelsey asked if, as far as he knew, Mrs Franklin had had any thought of remarriage.

He tilted back his head. 'She did ask me once, about a year ago, what would be the financial situation if she remarried. She didn't come especially to consult me about that, she came on another matter, a minor dispute with a garage over some repairs to her car. She raised the question of remarriage casually as she was about to leave. I didn't get the impression she was seriously considering the notion but just wanted the information if the matter should ever arise.

'I told her the partnership monies would be in no way affected. Franklin would undoubtedly ask the court to take another look at the maintenance payments; the result would depend on all the circumstances at the time, including the financial situation of her new husband. Her own alimony would probably cease, or be reduced to some purely nominal amount. The question of what would happen to the cottage would probably be resolved by agreement. Assuming that her new husband would be providing a home for herself and the two children, the most likely outcome would be that Foxwell Cottage would be sold, the mortgage paid off and the remainder of the proceeds divided equally between herself and Franklin.'

'What did she say to all that?'

'She treated the matter lightly. She said she thought she'd stick to her freedom, she knew when she was well off. As long as her income was coming from Franklin she felt her position would always be secure. He couldn't help working hard, it was in his nature. He was bound to keep expanding the business, he wouldn't be able to stop himself.'

'What did she mean by that? Why would he want to stop himself expanding the business?'

'To keep the profits down, to keep down the amount he had to pay over to her. It would be cutting off his nose to spite his face, of course, but you'd be surprised how many men in Franklin's situation, shrewd, sensible men in every other respect, take precisely that attitude after a divorce.' He looked dispassionately at Kelsey. 'It goes very hard with a man like Franklin to know that the harder he works the more he has to hand over. And I've yet to meet a shopkeeper who likes parting with money.'

CHAPTER 6

Wednesday was half-closing day in the Northwick Road area. Jane Franklin was out at work and her husband busy in his workshop when the two policemen called.

'Jane should be back any minute now,' Franklin told them as he took them up to the flat, into a small living-room next to the kitchen. Kelsey glanced round as he sat down; a shabby, anonymous room, very clean and neat.

'Your wife works full time?' he asked.

Franklin nodded. 'The hours vary a lot. She's giving up her job, now there are the two children to look after, but she has to work out the full month's notice. She can't just leave, they're short-staffed as it is.' He offered them tea, which the Chief refused. Franklin seemed very sharp and alert today, his manner brisk and restless, the skin stretched tight over his cheekbones. He'll look like a death's head when he's an old man, Sergeant Lambert thought.

'You don't mind if I make a cup of tea for myself?' Franklin said. 'I get parched down in the workshop.' During the next few minutes he darted in and out of the kitchen, replying to the questions shafted at him by the Chief.

'How are the children now?' Kelsey asked.

Franklin appeared in the doorway. 'Hard to judge how they've taken it. They seem right enough on the surface. They don't talk about it at all, or at least not to us. I've no idea if they talk about it to each other.' He vanished into the kitchen. They heard him clattering crockery, clicking open the fridge. 'Of course we've been very careful about what we've told them,' he called back. 'We've given them only the barest outline of what's happened.'

He reappeared in the doorway holding a milk bottle. 'We thought it might be best to break it to them very gradually, keep the worst of it from them altogether—as far as that's possible.' He levelled a glance at the Chief. 'I'd value your opinion on that.'

'You certainly won't be able to keep them in ignorance of the whole thing for ever,' Kelsey said. 'Or even for much longer. You won't be able to shield them from what they'll hear at school. I think perhaps what children can't cope with is the unknown—or the half-known. It breeds fantasy and fear. I believe they can cope much better with reality, however terrible it is.' But he couldn't be sure, he'd never had children of his own.

'We're keeping them away from school for the present,' Franklin told him. 'The headmistress is very good, very understanding. She advised keeping them at home for a few days, till the worst of it's died down.' Behind him the kettle uttered a shrill whistle and he vanished again.

'You realize we shall want to talk to the children?' Kelsey called out. 'We'll try not to upset them too much, we'll make it as brief as possible. And of course you and your wife will be present.'

Franklin came into the room, carrying a cup of tea. He perched himself on the arm of a chair and began to drink. 'Yes, we realize that. They're out in the local park just now, with Sharon—the girl who's helping to look after them while Jane's still working. Sharon's a good, sensible girl, she's the daughter of a neighbour.'

'We thought you'd want to know the results of the post mortem,' Kelsey said. Franklin stared down at the ancient carpet as the Chief gave a brief summary. 'It all goes to confirm the time of death,' Kelsey concluded. 'It must have taken place very soon after you left with the children.'

Franklin made no comment beyond a couple of nods. He drew a little trembling breath, raised his cup and drained it.

'One or two points you can help us with,' Kelsey added. 'In the way of general information. It all goes to build up the picture.'

'Any way at all I can be of help,' Franklin assured him.

Kelsey asked if he had known Venetia long before he married her.

He shook his head. 'It was rather a whirlwind affair. I met her at a dance. We were married a few months later.'

Kelsey asked if he recalled the names of any boyfriends Venetia might have had before he came on the scene. Franklin pondered. 'I can't recall anyone in particular, no one she was serious about. She was a popular girl, very pretty, she had a lot of boyfriends around her own age.' He looked all at once as if he might burst into tears.

'After the divorce, when she opened a new bank account, do you know of any particular reason why she should choose

64

the Allied Bank? Perhaps she knew a member of staff? Or the manager?'

'Not that I know of.' He appeared steady again now. 'Colborn, isn't it—the Allied manager? Springfield House chap, his wife's always in the local paper. I suppose Venetia might have come across him or his wife at some charity do, but that would be about all.'

'I'd like you to take your time and think very carefully about this next point,' Kelsey said with emphasis. 'It's extremely important. I'd like you to wipe from your mind what you've already told us about it, what you may have thought about it since Monday, and consider the matter again, completely afresh: At exactly what time did you drive away from Foxwell Cottage with the children on Friday afternoon?'

Franklin lowered his head and closed his eyes. He remained silent for some little time before he spoke, still with his eyes closed, his head lowered. 'I left the shop at four-thirty and came up here. I made a cup of tea and had a wash, then I drove out to Foxwell. The traffic wasn't exceptional in any way. I didn't look at my watch or check the time when I got to the cottage and Venetia didn't make any comment on the time. I think it must have been pretty close to five, say five minutes either way. I can't see that I could have spent more than ten minutes at the cottage, fifteen at the outside. I didn't check the time when I left but I think it would have been between five-five and five-twenty.' He opened his eyes and sat up. 'That's as near as I can make it.'

'I'm much obliged to you,' Kelsey said. 'We'll check with your assistant about the time you left the shop—purely routine.'

'By all means,' Franklin said. 'He's not here just now, of course, early closing.' Kelsey asked for his address and Franklin gave it.

The phone rang suddenly on a table by the wall. Franklin went over and lifted the receiver. 'Oh—it's you,' he said after a moment on a wary note. He put a hand over the mouthpiece and glanced at the Chief. 'Mrs Norton, Jane's mother.' His tone and the expression on his face suggested no excess of warmth towards the lady.

He removed his hand from the mouthpiece. 'It's very good of you to offer,' he said into the phone, 'but we're managing pretty well. Sharon's a great help, she's very reliable, very good with the children.' There was an appreciable pause during which he drew a long soundless sigh and glanced again at the Chief, with a look of weary resignation.

'It's very kind of you,' he said into the phone, 'but running you back and forth in the car every morning and evening would take up a great deal of time, and I'm afraid that's one thing we're never very well blessed with, even at the best of times.' After another interval he said crisply, 'I'm sorry but I'll have to ring off, I've got the police here, trying to talk to me . . . Yes, yes, I'm sure Jane will ring you later and let you know what's happening.' He replaced the receiver and blew out a long breath, he stood shaking his head. 'She's a bit of a trial,' he said. 'She'd talk the hind leg off a donkey, given half a chance.' He went back to his chair and dropped into it. 'She's a widow, her husband's been dead some years. She's still got plenty of energy, she gets out and about, belongs to this and that, but what she'd really like is to get tangled up in our lives, and I'm certainly not having that.' He grimaced. 'Fortunately she hasn't got a car, that's one almighty blessing. She never learned to drive and now she feels it's too late to start, thank the Lord. If she had a car she'd be over here every five minutes, there'd be no way on God's earth we could stop her.'

'Does she live near?' Kelsey asked.

'Near enough,' Franklin said with fervour. 'Strettisham, on the outskirts. A pleasant enough area, the Orchard Way development, built between the wars, nice, solid, little houses. Jane was born there, she grew up there. We go over now and then and we have her over here sometimes. Fortunately she detests travelling on buses, they make her feel sick, so she's forced to rely on being picked up by me.'

Down on street level there was the sound of a door opening and closing. Franklin sprang to his feet. 'That'll be Jane now.' He crossed the room and opened the door leading into the passage. 'Up here,' he called down. A minute or two later when there were steps on the stairs he called out again. 'I've got Chief Inspector Kelsey here.' Sergeant Lambert tried to detect any warning note in his voice but couldn't be sure.

Jane came into the room carrying her crash helmet. Lambert ran his eye over her with interest; she looked as if she might have captained the school hockey team in her day. She acknowledged the introductions with a set, unsmiling face. There was about her a marked air of strain and tension. Her eyes looked heavy, faintly bloodshot, as if she were short of sleep.

'I take it the children aren't back yet?' she asked her husband.

'No sign of them.' He explained that the Chief Inspector wished to speak to the children in their presence. 'And afterwards I'd like to speak to the two of you together,' Kelsey put in.

'In that case I'll ask Sharon to stay on and take the children into the garden after you've spoken to them,' she told the Chief. 'I don't like them to be on their own for the present.'

They all took their seats, Jane sitting tense and erect on a straight-backed chair. 'You've just missed your mother,' Franklin said. 'She was on the phone, wanting to come over.' She turned her head towards him with a frowning question in her look. 'It's all right,' he assured her. 'I put her off. I said you'd phone later.'

She gave a little nod, her face relaxed fractionally.

Downstairs a door opened and closed. 'That'll be the children.' Jane got slowly and heavily to her feet. 'I'll go down and have a word with Sharon.'

No one spoke after she left the room. Sergeant Lambert glanced idly about. No pictures, no photographs, no ornaments, no mirrors, no plants or flowers. The place had the air of some temporary habitation. But no dust or smears either, everything polished to a gleaming finish. A single good item took his eye, a clock on the mantelshelf, old-fashioned, handsome, with a silvery face and a mellow tick.

Jane came back into the room with the two children. They appeared self-possessed, behaved with impeccable manners when she introduced them. Simon was tall for his eight years, slightly built and fine-boned. His face wore a closed, wary look. Katie, two years younger, was short and chubby, very pretty, fair-haired and blue-eyed, with a friendly manner and an artless, confiding smile.

Franklin explained that the Chief Inspector would like to talk to them about last Friday afternoon. Simon gave a series of little nods in reply; Katie merely smiled again, looking up at the Chief with curiosity and interest. She sat down near Jane, on an old leather pouffé. Simon sat near his father, his hands tightly clasped on his knees, his shoulders hunched, his arms close to his sides.

'Don't worry,' the Chief said gently. 'There aren't any right or wrong answers. Just tell me what you remember, as best you can.' Simon gave another series of little nods. Katie tilted her head back, smiling cheerfully up at Kelsey.

He took Simon through Friday afternoon, from the time when Venetia had picked them up at school. In a flat monotone Simon described their return to the cottage, tea on the terrace, what his mother had said and done, how he and Katie were looking forward to the weekend in Northwick Road.

Katie began to get the hang of what was going on, she started to join in. She had been looking forward to the funfair, she told the Chief, particularly to riding on the roundabout with the horses, and driving in the Dodgem cars. The Chief displayed encouraging interest. Simon's manner began to relax as Katie chatted, he began to open up. 'When we finished tea,' he said in a lighter, easier tone, 'Daddy came in the car to pick us up.' He described how he and Katie had run into the cottage, had gone upstairs to wash, how they had been as quick as they could, had run downstairs again. 'Daddy put the cases in the car. Mummy came over to the car with us. We got in and she waved as we went off.' He displayed no agitation. 'I looked back and waved at her. I saw her go back to the terrace.'

'Then Daddy stopped the car,' Katie said, smiling

broadly. 'He told us to stay in the car, we mustn't get out. He said he wouldn't be long. Then he got out of the car and went back to the cottage.'

CHAPTER 7

The room grew very still. On the mantelshelf the clock ticked loudly. The sound of traffic floated up from the road; down on the pavement a lad went by, whistling. Franklin jerked himself up in his chair. Without looking at him, Kelsey motioned him not to speak.

'Was your father away long?' he asked Katie.

She pondered. 'Quite a bit,' she said at last. 'While he was away I told Simon about cutting out the coloured paper at school and all the shapes I made with it. And he told me about his picture being the best in the class and it was going to hang on the wall for a whole week.'

'What happened when your father came back to the car?'

She pondered again. 'Nothing happened. He just said he was sorry he'd been so long. He got in and we went to the fair. When we got there he bought us some ice-cream. I had strawberry and Simon had vanilla.'

Simon's cheeks had grown flushed, his eyes very bright. He turned fiercely on Katie. 'That wasn't last Friday, that was the time before.'

She was in no way abashed. 'The fair was last Friday, I know it was.'

'Yes, of course the fair was last Friday, but the other bit, about Daddy getting out of the car and going back to the cottage, and you and me sitting in the car talking about school, that was the time before when we came here for the weekend. There wasn't any fair that weekend. When Daddy got back in the car that time he brought us straight here.'

Katie began to look confused. She turned her head from side to side, looking down at the carpet, her face puckering. Simon looked across at the Chief. 'She's got it mixed up with the time before,' he said earnestly. His fists were tight

69

clenched, pressing down on his knees. 'Last Friday Daddy drove straight away from the cottage, he never went back there. We didn't stop anywhere till we got to the fair.'

Katie's face cleared. She raised her head and smiled at the Chief. 'I got it mixed up with the time before,' she echoed. 'But I can remember when we came back here after the fair. Jane was in the bedroom, lying down. Daddy went in to see her. He came out again and said she was tired, she'd been having a little sleep, she had to work very hard. After a bit she came out of the bedroom and I helped her to lay the table.'

Kelsey asked Simon if he knew of anyone hanging round the cottage in recent weeks, if he had noticed anyone himself or if his mother or any of the neighbours had mentioned anything. Simon shook his head; no, there had been nothing.

'I don't think we need keep the children any longer,' Kelsey told Jane. Throughout she had sat upright and unmoving, looking straight ahead, her face set and blank.

'Oh—yes,' she said, as if jerked out of some absorption of her own. She stood up. 'Come along,' she said to the children. They followed her obediently from the room.

Kelsey got to his feet and walked over to the window. He stood looking down into the road, at the withered heaps of blossom along the gutters. His attitude didn't invite conversation.

Jane came back into the room and Kelsey turned from the window. She looked tired and pale. She took something from her shoulder-bag lying on a table. A small bottle, as far as he could see. She went into the kitchen without a word, closing the door behind her. He heard a tap running, the clink of a glass set down on the draining-board.

She came back into the room empty-handed and took her seat. She didn't glance at her husband or the two policemen, she simply sat waiting for everything to start again, with the air of someone who tells herself it must end some time, it can't go on for ever.

Kelsey sat down again. 'And now,' he said briskly to Franklin, 'did you in fact stop the car and go back to the cottage last Friday afternoon?' He held up a hand as Franklin opened his mouth. 'Think carefully before you say anything. You may have gone back for some perfectly good reason, something entirely trivial perhaps, or something less trivial but still entirely harmless, perfectly understandable.'

'I did not go back,' Franklin said clearly and firmly, without hesitation. 'For any reason at all. Simon's quite right, Katie has got last Friday mixed up with the time before when I brought the children here for the weekend. I did go back to the cottage that time.'

'Why was that?'

'We had a clock here in this room, a cheap modern thing, unreliable. It finally packed up. I told Jane I'd ask Venetia if she'd mind if I took that clock from the cottage.' He indicated the handsome clock on the mantelshelf. 'It belonged to my father. When he died my mother went down south to live with an old friend, she got rid of most of her household stuff. Venetia and I were living at Foxwell, we'd already furnished the cottage. We could only take one or two pieces and the rest was sold. I kept that clock. I always liked it, and it reminded me of my father. When we were divorced everything at the cottage went to Venetia. That previous Friday, when I was driving off from the cottage with the children, I suddenly remembered the clock, I'd intended asking Venetia about it. So I stopped the car and went back. I asked Venetia if I could take the clock and she said she'd have to think about it. The following week I went over there on the Sunday to take the children out for the day. She said I could have the clock so I took it then.'

'To get back to last Friday,' Kelsey said. 'It would have been perfectly natural for you to go back to the cottage to speak to Venetia about the letter you had received from her solicitor. I doubt if you'd want to discuss that kind of thing in front of the children.' Lambert saw the tiny movement of Jane's head as she noted the fact that they had spoken to Venetia's solicitor. 'It would have been easy for an argument to start up on that kind of topic,' Kelsey went on. 'Easy for you to lose your temper.'

I did not get out of the car and go back to the cottage last Friday,' Franklin repeated stubbornly. 'You surely can't pay serious attention to what a six-year-old child thinks she remembers about something that happened last week.'

We can't entirely disregard it either, Kelsey thought. He stood up and walked across to where Jane sat, still gazing straight ahead. She didn't register his approach by any glance or movement. He suddenly produced the brown paisley scarf in its plastic wrapping and held it out before her.

'Do you recognize this scarf?' he asked.

She didn't flinch or gasp, she appeared in no way surprised. She displayed none of the avid curiosity or fascinated repulsion the scarf had evoked in others. She gave it a detached, clinical glance. After a moment she shook her head slowly.

'You're certain?' Kelsey pressed her.

She looked down again at the scarf. 'Quite certain.' Her voice was steady, she seemed controlled and armoured.

Kelsey looked across at Franklin. 'We'll need statements,' he told him. 'And fingerprints.'

'You won't need Jane's fingerprints,' Franklin said at once. 'She's never been inside the cottage. She never even met Venetia.'

The Chief looked at him in silence. There was no reason to suppose that whoever killed Venetia had ever set foot inside the cottage. It seemed certain that she had been killed on the terrace. The fracture at the back of the skull was consistent with a fall on the flagstones caused by the blow to the chin. Particles of soil, gravel, dust, had been driven into the scalp abrasions, into her hair, the fibres of her shirt and jeans. But the Chief said nothing of this now to the Franklins. He glanced down at Jane who continued to stare ahead.

'Were you in fact ever inside the cottage?' he asked her. 'If you were—for whatever reason—we'll need to know. It's to your own benefit to tell us the truth.'

There was a brief pause. She did go inside the cottage at some time, Lambert thought. She doesn't know if we know or not, she doesn't know if Venetia mentioned it to her solicitor and he mentioned it to us.

Franklin looked across at Jane with a frown. 'I did go inside once,' she said at last. A look of consternation flashed across Franklin's face.

'When was that?' Kelsey asked.

'Last Thursday lunch-time, about half past one.' Her voice was steady, tensely controlled. At close quarters Kelsey saw that the skin of her forehead was lightly patterned with a rash, tiny rosy spots. 'She knew who I was,' Jane added. 'She looked surprised to see me.'

'What did she say?'

'She said: "Well, hello, look who's here." She asked me why I'd come. I told her I wanted to speak to her, woman to woman, that writing solicitors' letters was no good, nothing that mattered ever got said that way.' She began to swallow convulsively. She fell silent, then managed to get a grip of herself again and continued. 'She said I'd better come inside. She'd been having her lunch in the kitchen, she'd just about finished. She gave me some coffee. We sat down at the table and talked.'

'What about?'

'I explained about wanting to start a family of my own, that I wasn't getting any younger. I hoped she might understand, having children herself. I told her I knew she was legally entitled to all she got from Roy, but she had a good standard of living, a good deal better than we have, perhaps she wouldn't mind reducing it a little to help another woman.'

'What did she say to that?'

She clasped her hands tightly on her lap. 'She listened quietly, she didn't interrupt. At the end she stood up and took the coffee cups over to the sink. She said: "You've said what you came to say. I can only tell you I'm sorry for you, but it's your problem, not mine. It's nothing whatever to do with me." I said I knew that, but she could help me solve my problem if she would. She said: "There's no earthly reason why I should. The only reason our paths ever crossed is because you went to bed with my husband while he was married to me. I can't see how that gives you any claim to my assistance." She said she had nothing to add to what

73

her solicitor had said in his letter. I realized Roy was right, it was a waste of time trying to talk to her, so I left. She came to the door with me and watched me go. She said: "I advise you not to come here again. If you have anything further to say to me, it must be said through my solicitor." She sounded very cold. I got the impression the only reason she'd asked me inside was pure curiosity. She'd never had the slightest intention of considering what I'd come to say.'

'You appear to have behaved in a very restrained fashion,' Kelsey observed. 'Didn't you resent her attitude?'

The muscles stiffened along her jaw. 'It would have been very easy to lose my temper but that would only have made things worse. So I controlled myself and left. There was nothing else for it.'

The Chief remained standing by her chair. He looked across at Franklin. 'Did Jane tell you she had gone to see Venetia, and the kind of reception she'd got? Was that why you got out of the car and went back to the cottage? To tackle Venetia about it?'

'I did not get out of the car and go back to the cottage,' Franklin repeated wearily. 'I had no idea Jane had been to see Venetia. This is the first I've heard of it.'

'Venetia could have mentioned it to you when you came to pick up the children.'

'I particularly asked her not to tell Roy about it,' Jane put in. 'I'd told him I thought of going over to see her but he wouldn't hear of it. I still thought it was worth a try, so I decided to go without telling him. If it worked, he'd be delighted; if it didn't, he needn't know.' She talked rapidly now, looking earnestly up at the Chief. Her face had lost its set, blank look.

Kelsey stood looking down at her. 'Perhaps you were tempted to return to the cottage, to make some fresh appeal.'

She shook her head. 'Once was enough. There would have been no point in going again. I could see there'd be no shifting her, she'd made up her mind.'

'I put to you a possible course of action. You went over there again on Friday afternoon. You waited on the common, under the trees, till you saw your husband leave with the children. Then you went down to tackle Venetia again.'

She looked appalled. She said nothing but shook her head with force.

'That's a monstrous suggestion,' Franklin said. He didn't sound agitated or fiercely angry, only immeasurably fatigued. He closed his eyes and leaned back in his chair. His features looked very sharp and bony. Sergeant Lambert had the strong feeling of the two of them being a pair, united, disciplined, extremely wary.

'How did you spend Friday afternoon?' Kelsey asked Jane.

'She was working,' Franklin broke in at once.

The Chief gave him a quelling glance. 'If you'd let your wife speak for herself.' Franklin subsided, biting his lip.

Jane gave the Chief the address of the agency client with whom she had spent the greater part of Friday afternoon; the address was a good five miles from Foxwell Common. 'She's an elderly woman,' she added. 'She broke her arm in a fall, it's in plaster.' She went there two afternoons a week. 'I left at five and did some shopping, then I came back here.'

Kelsey asked for the addresses of the shops she had visited.

'I didn't visit any shops,' she told him. 'I bought fruit and vegetables, and eggs, at stalls in the open-air market.' She halted. 'Oh yes—I did call in at one shop, a shoe shop, to ask if Roy's shoes were ready. I'd taken them in to be mended, they were supposed to be ready by Friday. I called in just before closing time. The girl told me the shoes weren't ready.' She smiled faintly. 'I think she'd remember me, I made rather a fuss about it.' She gave him the address of the shop. 'I got back here just after six. One of the repairmen was pulling up in his van. I spoke to him for a moment, I asked after his little girl, she'd been off school with a cold. Then I came up here and made a cup of tea. I prepared the supper, then I went into the bedroom to have a nap before Roy got back with the children.'

'Do you often take a nap at that time of day?'

'I very rarely take a nap at any time of day,' she retorted.

'But I'd been on late shifts two or three times recently. I wanted to be fresh for the children.'

Kelsey glanced from Jane to Roy. 'You both benefit considerably by Venetia's death,' he observed.

Franklin said nothing. He made a weary gesture as if to say: That doesn't mean we had anything to do with her death.

Silence fell, deepened. The atmosphere was filled with growing tension.

'Why did you take Jane with you in the car on Monday afternoon when the school phoned about the children?' Kelsey suddenly asked Franklin. 'You told us that Jane had never met Venetia, had never wanted to meet her. Perhaps you knew there was no longer any possibility of the two women meeting. You needed Jane to drive the children home from the cottage. You knew you would have to stay there, phone the police, wait till they arrived.'

'It was entirely my idea to go in the car with Roy to the school,' Jane put in before Roy had a chance to answer. 'He wanted me to stay here to give a hand in the shop while he was gone.'

'Then why did you insist on going? Was it because you knew what he would find at the cottage? You wanted to be there to drive the children home, away from it all?'

She shook her head again, with agitation. 'It was just that I was worried. I was afraid something was wrong. It was the first time Venetia had failed to collect the children.'

The Chief glanced across at Franklin. 'When you reached the cottage, why did you tell Jane and the children to stay in the car? Did you know what they were likely to discover if they went over and looked in Venetia's car?'

Franklin gazed at the Chief with infinite languor as if he could scarcely any longer be bothered to explain, to defend himself. 'As soon as I drove in and saw Venetia's car,' he said in a flat, dull tone, 'I knew something wasn't right. If she was back from her weekend why hadn't she driven straight to the school, or at least phoned them to explain what was happening? Why hadn't she answered the phone when the school rang? It was simply instinct, to keep the children in the car till I'd had a chance to look round, see if there was something amiss. Jane had to stay in the car to make sure the children stopped there.'

There was another tension-filled silence. 'You told us,' Kelsey said to Franklin, 'that after the divorce relations were always amicable between yourself and Venetia, there was no hassle, no conflict. Now it seems things were otherwise.'

Franklin gave a slow shake of his head. 'No, not really. Jane's thirty-fifth birthday was coming up. She seemed to feel it was a landmark, that if she didn't start a family soon, it would be too late.' He attempted a grin. 'You know what women are like when they get broody.' His glance invited understanding and support from Kelsey, the rational-minded male against the whims and moods of the female. Kelsey gave him back a blank stare.

'You took Jane's attitude sufficiently seriously to write to Venetia about it,' he said.

Franklin grimaced. 'Why not? I had nothing to lose. If Venetia wouldn't agree, I intended asking my own solicitor to apply to the court for a reduction in the alimony. I thought we'd probably get it if I explained how things stood. At the time of the divorce my solicitor told me not to worry about the size of the settlement. He said: "You can try for a reduction in a year or two, everyone does. You can tell them the tale."'

'I put it to you that far from not worrying about it, you bitterly resented the amount you were compelled to pay over to Venetia.'

'I did not resent it.' Franklin's tone grew warmer, more energetic. 'I wasn't overjoyed but I accepted it, it's the way the system works. Everyone knows it's loaded against the male, it's no use getting steamed up over it.' He moved his head. 'Actually, I thought Venetia behaved very well over the divorce, a good deal better than most women do. She looked after her own interests of course, she'd have been a fool not to.' He gave the Chief a level look. 'And in any case, I was sure she'd marry again before long.'

'I put it to you,' Kelsey said, 'that you knew she had no

intention of marrying again, that she had made it plain to you. Made it plain that she knew when she was well off, free and independent, with a secure income paid over by you.'

'She never said anything of the kind to me. We never talked about her remarrying. I wouldn't have dreamed of raising the matter, and I'm sure she wouldn't have discussed it with me if I had.'

As they got back into the car a little later Kelsey said sourly, 'The only thing all that goes to prove is that we can take with a hefty pinch of salt anything Franklin tells us about the time he left Foxwell Cottage on Friday afternoon.' He glanced at his watch. He intended nipping over to Strettisham, having a chat with Mrs Norton, Jane's mother, that lonely chatterbox. But first he wanted a word with Franklin's assistant, see what he had to say about Franklin's movements.

The address Franklin had given them turned out to be that of a large old house let out in bedsits. The assistant, a pimply, gangling youth of eighteen or nineteen, was getting ready to go out. When the two policemen paused outside the door of his room he was standing in his underpants in front of his wardrobe, freshly washed and shaved, drenched in cologne, trying to decide between the merits of two pairs of trousers. At the sound of the Chief Inspector's peremptory rap he sprang into the pair he was holding and went to the door. He gazed out at Kelsey without speaking, he didn't appear at all surprised. His chin was bedecked with tufts of bloodstained cottonwool.

Kelsey revealed his identity and asked if he might step inside. He explained his errand.

Yes, the assistant recalled Friday afternoon. Mr Franklin had left the shop to go upstairs to the flat at four-thirty, he remembered that clearly.

'Why is that?' Kelsey wanted to know, 'What makes you remember it so clearly?'

He appeared taken aback. 'I don't know,' he mumbled after a moment or two. 'I just do remember it.'

'I wondered,' Kelsey said blandly, 'if it was because Mr Franklin rang you just now to remind you of it.'

A tide of red flamed suddenly in the assistant's face. The effect, in conjunction with the cottonwool sprouts, was striking. He seemed bereft of speech.

'Mr Franklin did phone you just now?' Kelsey said in the same bland tone.

The assistant recovered his powers of speech. 'Yes, he did. To remind me to be specially early in the morning,' he added on a note of inspiration. His face relaxed, he looked pleased with himself.

'And why must you be specially early in the morning?' Kelsey wanted to know.

The inspiration didn't appear to have taken him as far as that. His face fell again, he glanced nervously about the room. 'It could be a busy morning,' he mumbled at last.

'When Mr Franklin phoned you just now,' Kelsey said relentlessly, 'he did remind you about the time he left the shop on Friday afternoon?'

Again the assistant glanced around. The tip of his tongue darted about his lips. 'He may have mentioned it,' he conceded. 'Just in passing.'

'And without all this phoning and prompting,' Kelsey said, suddenly menacing, 'what precisely do you yourself remember of last Friday afternoon?'

But the assistant had got his second wind by now. 'Mr Franklin left the shop at half past four,' he repeated stubbornly, without hesitation. The Chief regarded him in silence and he gave back an unwinking, mulish stare.

The Chief wasted no more time on him. He turned without another word and left the house. 'Ridiculous booby,' he said to Lambert as they went down the path to the gate. He abruptly dismissed the booby from his thoughts. 'Over to Strettisham,' he instructed. 'Orchard Way.'

The telephone directory disclosed only one Mrs Norton living on the Orchard Way estate. It was turned six when Lambert drew up before the house, a nice, solid, little dwelling, as Franklin had said, the front garden bright with tulips.

Mrs Norton was watching television. She came hastening to the door the moment she heard the bell, delighted to see them, to see anyone. A short, stocky woman in her late fifties, with an air of boundless, restless energy. When Kelsey introduced himself and Lambert her broad, pudgy face glowed with pleasure.

Kelsey explained that he had happened to be in her son-in-law's flat when she had phoned just now. He added, in a matey tone overlaid with unsubtle flattery, that it had occurred to him that a lady of her maturity might very well be able to offer some useful observations, the kind of insight that couldn't be expected from younger folk.

She clasped her hands before her impressive chest. 'Anything at all I can do to help,' she cried. 'You're more than welcome.' She flung the door wide, her face creased in smiles. She took them into a sitting-room, chintzy and ingle-nooky, furnished and decorated to an extent that Kelsey would scarcely have believed possible. The furniture shone like glass. A vast arrangement of flowers screened the hearth. In every direction the eye was met with festoons and swags, ruches and frills. Every horizontal surface was crammed with ornaments, the walls were crowded with pictures, photographs, calendars. Lambert felt an imminent threat of claustrophobia.

'What a dreadful business!' Mrs Norton said as they all sat down. Her face took on a brief ritual look of appalled horror and then resumed its expression of lively pleasure and keen curiosity.

'Of course, as I told Roy over the phone, the moment I heard of it,' she declared with total conviction, 'it's someone from Chelmwood who did it. I'll lay you any money you care to name. I've said to Jane, many a time, that hospital should never—'

'Forgive me,' Kelsey broke in, 'but I think it better not to speculate. I'm sure you understand.'

She was brought up sharp. 'Oh—yes—of course,' she said in a tone of profound disappointment. She recovered swiftly. 'I do think they ought to let me go over to the flat to lend a hand. I know Jane's very competent but she's not made of iron. There's a limit to what any one human being can be expected to do. I bet you anything you like she comes out in that rash of hers before many days go by, she always gets it when she's overstressed. It got that bad a couple of months back, she had to go to the doctor with it. Depression and anxiety, he said it was—and doing too much. It came out all over her face and neck.'

Kelsey asked her if she had ever met Venetia.

She shook her head with vigour. 'No, never. Nor did Jane. Nor ever wanted to, either. Jane was so certain—at the time of the divorce—that Venetia would marry again, a young woman with her looks. She never thought they'd have to go on paying out all this alimony as long as this.' She leaned forward. 'Jane didn't even know about the partnership business till they were all well on the way to the divorce court and it was a bit late to think about pulling out. Even then she didn't quite realize all it would mean for her, that they wouldn't be able to afford a family of their own.'

She gave the Chief a look full of significance. 'I don't know that Jane would ever have got into the situation in the first place if she'd realized all that.' She jerked her head. 'But what really riled her, what made her hopping mad, was the way the court takes the second wife's earnings into account when they fix the maintenance for the first wife. Can you credit that? One woman working to help support another woman younger than herself! In this day and age! Jane scrimping and saving, working like a galley-slave, and Venetia swanning about spending money like water and looking for more.' She flung out a hand. 'That's not the whole of it, either. Did you know Roy has another lot of money to find every month, to pay over to his mother?'

No, Kelsey didn't know.

'It was in his father's will,' Mrs Norton explained with relish. 'Roy inherited the business on that condition. His mother lives down south now, with some woman friend. I've never met her, of course, but Jane has, and she wasn't very taken with her. She and Roy go down to see her every so often.' She pulled a face. 'I gather she's one of these women who practically live at the doctor's, make a hobby out of aches and pains. Pills for this, that and the other.'

She gave a long sigh. 'At least some good will come out

of all this. Jane and Roy can buy a proper house at last, instead of living in that dreadful flat.' She pursed her lips. 'It's my opinion that marriage would have folded up if things had gone on like that for much longer. Young women, they fall in love, they think that's all there is to it. They haven't the foggiest notion what they're letting themselves in for when they take on a man that's been married before, that's got the first family hanging round his neck.'

CHAPTER 8

The inquest on Venetia Franklin was set down for eleven o'clock on Thursday morning. At twenty minutes to eleven Chief Inspector Kelsey was still closeted with the Superintendent, discussing various aspects of the investigation. Downstairs in the front reception area Sergeant Lambert sat waiting, glancing through a copy of the local weekly paper, the *Courier,* that someone had left on a table. The paper came out on Thursdays; today it carried a long account of the case. He skimmed rapidly through it but was disappointed to find no mention of his name.

He looked through the pages a second time, more slowly. A double centre spread gave a detailed report of the ceremonies last Friday at Polesworth. Photographs of local worthies, the Viscountess dignified and smiling, the children important and resplendent in new outfits, their hair gleaming, handing over the purses. Standing a little to one side, Ruth Colborn, handsome and elegant, guiding the children, looking down at them with a protective, proprietorial air.

Five minutes later the Chief Inspector came out of the Super's office. On his way downstairs he encountered a constable he had earlier despatched to check Jane Franklin's account of how she had spent Friday afternoon. Kelsey asked how the constable had got on. No problems, it seemed, everything checked. Jane had left the home of the elderly woman patient on the dot of five. The patient had signed the agency card as she always did. She had looked up at the clock and noted down the time on the card; she was always most particular about this, she had no intention of being overcharged. The constable was positive her memory could be relied on. 'She's very much on the ball,' he assured the Chief. 'Not in the least senile or dotty.'

The shop assistant remembered Mrs Franklin calling in just before closing-time, at five-thirty; she clearly recalled the somewhat heated exchange about the shoe repairs. And Franklin's service engineer was equally positive about his conversation with Jane a few minutes after six.

Sergeant Lambert had abandoned his newspaper and was pacing up and down, glancing at his watch, when at last the Chief came striding into the hall. Mercifully the traffic was light and they reached the courthouse with a minute or two to spare.

The proceedings were brief and formal, the inquest being opened and adjourned. The body was released for burial and Roy Franklin had a word with the Chief about this afterwards. He wanted to arrange the funeral as speedily as possible, for next Monday, if he could. Mrs Stacey, Venetia's mother, had not attended the inquest. She was leaving all the arrangements for the funeral to Franklin, her only stipulation being that it should take place as quietly as could be managed. Franklin had decided on cremation and the Chief told him there was a crematorium in a town some twelve miles the other side of Wychford, far enough from Cannonbridge to keep the curious and sensation-seeking away, and reasonably convenient for Mrs Stacey to attend.

Jane Franklin stood silently by while Roy spoke to the Chief. Sergeant Lambert looked up at the little group as he waited at the foot of the courthouse steps. Jane held herself rigid and motionless, her gaze lowered, her face pale, set in lines of deep weariness. She was very soberly dressed and looked older and plainer. Franklin, by contrast, in spite of his dark suit and black tie, had a lively, darting look, an alert, businesslike air. His exchange with the Chief was briskly matter-of-fact. He might have been an undertaker making arrangements for the funeral of some total stranger.

There had been no sign of Philip Colborn at the inquest

—not that the Chief had expected him to appear. When the Franklins had gone off to their car Kelsey went slowly down the steps. Without haste or enthusiasm he walked with Lambert to the car park. It was back to the station now, back to the tedious, time-consuming business of attempting to compose as complete a picture as possible of Venetia Franklin's lifestyle over the last few months. Friends and acquaintances still to be talked to; clubs, organizations, travel firms to be questioned. Every address book and phone book in Foxwell Cottage, every item of correspondence in desk and drawer, to be minutely gone through. Out of the whole mass of it possibly nothing at all. But possibly also, the one, tiny, invaluable, diamond point of fact that would light up the entire investigation.

At this stage of a murder investigation the Chief made little distinction between the Sabbath and the other six days of the week. This Sunday his lunch consisted of a cup of coffee and a sandwich. By a quarter past two he was behind his desk again, contemplating the results of the activity of the last few days.

It would seem that after the divorce Venetia had almost completely withdrawn from even such sketchy community activities as she had engaged in during her marriage. The married couple who had sent her the postcard had returned from their Italian holiday yesterday evening and the Chief had spoken to them this morning. They were a childless couple, a good deal older than Venetia, living in a flat in a superior residential suburb of Cannonbridge. An earnest, high-minded couple, active in local church and community work. They had strongly disapproved of Roy's conduct over the divorce and had tried afterwards to take a helpful, supportive interest in Venetia. The wife had done her best to persuade Venetia to join various groups, take up voluntary work, begin some kind of training for a job, but all without success. Venetia had seen less and less of the pair and they hadn't laid eyes on her for the last two or three months. She had never at any time discussed her private life with them; they knew nothing of any men friends.

Kelsey sat back in his chair and stared at the wall. In all the inquiries so far no one had recognized the Paisley scarf. No one had shed any significant light on the crime. He sighed and returned his attention to the papers before him.

The two payments recently made by Venetia, to a singles club and a travel agent, both in Strettisham, had now been looked into. The club payment had been for a month's trial subscription; the month had expired a day or so after Venetia's death. She had, it seemed, visited the club two days after paying her subscription, and again, a few days later. No one recalled her, no one recognized her photograph. Her attendance could be deduced only from the fact that on both occasions she had signed the book.

The club was popular and well conducted. There were over three hundred members, more than half with addresses in Strettisham, and the rest from neighbouring towns and villages, a few from as far afield as thirty miles.

The payment to the travel agent was for a singles weekend at a London hotel, arranged by a reputable travel firm. The weekend included a sightseeing tour and steamer trip, visits to a show and a jazz concert. The hotel confirmed that Mrs Franklin had actually spent the weekend under its roof but no one on the staff could now recall her—or, for that matter, any other member of the party. The travel firm had supplied a list of those who had gone on the weekend, some eighty in all, with slightly more men than women. Most of them came from within the county borders but a few from more distant parts of the country. The long process of interviewing everyone on the list was now under way, so far without significant result.

The phone rang on the Chief's desk. He picked up the receiver and heard the voice of the desk sergeant: a young man had just come into the station, asking to speak to the Chief. His name was Harcup, he had a Cannonbridge address, he thought he might possibly have some information that could conceivably be of use in the Franklin case.

And the young man sounded no less hesitant and apologetic when a constable showed him into the Chief's office a few minutes later. A very presentable-looking young man, twenty-two or -three, a fine head of hair, thick and shining, cut in an up-to-the-minute style.

He feared he could be wasting the Chief Inspector's time but his mother had insisted he came along. He had mentioned the matter to her over lunch—he always went to his mother's for Sunday lunch. She had told him to get over to the police station without delay and ask for the Chief Inspector.

'I'd be very interested to hear anything you have to tell me,' Kelsey assured him in as mild and unthreatening a manner as he could muster.

Harcup relaxed slightly. 'I'm a hairdresser,' he told the Chief. 'Mrs Franklin was a customer of ours. I did her hair on the Friday afternoon, the eleventh of May. She had an appointment for two-thirty, shampoo and set.'

He worked in a high-class salon near the centre of Cannonbridge; Mrs Franklin had been a customer for the past year. That Friday she had sat reading the county newspaper under the drier. When he went to comb her out she mentioned an ad in the paper for a nightclub in Ellenborough, a town some forty-five miles away, roughly twice the size of Cannonbridge. A singer and a comedian, both well known on television, were currently appearing at the club. Mrs Franklin asked Harcup if he had seen the show. He said he hadn't but some of his customers had mentioned it, they thought it very good. 'She told me she was going to see the show the following evening, Saturday.' He fell silent, gazing earnestly at the Chief who waited for him to continue.

'That's all,' Harcup said apologetically. 'Just that she was going to see the show on the Saturday. I knew I'd be wasting your time,' he added bleakly. 'I should never have come.' He pushed back his chair.

Kelsey waved him back into his seat. 'You're very far from wasting our time. That's the best piece of information I've come across all day.'

A relieved smile appeared on Harcup's face. He settled back in his chair.

'Did she actually say she was going to Ellenborough for the weekend?' Kelsey asked.

'Not exactly.' He spoke now with more confidence. 'When she booked the appointment—she called in on the Wednesday morning to book it—she had a word with me then. She said she was going away for the weekend, she wanted to look specially good. She grinned and said: "For the new boyfriend." I told her I'd do my best. Then on Friday when she spoke about going to see the show in Ellenborough, I took it that was where she would be spending the weekend, but she never actually said so.'

'Had she mentioned this new boyfriend before?'

'Yes, once or twice. A few weeks back she told me she was off to London on a singles weekend. She had the full works that time, shaping, tinting, conditioning. She seemed excited about the trip, she was really looking forward to it.' He tilted his head to one side. 'You often get women like that, after a divorce, they suddenly start breaking out. We see a lot of that in our line. The next time she came in, after the London weekend, I asked her if she'd had a good time and she said yes, fabulous. She said she'd met this man, he was on the weekend too. "This gorgeous guy," she called him.'

The Chief pressed him but he could recall nothing else that Venetia had said about the new boyfriend. Kelsey asked if he knew of any other boyfriends of Mrs Franklin's.

'Just the one she always called Loverboy.' He grimaced. 'We get all that sort of chat, you get used to it. He was in the picture when she first came to us but I don't know how long she'd known him before that. She used to say: "Make me look nice today, Loverboy's coming over," but after a few months it got to be: "Just the usual today, it's only Loverboy."'

Kelsey asked if he knew any details of Loverboy but he shook his head.

'Did you get the impression Loverboy was aware of the new boyfriend?'

'I'm sure he was, Harcup said at once. 'When she told me she was going to London on a singles weekend I asked her what Loverboy had to say about that. She said it was none of his business, she was a free agent. She said she'd told him straight out where she was going and he'd gone off in a fit of the sulks. She laughed and said: "He'll be back, you can lay money on that." Then after she came back from London, one day when she was talking about the new boyfriend, I asked her if Loverboy knew about him and she said yes, he did. I asked how he'd taken it. She laughed and said: "He wasn't exactly over the moon."'

'Now I'd like you to think very carefully about this,' Kelsey said. 'Did she definitely say that Loverboy knew she was going off last weekend to see the new boyfriend?'

Harcup pondered. 'No, she never said exactly that, not in so many words. I certainly had the impression she'd told Loverboy, but that's all it was, an impression, she never actually said so.'

Kelsey asked if she had ever talked about her ex-husband but he shook his head. 'Sometimes she mentioned that he was taking the children for the weekend, but that was all.' She had never talked of any other friends, male or female.

'Did she ever talk about money? Her financial situation?'

'No, never. She certainly never seemed short of money. She spent a lot in the salon. She never asked how much a treatment would cost before she decided to have it, and she always tipped well.' She had never spoken of worries of any kind. 'She didn't seem the sort to worry,' he added. 'She was always pleasant and good-tempered. She seemed to enjoy life, not to take it too seriously.'

'Ellenborough,' the Chief said aloud a few minutes later when the door had closed behind Harcup. He picked up the list of names supplied by the travel firm. Three names with an Ellenborough address, one woman and two men. He stabbed his finger at the name of the second man: Derek Wilesmith. 'That's the one!' he said with certainty. On the cover of the phone directory in the sitting-room at Foxwell Cottage several phone numbers had been jotted down: one was an Ellenborough number with the initials D.W. beside it, number and initials boldly encircled with a pencilled ring.

CHAPTER 9

Ten minutes later the Chief was sitting in the car beside Sergeant Lambert, headed for Ellenborough. A fine, sunny, Sunday afternoon, the family cars out on the road, bound for picnics on the commons, tea at auntie's. They drove past a stretch of river with fishermen strung out along the banks in the shade of drooping willows, past a village cricket match, jocose and lively, a reservoir where canoeists paddled, sailboats tacked and veered.

Wilesmith's address turned out to be the basement flat of an Edwardian villa in a pleasant enough suburb. Lambert pressed the bell and a young man, twenty-six or -seven, came to the door. Tall, well built, broad-shouldered, handsome in an unsubtle, macho way. Dark hair trendily cut, deeply tanned skin, light green eyes, restless and darting. He had a very strong physical presence, he held himself in a poised, alert stance. He wore expensive-looking casual clothes, an open-necked shirt, jeans cut skin-tight over a spectacularly flat stomach and narrow hips. An ornate medallion on a long chain nestled among the dark curly hair sprouting from the bronzed expanses of his chest.

He said nothing but gave them a questioning look. In one hand he held a lit cigarette; he raised it to his lips and took a long draw. His hands were well manicured but not the hands of a man who sat all day at a desk. His fingers were deeply stained with nicotine.

When the Chief revealed his identity Wilesmith made no response, gave no sign of surprise, but stood waiting like a coiled spring for him to continue. The Chief told him they were calling in connection with a case they were working on: the death of Mrs Venetia Franklin at her cottage in Foxwell, outside Cannonbridge.

Wilesmith gave a brisk nod, as if he'd been expecting the visit.

'We'd like to come inside,' Kelsey added when Wilesmith

still said nothing, still made no move to admit them. 'We believe there are one or two matters on which you might be able to help us.'

'Oh—yes—right,' Wilesmith said with an offhand air. He led the way along the hall into a sitting-room furnished in a very modern, totally anonymous, chainstore fashion. There appeared to be no shortage of funds but very little sign of taste or individuality. The room was tidy enough except for half-a-dozen Sunday newspapers scattered on the carpet beside an easy chair. On a nearby table stood an empty coffee beaker, an empty beer glass, a couple of empty beer cans, a packet of cigarettes and a lighter. In a corner a TV set showed a darts match.

'I didn't know anything about what happened to Venetia till today,' Wilesmith said in a matter-of-fact tone. He jerked his head at the newspapers, one of them a regional paper carrying a long account of the case. 'I've been reading about it in that.' He switched off the TV and waved a hand at a couple of chairs. 'I was just going to make more coffee. Do you want some? Or there's beer, or lager.' Kelsey shook his head. 'I won't be a minute,' Wilesmith told them. 'I've a bit of a head today.' He gave a ritual grin. His teeth were stained with nicotine. 'I had a heavy night.' He went out to the kitchen, closing the door behind him. At once the room seemed empty and tranquil. Kelsey picked up the paper Wilesmith had indicated. He glanced over the report.

A few minutes later Wilesmith came back with a coffee-pot. Again Lambert was struck by his intense physical presence. Wilesmith poured himself some coffee and set the pot on the floor.

The Chief laid down his newspaper. 'You knew Mrs Franklin?' he said.

'Very slightly.' Wilesmith began to drink the scalding coffee. 'I met her a few weeks ago, on a singles weekend in London.' He gave the Chief a look edged with challenge. 'But you know all that or you wouldn't be here.' He stubbed out his cigarette and at once lit another, inhaling deeply.

'You expected her here a week ago last Friday, May the eleventh?' Kelsey asked.

'Yes, it was all fixed. She rang me on the Monday evening and suggested it.'

'She rang you?'

He gave an impatient nod. 'Yes, she was the one who made most of the running.' He drew on his cigarette. 'I'm not short of girlfriends.'

'That Friday—did she phone to tell you she couldn't make it after all?'

'No, she didn't. I heard nothing more from her after the Monday. I definitely expected her on the Friday.'

'What time did you expect her?'

'She said between seven-thirty and eight.'

'Had you seen her since the London weekend?'

'Yes, once. She rang and said how about meeting. I said OK. She said she could make it the following Saturday, her husband was taking the kids out for the day. She came over here in the morning, around eleven o'clock. She left again about six. She said she'd try to make it a whole weekend next time, she'd fix it with her husband to have the kids.'

'That Friday, the eleventh,' Kelsey said. 'The arrangement was that you should go over to the cottage to pick her up.'

Wilesmith frowned. 'No, you've got that wrong. I've just told you, she was coming over here, in her own car.'

'Maybe you decided on the spur of the moment to leave work early, surprise her, drive over there and pick her up.'

His frown deepened. 'Why on earth would I want to do a damnfool thing like that? I'd have had to run her back on the Monday afternoon as well, I'd have had to take time off work. She was going to spend the Monday morning shopping in Ellenborough after I'd gone to work. She didn't intend driving back to Cannonbridge till after lunch, in time to pick the children up from school.'

Kelsey regarded him for some moments. 'Did you have any feeling for her?'

He shrugged. 'I can't say I did. She was all right, nothing special. Those singles weekends are just glorified pick-ups when you come down to it.'

'Why did you bother with her at all?'

Again he shrugged. 'Why not? She was pretty keen. I just took what was offered. She seemed to have plenty of cash and she didn't mind spending it.' He grimaced. 'Made a change from some of these young girls, they expect you to spend the earth on them.'

'Do you live here on your own?'

Wilesmith gave a nod.

'When she didn't turn up on the Friday evening, what did you do?'

'I hung round here for a bit. I thought maybe she'd run into heavy traffic, she'd be along soon. I had a drink, watched TV. When it got to half past eight I rang the cottage but there was no reply. I rang again about twenty minutes later.' He grimaced again. 'I thought: What the hell, she's changed her mind, she's not coming. I was a bit irritated, I thought she could have let me know. So I went out. I'd intended taking her to a club, the food there's pretty good, so I went along there. I met up with some friends, had a meal, stayed till around half past twelve.' He gave the Chief details of the club and the friends he had met. 'Then I came back here and went to bed. I thought I might hear from her over the weekend to say what had happened, I thought she might still show up.' He had gone shopping on Saturday morning, watched football on TV in the afternoon. On Saturday evening he went to see the nightclub show with a friend he phoned on Saturday afternoon. Again he supplied details.

'When you read the papers this morning,' Kelsey said, 'were you surprised?'

'That's putting it mildly. I was knocked sideways.'

'Can you make any sort of guess about what's happened? Anything she said that gives any kind of clue?'

'No, nothing at all. As I said, I hardly knew her.'

'Did she mention any man friend who might be jealous of you?'

He shook his head. 'We didn't sit around discussing her men friends.'

'After you read the papers this morning, why didn't you get in touch with us? To let us know about last weekend?'

'I don't see how that would have helped you,' he said with surprise. 'Telling you she was supposed to come over here and didn't—that wouldn't have got you much further.'

He's certainly not stupid enough to believe that, Sergeant Lambert thought.

'It would have saved us a good deal of time and effort,' Kelsey said brusquely. 'We've spent a good many man-hours trying to find out exactly that, where she intended spending last weekend.'

'Sorry about that,' Wilesmith said casually. 'Never occurred to me. Anyway, you got here in the end.'

'We'll need your fingerprints,' Kelsey told him.

His head jerked up. 'What for? I was never over there.'

'Just for the record,' Kelsey said blandly. 'Got to be done.' Wilesmith made no further protest and allowed Lambert to proceed. When the sergeant had finished Kelsey asked Wilesmith how he had spent the afternoon of Friday, May 11th.

'I was at work of course,' Wilesmith answered with irritation. 'Where else would I be? I had nothing to do with the murder. I scarcely knew the woman. What possible reason could I have for choking her to death?'

'I'm not suggesting you had anything to do with it,' Kelsey said patiently. 'These questions are simply routine. What is your work?'

'I'm a methods engineer.' He mentioned a large factory on the edge of Ellenborough; Lambert remembered seeing it on the way in.

'What time did you leave work that Friday? I'd like you to be as precise as possible.'

'I left at ten to five,' Wilesmith answered at once. 'The factory closes at five. I wanted to get out ahead of the rush, to catch the shops on the way home.'

'Is there someone who can confirm the time you left?'

He pondered. 'I can't think of anyone.'

'What were you doing immediately before you left?'

'I'd been down on the shop floor. I went back to my office at about a quarter past four to clear my desk, ready for Monday morning.'

'You have a secretary?'

'I share one.'

'Can't she confirm what you've told us?'

'She wasn't in that Friday. She'd been at home for a couple of days with a bad cold.'

'Did anyone ring you in your office just before you left? Maybe someone looked in and spoke to you? Or you had a word with the doorkeeper on your way out? Perhaps you spoke to someone in the car park?'

Wilesmith stared about. He put up a hand and rubbed his lip. 'I can't think of anyone,' he said again.

'Can you tell us what shops you called at on your way home? Did you see anyone you know while you were in there?'

Wilesmith mentioned the name of a large supermarket. 'I got what I wanted, paid for it and left. I didn't stand round chatting. The checkout girl wouldn't know me from Adam, I certainly don't know her.' He hadn't seen anyone he knew.

Kelsey contemplated him. 'When you came up from the shop floor at a quarter past four, would anyone have been any the wiser if you had left the factory then?'

There was an appreciable pause before Wilesmith answered. 'I suppose not.' He flung out a hand. 'I'm telling you again, I had nothing to do with what happened.' Anger shook his voice. He stopped and took a grip on himself. He continued in a calmer tone. 'I can understand the way your mind's working, but you've got it all wrong.' He gave a short, mirthless laugh. 'This is like something out of the movies. You never think it'll happen to you.'

'You never think what will happen to you?'

Wilesmith's air of determined reasonableness vanished abruptly. 'You never think you'll find yourself sitting in your own flat,' he said ferociously, 'trying to convince some stupid berk—' He broke off and drew a long breath. 'I'm sorry. You've caught me at a bad moment. I didn't get to bed till very late, I've got one hell of a head.' He poured a beaker of the cooling coffee and drank half of it in a single gulp. He lit a cigarette with hands that seemed a good deal less than steady. 'I suppose you're only doing your job.'

'That Friday evening,' Kelsey began again. 'At precisely what time did you arrive back here after you left the supermarket?'

Wilesmith drained his coffee and took a long drag on his cigarette. 'At a quarter to six.' He strove to keep his voice level and calm. 'I noticed the time because of Venetia coming.'

'Did you speak to anyone as you came in? One of the other tenants, perhaps? Or maybe some neighbour saw you getting out of your car?'

Wilesmith shook his head. 'There are two other flats here. There's a married couple on the ground floor, but they weren't here that Friday. They're moving away soon, he's retiring, they're going to Cornwall. They went down there for a few days, house-hunting.' He took another pull on his cigarette. 'The woman in the top flat—she's a widow, middle-aged—she's always out at work at that time. She works in a local pub, in the kitchen.' He massaged his cheek. 'I didn't see any neighbours. I don't know any of them, I never bother with them.'

'How long have you lived in this flat?'

Wilesmith's fingers suddenly ceased their kneading. 'About eighteen months,' he answered after a pause.

'Where did you live before that?'

There was a longer pause. He drew on his cigarette, tilted back his head, expelled the smoke in a long stream. Then he gave them an address, in the same district of Ellenborough.

'Was that another flat?' Kelsey asked.

Again an appreciable pause. 'No, it was a semi-detached house.'

'Did you own the house?'

Another pause. 'I was buying it on mortgage.'

'You lived there on your own?'

This time the pause stretched on.

'It won't take us long to find out,' Kelsey said. 'Did you live there on your own?'

A light dew broke out on Wilesmith's brow. 'No, I didn't.' He leaned forward and stubbed out his cigarette with force, immediately lit another and took a long pull.

'Are you a single man?'

He stared down at the carpet. 'I'm divorced. I lived there with my wife.'

'Where is your wife now?'

'I have no idea. I moved here after we split up. She went into digs locally but she didn't stay there long. I don't know where she went from there.'

'We'll have the address of those digs,' Kelsey said, and Wilesmith gave it to him. 'Do you never see her around town?' Kelsey asked. Wilesmith shook his head.

'Do you pay her alimony?'

'No. She didn't ask for any. She's always had a job. And we didn't have any children.'

'Where does she work?'

'I have no idea.'

'Where was she working at the time you separated?'

He gave them the name of a firm of builders in Ellenborough. 'But she's definitely not there now.'

'How do you know?'

'I—' He broke off and then said after a few moments, 'I had to get in touch with her, to ask her something. I went along there but they told me she'd left.'

'Didn't they tell you where she'd gone?'

'No. They said it wasn't their policy to give that information.'

'What kind of work does your wife do?'

'Secretarial and receptionist.'

'The digs that she went to after you split up—did you call there to ask for her new address?'

'Yes, but they wouldn't give it to me.'

'Did you approach her family? Her parents?'

He gave a short laugh. 'I'd hardly be likely to do that. I was never on very good terms with them. Anyway, they don't live locally.' He mentioned a small town several miles away. Kelsey asked for her parents' address and he gave it.

'What about your wife's friends?' Kelsey asked.

'I didn't bother any of them. It wasn't that important.'

'What did you want to ask your wife?'

96

'Some cassettes I had—I looked for them not long after I moved in here. I couldn't find them, I thought she might have taken them by mistake.'

Kelsey asked for his wife's Christian names and he gave them: Ann Marie.

'You told us earlier,' Kelsey said, 'that you're not short of girlfriends.'

'I've a fair number.'

'Anyone in particular at the moment?'

He shook his head.

'Do you intend to marry again?'

He gave a sound between a laugh and a snort. 'I most certainly do not. If there's one thing I've learned over the last few years, it's that I'm definitely not the marrying kind.'

The Chief suddenly produced the Paisley scarf and asked him if he had ever seen it before.

Wilesmith looked down at it with no sign of surprise or agitation, no show of interest. He didn't ask what it was. 'No, I've never seen it before,' he answered after a few moments.

'Do you sometimes wear a scarf in the neck of a shirt?' Kelsey asked.

'Yes, sometimes, but that's not one of mine.' He looked and sounded calmer and more steady than at any time during the last few minutes.

CHAPTER 10

The house where Ann Wilesmith had stayed immediately after separating from her husband was a neat redbrick semi in a housing estate near the firm of builders for whom she had worked. The sound of the television news drifted out through an open front window as Kelsey and Lambert walked up the path. Before Lambert's fingers pressed the bell the sound abruptly ceased. The echo of his ring had barely died away when the door was flung open. A short, plump, motherly-looking woman confronted them, her face creased in anxiety.

'It's my lad,' she said, staring up at them in anguish. 'He's had an accident.'

'As far as we know, no one's had an accident,' Kelsey assured her.

'You are police?'

'Yes, but we're not here in connection with any member of your family.'

She drew a long tremulous breath and closed her eyes in relief. 'Every time he goes out on that motorbike I'm on tenterhooks till he gets back safe and sound.'

The Chief disclosed his identity. 'We understand you had a young woman staying with you—'

'Ann Wilesmith,' she broke in, her face full of tension again. 'He's done something to her.'

'As far as we know,' Kelsey assured her again, 'nobody's done anything to her. We'd just like a little information about her, we think you might be able to help. It could have some bearing on a case we're working on.'

'Oh, I'm sorry.' She gave her head a brisk little shake. 'That's me all over, always jumping to conclusions. You must think me very stupid.' She held the door back for them to enter; she took them along the passage into a sitting-room.

'I understand Mrs Wilesmith was in digs here with you some little time back,' Kelsey said.

'You couldn't exactly say she was in digs here,' she told him. 'I don't take lodgers in the ordinary way. She's the only person who's ever stayed here like that. When she left her husband she asked me if I could take her in for a week or two, till she got herself fixed up.'

'It was she who left her husband?'

She gave a vigorous nod. 'And left him in a hurry, too. I'm a cook in the canteen at the builders where she used to work. We always got on well, we used to have a chat and a bit of a laugh. That morning, a Monday morning it was, she came running down to the canteen the moment she got here. I'd barely had time to get my cap and overall on. She was in a terrible state, very strung up, she was shaking and crying all the time she was talking to me. She said she was leaving her husband, leaving right away, that very day.'

'Did she say why?'

'No, and I didn't ask her, she was in no state to talk about it. She said she was going up to tell the boss she wouldn't be in to work that morning, then she'd get a taxi and go back home, pack her things and clear out. I asked her if she'd stopped to think what she was doing—if it came to a divorce she might lose her claim to the house and furniture if she'd just walked out. She said it would come to a divorce all right, the sooner the better. She didn't want the house or furniture, he was welcome to the lot. All she wanted was to be shut of him.'

'Did she ever tell why she'd left?'

'No. She wasn't here long, no more than a couple of weeks. I never asked her and she never talked about it. A few days after she came here her husband started hanging round the works in the evening, when we were knocking off. She spotted him one day, she ran back inside and went out by another door. After that she always looked out first, it made her very nervous. Of course it didn't take him long to find out she was staying here. He turned up on the doorstep one evening, asking to see her. She was up in her room at the time. I went up and told her he was here but she wouldn't even come to the door to speak to him. She started shaking like a leaf, so I went down and told him she wouldn't see him, and he'd better not come round here again, it wouldn't be any use. He didn't make a fuss, he just left.

'As soon as he'd gone she came running downstairs to tell me she'd be leaving as soon as she could find somewhere, it wasn't fair to involve me and anyway she wouldn't be able to rest easy in the house any more, him turning up like that. She went a few days later. She explained everything to the boss. He was very good about it, he gave her a first-class reference. She knew she'd have no difficulty getting another job. She had very good qualifications, she was very efficient, always pleasant with the customers, everyone liked her.'

'Where did she go?'

'I've got the address.' She mentioned a town some twenty miles away. She went over to a bureau and looked out the address for him. 'She's got a little flat there, she's renting it. She works for an estate agent, in the front office. I can't give you the exact address of the estate agent but I know it's right in the middle of town. She picked that particular town more or less out of a hat. She said she didn't know a single soul there, he'd never think of looking for her there.' She jerked her shoulders. 'It seems to have worked. He did call here once after she'd left, wanting her new address, but of course I wouldn't give it to him.' She suddenly thought of something. 'She doesn't call herself Wilesmith any more. She went back to her maiden name, Rowberry. Miss Ann Rowberry, that's what she calls herself now.'

The Sunday-evening traffic was fairly light and half an hour later Sergeant Lambert halted the car outside a large Victorian house divided into flats. He rang the doorbell of Ann Rowberry's flat but there was no reply. As he pressed the bell again an elderly woman came down the stairs.

'Miss Rowberry's not there,' she called out. 'She's gone to the coast for the day with some friends, she won't be back till late this evening.' Kelsey asked if she knew the name of the estate agent Miss Rowberry worked for and she was able to tell him.

'We'll look in there tomorrow morning,' he said to Lambert as they left the house. 'After the funeral.'

Venetia Franklin's funeral took place at ten o'clock on Monday morning. Roy and Jane Franklin were there, Roy very much in charge of the proceedings, directing, shepherding, greeting, chatting. Jane's manner was in marked contrast; throughout she stood silent and rigid. Dressed once again in a severely tailored dark suit, she looked even paler and plainer—though less deeply fatigued—than at the inquest. Neither of the children was there, but among the wreaths and sheaves Sergeant Lambert noticed a separate offering in the name of each child.

Venetia's mother, Mrs Stacey, was present, supported by

a small group of relatives, all much of her own age. She looked old and frail, her face blank and set, as if resolutely distancing herself from all that was going forward. Nearby stood Megan Brewster, composed and elegant.

Philip Colborn was nowhere to be seen, nor could Lambert discover any flowers from him.

Afterwards Lambert drove the Chief over to the estate agent's where Ann Rowberry worked. The premises had recently been modernized and the whole of the front office was visible through the large window. Two young women sat behind desks. One, a brunette, was talking into a phone; she had a merry, lively face. The other girl was looking through a file. She was younger, shorter, slimmer, with a quiet, disciplined air. She had blonde, curly hair, delicately pretty features. At the other end of the office a young couple studied the particulars of properties on the display boards.

Kelsey pushed open the door and went inside. The blonde girl looked up with a smile of professional welcome as he came up to her desk.

'Miss Ann Rowberry?' he said in a discreet tone. 'Formerly Mrs Derek Wilesmith?'

Her smile vanished. The colour drained from her face, she looked as if she might faint. The other girl glanced over at them.

'There's no need to alarm yourself,' the Chief added in the same discreet tone. He told her who he was. 'We'd like a word with you about your ex-husband. Is there somewhere we could talk in private?'

She stared up at him with a stunned, helpless air. The other girl left her desk and came over. 'The manager's not in,' she told the Chief. 'He won't be in for some time. But I'm sure he wouldn't mind you using one of the alcoves.' She glanced at Ann Rowberry. 'I'll hold the fort.'

Ann led them through an archway into an area partitioned into alcoves. She chose the furthest alcove and the two men took their seats opposite her.

'What do you want to know about Derek?' Her eyes were filled with anxiety.

'It's in connection with a case we're working on,' Kelsey began.

'Has he done something?'

'Not as far as we know.' She scanned his face, saw he wasn't going to enlarge.

'I'd like to ask you about your marriage,' Kelsey went on. 'Why you left your husband, what kind of man he is.'

She clasped her hands on the table in silence.

'You haven't married again?' Kelsey asked in a conversational tone.

'No.' She gave a shudder. 'I'm not likely to.'

'Why not?'

She began to speak in a rush. 'It's terrifying to be shut up in a house, at the mercy of another human being, bigger and stronger than you, someone who seems to hate you —for some reason you can't fathom. It's like a horrible nightmare.'

'You were frightened of your husband?'

'In the end I was absolutely petrified. I made a bolt for it.' She gave another shudder.

'Did he assault you physically?'

She shook her head. 'I was sure he was going to, right at the end, but I ran upstairs and he didn't come after me. It was his attitude that frightened me, the way he spoke to me, looked at me. I couldn't understand it.' She made an effort to speak calmly, in an orderly fashion. 'My parents never wanted me to marry him, but they couldn't give me any good reason. He had a good job, he always behaved well towards them, but they never liked him.'

She gave a trembling sigh. 'I was crazy about him, I wouldn't hear a word against him. I'd never had many boyfriends, I was always shy and quiet, and he wasn't like any of the other boys I'd known. He was good-looking, but it wasn't just that. He was so—' She stared at the floor. 'He always seemed so alive, I can't really explain.'

She looked up at the Chief again. 'Anyway, we did get married. It was marvellous at first, I was very happy. Then he started to change. He began to drink a lot more—he'd always a drunk a fair amount but it hadn't seemed to affect him before, not in the way it did later. It seemed to put him in a terrible mood.' She shuddered again. 'A black, horrible mood. I couldn't talk to him, couldn't get through to him. I soon learned to keep out of his way when he was like that.'

She drew a long breath. 'Then I found out he was being unfaithful. It didn't take much finding out, he didn't really try to hide it, he didn't seem to care if I knew or not. I tried to say something about it once or twice but he just flew into a rage and told me to shut up, it was none of my business.' She bit her lip. 'I couldn't say anything about it to my parents, not after the way I'd refused to listen to them. Things went on like that. Sometimes they'd be a bit better, he'd be in a good mood, he wouldn't drink so much, it would be more like it was in the early days. I would start to hope it would be all right again. I'd tell myself he'd just been going through a bad patch, he was getting over it.'

She fell silent for a moment. 'Then it would all flare up again, in an instant, out of the blue. He was so unpredictable. I think that was the worst part of it, never knowing what to expect, it tore my nerves to shreds. One Sunday evening, he'd been drinking all day, he was in a terrible mood—we'd been married about two and a half years by then—he blew up over some little trifle and he came at me. That was the first time I really thought he was going to attack me, I actually thought he might kill me, the way he looked. I ran upstairs into the bathroom and locked the door. He didn't come up after me.

'After a while I crept out of the bathroom and locked myself in the spare room. About midnight I heard him come upstairs and go to bed. He didn't come near me. I didn't dare close my eyes all night. In the morning I stayed where I was till I heard him leave the house to go to work. I went straight out to the place where I worked and asked a woman I knew there—' Tears came into her eyes. 'She was so kind to me, she let me stay with her till I found somewhere. I never properly explained anything and she never asked any questions. I don't know what I would have done without her.'

Kelsey produced the scarf and asked if she had ever seen

it before. She looked down at it with a puzzled air, then she shook her head. She glanced up at him with anxiety. 'Why do you want to know about Derek?'

'A case over in Cannonbridge,' Kelsey said. 'You may have read about it yesterday in the Sunday papers.'

'I didn't read any papers yesterday, I was out all day.' Her look of anxiety deepened. 'What sort of case is it?'

'A woman your ex-husband met recently,' Kelsey said in an expressionless tone. 'She had intended spending the weekend with him. She was found dead last Monday.'

She put a hand up to her face. She was very pale. 'How did she die?'

He gave her the bare facts in bleak outline.

She stared up at him, her eyes enormous. 'Do you think he could have had something to do with it?' Her voice was barely above a whisper.

'Do you think it's possible?' Kelsey countered.

She was silent for several seconds, then she said, 'If you'd asked me that on my wedding day I'd have thought you were mad, or joking. Now all I can say is: I just don't know.'

On the way back to Cannonbridge Kelsey settled himself against the upholstery and closed his eyes. I'll definitely get away in good time this evening, he promised himself, I'll get an early night. His thoughts began to swim and dissolve. The next thing he knew was that the motion of the car had ceased. He opened his eyes and gave a vast yawn. They were on the forecourt of the police station.

'Coffee,' he said. 'Strong black coffee.' He levered himself up and out of the car. The rest of the day rose before him, an endless uphill slope.

Half an hour and two coffees later he had totally forgotten the early night. It was after ten when he eventually put the key in the door of his flat. It was as much as he could do to get his clothes off before he fell into bed.

It was a fine, mild night. The hills above Cannonbridge slept under a calm, unclouded sky, moonless and starless. Beneath an overhanging ledge of rock in a dip of the hills, screened by thick bushes, old Ben Cresswell sat at ease, drinking rough cider. He had been drinking in various lairs on the hills for the best part of fifty years. He had been a farm hand until he retired, often crossing the hills in search of strayed sheep. He had formed the habit then of secreting a bottle here and there, to refresh himself in the long summer days. He had never married, had lived at home in an ancient stone cottage at the foot of one of the hills, with his fierce old mother, a sternly religious woman. Ben could never take a bottle home, she would never have allowed alcohol into the house, so he drank it on the hills, two or three evenings a week.

His mother had lingered on into ripe old age, had died a few years ago after a fall, gathering firewood on the grassy slopes. Ben, master of the cottage at last, governed now by habit as rigorously as ever he had been governed by his mother, went on drinking as before, except that now on warm, still nights he no longer bothered to creak back into the cottage around midnight, but bedded himself snugly down in one of his little caverns on a couch of dried bracken, sleeping deeply and peacefully till the sunlight stole through the branches and the song of birds pierced his dreams.

Shortly after four o'clock on Tuesday morning, long fingers of light began to ray out above the horizon, a bird stirred in the branches of a rowan. By six the joggers were pounding over the hill paths, by seven the dog-walkers appeared.

Around half past seven the sound of all this activity penetrated to Ben's ears. He opened his eyes, yawned and stretched, raised himself up and drained the last swig of cider he always saved for morning. He tucked the empty bottle into a deep inside pocket of his old tweed jacket, parted the bushes and crawled out, restoring the branches carefully afterwards to their decent screening function.

He yawned widely again, got himself up on to his feet and stood surveying the shimmering morning. Across the hills the cuckoos called, hollow, echoing notes. He set off for home, up one long slope and down another. When he reached the top of a second grassy eminence he paused to draw breath. He stood looking down at the magnificent panoramic view, fields and woods, the distant river, the town spread out below, minute cars crawling along the roads.

He shifted his gaze nearer. His eye, still hawklike, accustomed over the years to detecting anything on the hills worth scavenging, made out a colour, a shape, under a group of trees, that at once suggested a coat or jacket forgotten or dropped. He set off down the slope towards it.

CHAPTER 11

Detective-Inspector Glover drove into the forecourt of the main Cannonbridge police station. A tall, spare man, hair tinged with grey. He got out of his car and walked without haste towards the entrance, towards whatever this sunny Tuesday morning might see fit to bring. Within hailing distance of retirement, already looking forward to the fishing and the rose-growing, he had long ago resigned himself to the fact that he would never rise above the rank of inspector. At the end of each working day he closed his mind as well as the door of his office, went home and kissed his wife, ate his meals with a good appetite, was on friendly terms with his children, dug his garden and slept soundly at night.

As he came into the front hall the desk sergeant was replacing the receiver on his phone. 'Body of a young man on Bracken Hill,' he told Inspector Glover. A motorist had just rung in. Old Ben Cresswell had found the body, had stopped a jogger and got him to run down to the road, flag down a car.

Inspector Glover stood inside the canvas screens erected on the hillside, waiting for the men to remove the body to the mortuary. Nothing about the body suggested that the young man had been sleeping rough, there were no signs of self-neglect. In his early twenties, medium height, well developed, well nourished, clean and well groomed, neatly enough dressed in a T-shirt and jeans under a camouflage jacket. An unremarkable face, clean-shaven, trim haircut, hands that were no strangers to manual work but well cared for.

According to the police doctor, he appeared to have died from a drug overdose although there were no signs of habitual drug misuse. In one of his pockets was a used disposable syringe, and a small, capped bottle holding a trace of liquid. He had been dead several hours, had probably died—at a rough guess—between six and nine the previous evening.

Among a few personal items in a zipped pocket was a used envelope from the Department of Health and Social Security. It was addressed to Martin L. Hynett, Hollymount, Grange Road, Wychford.

Detective-Constable Rudge turned the car into Grange Road, three-quarters of a mile from the Wychford police station. The road had an air of crumbling gentility, large detached houses, late-Victorian, all now turned into flats or split up into bedsits. He halted the car outside Hollymount.

Beside him, in the passenger seat, Inspector Glover sat looking out at the house. According to the Wychford police, Hollymount was owned and run by a man named Jopling, who lived on the premises. A bachelor in his fifties, formerly a regular soldier, a decent, law-abiding, hard-working man. The house was let off in bedsits, to male tenants only, mainly ex-mental patients or mentally handicapped, men with nowhere else to go, without family or friends.

The two policemen got out of the car and walked up to the gate. Glover's ring at the doorbell was answered by Jopling himself, a short, wiry man, still with something of a military air. Glover told him who he was and asked if he might step inside. Jopling took them into the front hall, spacious, comfortably furnished. Glover explained what had happened. Jopling showed no surprise; after fifteen years at Hollymount few things could still surprise him. Glover asked what he knew of Hynett's movements over the last day or two.

It all seemed straightforward enough. Hynett had left the

house at around six the previous evening. For some days before he had appeared troubled and depressed. Jopling had asked if he could help but Hynett had been unresponsive. Jopling had suggested he should see a doctor and had given him the name of a local man. To the best of his knowledge Hynett had followed his advice.

Hynett had said nothing to Jopling the previous evening about where he was going or when he expected to return. Jopling had no idea why Hynett should have gone to Cannonbridge; he knew of no connection Hynett might have had with the town, or of any friends he might have had there. This morning, when he discovered that Hynett had been out all night, he had questioned the other residents, but Hynett had said nothing to any of them about where he was going—Hynett was never very communicative. He was a comparative newcomer to Hollymount, had been there only a few weeks. Jopling had no previous knowledge of him, nor did he know of any family. Hynett had told him that he moved about a lot, that he had come to Hollymount from Devon.

Glover asked if Hynett had been a patient in a psychiatric institution. 'I believe so,' Jopling said. He didn't know any details but from what little Hynett had let fall he had gathered it was some time ago.

'We'll take a look at his room,' Glover said, and Jopling led them up to a pleasant enough single room at the top of the house, looking down on the back garden. 'I don't suppose we'll be very long,' Glover told him, and Jopling took himself off.

The room was adequately furnished, spotlessly clean, very orderly. The two men began a routine search. Constable Rudge paused to glance at the titles of the books neatly ranged in an open bookcase: a Bible, prayer-book, several works of a religious nature, biographies, thrillers. 'He seemed fond of reading,' he observed.

Glover made no reply. He was running his hand along the brass rail inside the wardrobe, feeling in the pockets of a raincoat, a jacket. He thrust his head into the wardrobe and ran his hand down the inside of the wooden panels on either side of the wardrobe door. He gave a grunt as his fingers encountered something half way down, on the left. He squinted along at it. A band of webbing had been secured with thumbtacks to the timber frame. A large plastic wallet had been slipped behind the webbing. He eased it out and stepped back into the room.

Inside the wallet was a birth certificate and a post office savings book opened fifteen years ago, both giving the same address in Strettisham; there was also a building society account book, opened six years ago, giving a different Strettisham address. There were some snapshots, old Christmas and birthday cards, and a lady's handkerchief that had been crumpled and smoothed out again, carefully refolded.

'Better take another look round,' Glover said. 'Might be something else stashed away.'

Rudge began examining the undersides of drawers, of the bed. He turned back the mattress, peered behind the heavier pieces of furniture, moved forward the lighter pieces.

He lifted off the top row of books and edged the bookcase out from the wall. Another strip of webbing, secured to the back of the shelves, held in place a long, rectangular book with thick pages. He took it out and opened it. It was a scrapbook one quarter filled with newspaper cuttings.

He passed the book to Glover who glanced through it. Rudge stood beside him, looking down at the cuttings which had been carefully pasted in. Every cutting was to do with the death of Venetia Franklin.

'Might not mean anything,' Rudge said. 'He could have been the type that gets a kick out of reading about brutal murders, particularly of women.'

Glover turned back the pages and looked at the first cutting, taken from the *Cannonbridge Courier*. A large photograph showed a group standing beside a homemade cake stall at a charity fair: two young women making purchases, another young woman serving them, some children nearby, all with their faces turned to the camera, smiling into it. The head and shoulders of one of the young women customers had been boldly encircled in ink. The column beside the photograph gave a report of the event, a bring and buy sale at Sunnycroft School. Underneath the photograph were listed the names of those in the group. The name of the young woman whose likeness had been ringed was Mrs Venetia Franklin.

In the margin at the head of the page was a small inked map, no more than a dozen strokes, showing, apparently, a road, a lane, some dwellings, one of them marked with a cross and the letters F.C.

Glover stabbed a finger at the top of the page, at the printed date. 'April 19th,' he said. 'Three weeks before Venetia Franklin was murdered.'

The clock on the kitchen wall at Hollymount showed a quarter to four. The kitchen was a large room where meals were eaten as well as prepared.

Chief Inspector Kelsey stood on the threshold, looking round. 'I'll see the men in here,' he told Jopling with massive geniality. His fatigue had evaporated, he was in the agreeable, stimulated frame of mind which he experienced only once or twice—if at all—in a case of any importance, when all at once an entirely fresh avenue opened up before him.

He took his stand at the head of the long table with Inspector Glover, Sergeant Lambert and Constable Rudge seated behind him. The men filed silently into the kitchen, a dozen of them, shepherded by Jopling, who took his seat at the other end of the table. The men already knew the bare facts of Hynett's death and there was a general atmosphere of interest. Some faces displayed nervousness, others showed chronic anxiety, one or two appeared apathetic and uncomprehending.

Kelsey's manner, when he addressed them, was friendly, his tone easy, his speech measured and clear. He asked if anyone had spoken to Martin Hynett yesterday on his way out of Hollymount or shortly before he left, if they knew anything about his state of mind at that time, if he had said where he was going, what he intended doing. He paused and glanced about at the row of faces, slack-jawed or suspicious, vacant or twitching. In the stillness someone let out a long,

110

noisy breath. A moon-faced young man suddenly dropped his arms on the table and sank his head down on his arms with his face turned sideways, staring up at the Chief. His neighbour gave him a nudge and he sat slowly up again.

Kelsey asked if anyone knew of any relatives of Hynett's or any close friends. No one spoke, no one stirred. One or two began to pull faces. He then came to the matter of the scrapbook. Had Hynett mentioned it to anyone? Had he spoken of his reason for keeping it? Again there was no response but now the men were showing signs of restlessness, jerking their heads about, blinking, grimacing.

The Chief dipped a hand into his pocket and produced a plastic envelope containing the lady's handkerchief that had lain among the personal belongings in the wallet inside Hynett's wardrobe. The handkerchief was displayed fully opened out; it was of excellent quality, fine white linen exquisitely embroidered in white, graceful sprays of lily-of-the-valley in the corners, the edges finished with drawn threadwork.

He held up the envelope. At once interest re-awakened, they stopped fidgeting. 'This is a lady's handkerchief,' he told them. 'Constable Rudge will take it round in a moment so that you can all get a good look at it. I want you to see if you can recognize it, if you have ever seen it anywhere before.'

Rudge took the envelope and walked slowly round the table, pausing at intervals to let the men stare down at the handkerchief. 'If you're not sure if you've ever seen it before,' Kelsey added, 'you can always take another look at it afterwards. Don't be afraid to come forward and ask one of us to let you see it.'

Rudge returned to the head of the table and laid the envelope down in front of the Chief. Kelsey dipped his hand into another pocket and brought out a second envelope. There was a stir of heightened interest as if he had suddenly turned into a conjuror capable of producing a succession of unusual objects.

This time the Chief held up the brown Paisley scarf. 'I'd like you to do the same thing with this scarf,' he told his expectant audience. 'Take a good look at it when Constable Rudge brings it round. See if you can recognize it, if you have ever seen it anywhere before, if you have ever seen anyone wearing it.'

There was less inhibition this time about craning forward to peer at the scarf, but still no one had anything to say. Again the Chief told them they might ask to see it again later. Again Rudge returned to the head of the table and laid down the envelope.

They all sat gazing at Kelsey with varying degrees of lively expectancy, waiting for the next trick. Sergeant Lambert looked along the twin rows of faces. Half of them have forgotten by now why they're here at all, he thought. They seemed to think now it was some sort of party, that at any moment the door would open to admit trolleys laden with tea and cakes, charitable ladies offering paper hats and a present for everyone.

'Right, then,' Kelsey said. 'That's about it.' He thanked them for listening and asked them to think over what he had said. 'If any of you remember anything at all that might be of use,' he added, 'even something very small, something that might seem very unimportant, we'd be very pleased if you'd come and tell us about it. We'll be here for a little while yet, and some of us will probably be back again tomorrow. Don't be afraid to come up and speak to one of us. If you prefer, you can always tell Mr Jopling about it and he can speak to us for you.'

As the men drifted out of the kitchen Kelsey signalled to Jopling that he'd like another word with him. 'While you're talking to Jopling,' Inspector Glover told the Chief, 'Rudge and I will take a wander round, give the men a chance to talk to us.'

Kelsey and Jopling sat down at the table. 'If you could cast your mind back ten days or so,' Kelsey said. 'A week ago last Friday, May 11th. I'd like you to try to remember anything at all about Hynett's movements that day.'

Jopling pushed back his chair. 'I'll take a look in my diary,' he offered. 'I make a note of everything that happens here.' He came back a few minutes later with a large desk diary. 'No problem,' he announced. 'I've got that day quite clear in my mind now.' He laid the open diary down in front of Kelsey. 'Take a look at it yourself. You'll see that one of the men had a touch of food poisoning, a meat pie he'd eaten when he was out the evening before. He was taken bad in the night, I had to get up to him. I went up to see him again in the morning, that was the Friday morning, the eleventh, to see if I should give the doctor a ring, ask him to look in.' He waved a hand. 'I didn't, as it happens, I decided he'd be all right inside twenty-four hours—and he was. Anyway, when I came out of his room I was standing on the landing, thinking about it, and Hynett came down the top flight of stairs, from his room.'

'What time would that be?'

'About a quarter to ten. He spoke to me as he went by, then he went off down the stairs and out of the house.'

'What did he say?'

'He asked me how he was—the chap in bed. That was all.'

'How was he dressed?'

Jopling closed his eyes and tilted back his head. 'T-shirt and jeans,' he said after a moment. 'His new camouflage jacket—he bought that at the army surplus store a few days before. And he had his binoculars in a case over his shoulder.' A pair of binoculars in a leather case hung at the back of the door of Hynett's room.

'Had he had the binoculars long?' Kelsey asked.

'I don't know. The first time I saw him with them was the day before, the Thursday.'

'Did he say where he was going—on the Friday?'

'No, but I imagined he was off to the same place he'd been to the day before, seeing he had the binoculars with him again.'

'Where had he been to the day before?'

'I can't tell you the exact place but he did say that day, the Thursday, that he was going birdwatching. I'd passed some comment about the binoculars.'

'What time did he leave here on the Thursday?'

Jopling pondered. 'In the middle of the morning, about eleven.'

'Had he gone birdwatching before while he was here?'

'Not as far as I know.'

'Had he ever mentioned an interest in birdwatching?'

'Not to me, but then he was never very chatty.'

'Did you notice anything unusual about his mood or behaviour when he returned to the house on either the Thursday or the Friday? Particularly on the Friday?'

Jopling thought for some moments, then he shook his head. 'I can't particularly recall speaking to him or noticing him on either of those evenings. He always stayed up in his room a lot, he was fond of reading. He went down to the library three or four times a week and he bought second-hand books from the market stall and the charity shops.'

'Did he go to the pubs? Did he join any clubs? Did he go to discos or singles bars? Anything like that?'

Jopling shook his head. 'He wasn't interested in anything like that,' he said with certainty.

'Was he interested in girls?' There was certainly no evidence of it in his room, no pin-ups, no girlie magazines.

'Not from anything I ever saw or heard. I don't allow any women on the premises.' Jopling made a face of distaste. 'You can imagine the antics they'd get up to if I did. I'm not having any of that under my roof. What they do outside these walls is their affair but I don't want to hear about it. I'm not interested in that kind of thing, never have been. Hynett was a bit of a fitness fanatic, he often went to a local gym in the afternoons. If there was any boxing on TV, he always watched that. And he went to chapel while he was here.'

'Did he talk about any religious experiences? Any visions? Did he hear voices?' No, Hynett had never mentioned anything of the kind.

Kelsey looked at his watch; he had to keep an eye on the time because of getting back to Cannonbridge for the results of the post mortem.

At the top of the house Inspector Glover and Constable Rudge were once again in Hynett's room after a fruitless twenty minutes spent strolling about the house and garden in the hope that one or other of the tenants might approach them with some nugget of information.

Glover began to open the drawers of the chest, the dressing-table again, this time searching minutely through the contents. Over by the wall Rudge looked through the books with closer attention, skimming through them, shaking them for any loose paper slipped inside. He picked up the Bible. It fell open where a red silk ribbon, secured into the binding, acted as a bookmark.

He glanced down at the closely printed columns: the second book of Kings, ninth chapter. A pencil mark ran down the margin beside the last six verses. He cast an eye over them: the story of Jezebel. He began to read with idle curiosity; years since he had come across the story, not since he left school. As he read he felt the hair begin to rise on his scalp . . . *So they flung her down and her blood splashed against the wall* . . .

At the end of the chapter he glanced back over the verses. The words: *Go forth now, seek out this accursed woman,* had been heavily underscored.

He went over to where the Inspector crouched before the dressing-table, searching through singlets and underpants. Glover glanced up as Rudge came over and then returned his attention to his task. Beneath the underwear at the back of the drawer he came on half a dozen pair of socks neatly rolled together in twos, each pair fastened into a tight ball. He undid the first pair, then rolled it up again. He began to undo the second pair.

Rudge held out the open Bible. 'I think you ought to take a look at this.' He stabbed a finger at the page.

In the toe of one of the socks Glover could feel something hard and round. He slipped his fingers inside and drew out a small object wrapped in a paper tissue. Rudge watched as the Inspector got to his feet and opened out the tissue.

Inside was a button, dark blue, many faceted. Attached to the shank by strands of thread was a tiny square of cloth with ragged edges. Fine cotton cloth, striped in blue and white.

CHAPTER 12

In the mortuary corridor Chief Inspector Kelsey and Inspector Glover stood talking to the pathologist who had carried out the post mortem on Hynett.

'A pretty easy death, as these things go,' the pathologist observed. 'He'd fall into a deep sleep almost at once, he'd slide from that into a coma, and then into death very soon afterwards. Ten, fifteen, twenty minutes, from the time he injected himself.' The injection had been compounded from an assortment of drugs, apparently selected at random. None of them hard drugs, all of the type regularly prescribed by any general practitioner. 'As if he had access to the pills of a dozen different patients,' the pathologist added. 'He crushed them up, made his little brew.' That could figure, Kelsey thought. Most of the Hollymount residents were on repeat prescriptions for a variety of conditions, physical or psychological, or both. The various medicaments were haphazardly kept, in bathroom cupboards and bedside cabinets, on kitchen shelves and dressing-tables.

'Does it suggest suicide?' Glover asked.

'It's certainly the first thought that comes to mind.' The random element, with its suggestion of abandon and desperation, chimed in with suicide. And the total recklessness of any consequences. 'He must have known he was taking a terrible chance with a mixture like that.' The pathologist shook his head. 'But it's just as likely, if not more likely, to have been sheer misadventure. People who are extremely disturbed can do very odd things. They certainly don't always intend the results of their actions, very often they're hardly aware in any rational sense of what those results are likely to be.'

He grimaced. 'It could even have been some bizarre experiment that went wrong.' There were no marks on Hynett's body suggesting other recent injections. 'But he might have tried minor experiments along the same lines some time ago, even years ago, perhaps when he was going through a bad patch. Mixing together anything he could get hold of. If he got away with it then, if he managed to put himself into a long, deep sleep without any really bad side effects, then he could have remembered that now. He may have thought: If mixing two or three pills produced a good result, then mixing ten or twelve might be even better.' He shook his head again. 'You can't attribute normal, logical thought processes to someone who is severely agitated and depressed.'

Physically Hynett had been in excellent shape. He had very good teeth, very well cared for. The pathologist always paid particular attention to the teeth, he felt they told him a lot. 'He came from a good home, poor devil,' he said. 'His mother ate properly while she was carrying him. Someone saw he ate the right foods when he was a child, someone taught him good habits, saw that he used his toothbrush.' Wherever the years had led Hynett he still ate properly, still took his exercise, still looked after himself. Whatever miserable end he had contrived for himself, by accident or design, he had to the last retained some of the habits of a well brought up and obedient child.

First thing on Wednesday morning Chief Inspector Kelsey set in motion a comprehensive and detailed inquiry among all Venetia Franklin's friends, relatives, neighbours, her known contacts of any kind, in an effort to discover any connection, however tenuous or fleeting, between Venetia and Martin Hynett.

A little after nine Sergeant Lambert again drove the Chief over to Wychford. They had an appointment with the general practitioner Hynett had recently consulted on Jopling's recommendation.

The doctor was an oldish man with a friendly, relaxed manner. He told the Chief that Hynett had consulted him on only one occasion, a few days before his death. He hadn't made an appointment, he had called in during morning surgery and asked to see the doctor. He had been very insistent and the doctor had spared him a few minutes.

He had complained of insomnia. The doctor asked how long it had been troubling him. 'He said not long, a few days. I asked if he had any physical problem that might be causing it, any pain or other symptom, but he said no, he was very fit, apart from the insomnia. I had to take his word for that. I had no time to examine him then and he certainly looked fit enough physically, though he did appear very tired and restless. He could hardly sit still and he stammered badly. I asked how long he'd had the stammer. He said he'd had it on and off since he was ten years old, it had more or less disappeared until recently.

'I asked if something had happened recently to bring back the stammer and cause the insomnia. That seemed to agitate him but he strongly denied the suggestion. I could see of course that he had something on his mind but there wasn't time to go into it properly and he didn't seem disposed to confide in me. He asked me to give him something to make him sleep. To knock him right out, he said, so he wouldn't dream. I asked if he was afraid of his dreams. He hesitated and then admitted he was having bad nightmares. It seemed to me that it wasn't so much a case of not being able to sleep as of being afraid to let himself fall asleep, having to stay awake to escape the nightmares.'

As soon as Hynett told him he was staying at Hollymount the doctor realized he was probably an ex-mental patient. Hynett didn't volunteer this information so the doctor asked him outright if he had ever been in any kind of psychiatric institution. After some reluctance Hynett told him yes, he'd been in Chelmwood Hospital several times in his late teens, the last time being about four years ago. He had never been in any other hospital and was currently receiving no treatment of any kind. Because of his wandering life he was not in fact on the books of any doctor; the last practice he'd been registered with was in Strettisham, his home town.

'I suggested that it might be a good idea to have further psychiatric help,' the doctor added, 'but he was strongly against the idea, he said he didn't feel it was necessary, all he wanted was the sleeping pills.

'There was no point in trying to persuade him to go back

to Chelmwood. It's more or less closed its doors now, all the old staff are gone. But we have a very good psychiatric department here, in the local hospital. I asked how long he intended staying in Wychford. He said not long. I told him that in that case it would scarcely be worth his while registering with me, I would treat him on a temporary basis. I wrote him out a prescription for some sleeping pills, nothing very powerful, but strong enough to give him a sound night's sleep. I told him I was prescribing enough for three nights. He seemed very disappointed and asked why he couldn't have enough for a couple of weeks.

'I told him he must come to see me again when the three days were up. He must make a proper appointment so that I could give him more time. If necessary he could have another prescription then. I also urged him to think over what I had said about getting psychiatric help, I could probably arrange for him to go along to the local hospital as an outpatient.

'He said he would make the appointment, he would come back in three days' time, and he would think about going to the hospital. He took the prescription and that was the last I saw of him. He never made an appointment.'

'Did you think he might be suicidal?'

'Not particularly. The idea is always there at the back of your mind when you're talking to someone like that, that's one of the reasons I prescribed the bare minimum of pills, but I certainly didn't feel any strong indication of suicide.'

As they walked out to the car Lambert suddenly said, 'Just as well we didn't take Jane Franklin's mother up on her offer. We'd have lost a packet.'

Kelsey gave him an abstracted stare.

'Mrs Norton,' Lambert said. 'She offered to lay us any money we cared to name that it was someone from Chelmwood Hospital who murdered Venetia.'

Kelsey's next appointment was with the minister of the chapel Hynett had attended while he was at Hollymount. The chapel was a bright, modern little building five minutes' walk from Hollymount; the minister was an amiable middle-aged man with a down-to-earth manner. He received the two policemen in the sitting-room of his small house next to the chapel.

'I spoke to Hynett more than once,' he told the Chief. 'The first time was when he came to the mid-week prayer meeting one Wednesday evening. I spoke to him again the following Sunday morning, when he came to the family service.'

He consulted a wall calendar. 'That would be Sunday, May 6th. I always stand at the door as the congregation leaves. I make a point of speaking to anyone new. If they show signs of wanting a longer chat I ask them to call in here, have a cup of tea. I suggest times when they're likely to find me at home.'

'Did Hynett take you up on that?'

'No. I got the impression he would have liked to come but was too shy. I didn't press him, I thought he might open up later on, when he got to know me better. He told me he was staying at Hollymount.' He moved a hand. 'Of course that told me he was a young man with problems.'

'Did he tell you anything about himself?'

'A little. He said he came from Strettisham, that he'd been brought up to go to chapel.'

'Did he mention any relatives over there?' The Strettisham police had called at the two addresses given in Hynett's papers, but at neither address did anyone know of him.

'I asked him about that,' the minister said. 'He told me there was nobody left. He gave me a very straight look and said: "I have no family now anywhere at all. Not a soul on the face of the earth."' The minister fell silent for a moment. 'It was a very bleak statement.' He sighed and shook his head. 'I told him about various groups and societies we run in the parish, different social events we have. I said he was very welcome to come to any of them. I'd look out for him, introduce him, see he wasn't left on his own. But he never showed up at anything.'

'How did he strike you?'

'Very quiet, intelligent enough. A very vulnerable type.

There seemed to be a good deal of tension there. His manner was always guarded.'

'Did you speak to him after Sunday, May 6th?'

'Yes, I spoke to him at Hollymount after that. When he didn't come to the next Wednesday prayer meeting or Sunday service, I called in at Hollymount on the chance of catching him in. Mr Jopling told me Hynett was up in his room. I said not to send for him to come down, I'd go up and have a word with him.'

'When exactly was this?'

'Tuesday of last week, May 15th. It was in the afternoon, about five o'clock. I knocked at his door and he called out right away, he said: "Hang on a moment." It was quite some time before he opened the door.'

'Did he look surprised to see you?'

'No. He looked very wary, defensive. He didn't ask me in. He didn't say anything, he just looked at me. I said I hadn't seen him at chapel, I hoped there was nothing wrong. He wasn't very forthcoming, he didn't show any friendliness, he seemed anxious to be rid of me. He said he was all right, there was nothing wrong. He was stammering so badly he could hardly get the words out. I'd never noticed any stammer before. I told him he'd always be welcome to call at my house, for a meal if he liked. If there was anything I could do to help him, I'd be only too pleased.'

'What did he say to that?'

The minister sighed again. 'He said: "What makes you think I need your help?" It wasn't very politely said. I felt sorry for him, he seemed so locked inside himself. I started to say I hoped we'd see him at the prayer meeting next evening, but he shut the door in my face.'

After leaving the minister Kelsey called in again at Hollymount. Jopling assembled his tenants in the kitchen as before. Sergeant Lambert detected a mild air of expectancy among the men, as if they were hoping for more conjuring tricks.

If so, they were disappointed. The Chief asked them to try to cast their minds back the best part of two weeks, to

Thursday and Friday May 10th and 11th. He attempted to identify the days in their minds by recalling that it was on the Thursday night that one of their number had been taken ill with stomach pains after eating a meat pie. He saw some of the men nod, flickers of recollection appear among the faces.

He asked if anyone knew where Hynett had gone that Thursday and Friday, what mood he had been in at that time, or indeed if anyone could recall anything of Hynett during those two days, however trifling. After a pause during which no one volunteered anything he asked if Hynett had told anyone where it was he went birdwatching. After another unfruitful pause he asked if anyone knew how Hynett had come by his binoculars, if he had brought them with him when he came to Hollymount or if he had acquired them later. He saw some movement at this, some exchanges of glances, but no one offered a direct response.

When he sat down he expected the men to push back their chairs and leave but they all remained seated, turning their heads to look at Jopling with an expectant air.

Jopling got to his feet and addressed the Chief from where he stood. 'The men would like me to ask you if Martin had enough money to give him a decent Christian burial. He doesn't seem to have had any family and the men don't want him buried on the parish. If there isn't enough money they'd like to make a collection among themselves.' He cleared his throat. 'I would be willing to make up any shortfall.'

Kelsey looked at the assortment of faces, united now in a common purpose. 'It's all right,' he told them gently. 'Martin had a building society account. There's enough money in it to give him a proper funeral. If we don't find any relatives, I'm sure Mr Jopling will help us to arrange the funeral in a way that will meet your wishes.'

When Kelsey and Lambert left the kitchen a few minutes later they saw two of the men talking earnestly to Jopling. At the sight of the policemen they fell silent. They stood watching as Jopling came over to speak to the Chief.

'They'd rather not talk to you themselves,' Jopling explained. 'They want you to know that Hynett bought the binoculars about a week after he came here. He asked them if they knew where he could get a good pair second-hand and they told him about two places locally, a pawnshop and a swap shop. Next day they asked him if he'd had any luck and he told them he'd found a pair he was satisfied with at the swap shop, he'd got them very reasonably.' The men hadn't asked Hynett why he wanted the binoculars and he hadn't volunteered the information.

Kelsey asked Jopling to thank the men for him. He asked if Jopling knew at which newsagent's Hynett had bought his papers. Jopling didn't know but he gave them the name of his own newsagent and of two or three others within walking distance of Hollymount.

The two policemen stayed another ten minutes, strolling casually about, but no one approached them. 'We'll look in at the newsagents,' the Chief told Lambert as they got into the car again. 'It'll probably turn out to be the nearest.'

And it was at the nearest that Hynett had bought his papers, waiting on the doorstep every morning for the shop to open, at seven o'clock. The newsagent identified him from a photograph. 'I certainly remember him,' he told the Chief. 'I never laid eyes on him before a couple of weeks ago, then one morning there he was, on the doorstep. He bought a copy of every daily paper, he started looking through them as soon as he got his hands on them, he was reading them as he left the shop. He came in several days running, same thing every morning, buying all the papers, reading them the moment he got them. Then a couple of days ago, finito, not a sight or sound of him. Hasn't crossed the threshold since.'

'When precisely did he start buying the papers?' Kelsey asked.

'Tuesday, last week. I know that because it was Freda who served him. She's a part-time assistant, she comes in five days on the trot, Friday to Tuesday. My wife gets up and does it the other two days.'

Kelsey asked if he could recall exactly what had happened, what was said.

123

'He practically ran into the shop the minute I opened the door,' the newsagent told him. 'He went up to the counter and said to Freda: "I'll take a copy of every daily paper you've got." Only he didn't say it straight out, he stammered it out, it took her a couple of minutes to make out what he was saying. Freda thought it was some kind of joke. She said: "It's a bit early in the morning for fun and games. What do you really want?" He didn't laugh, he seemed very serious, very strung up. He said it again, that he wanted a copy of every daily paper in the shop. Stammering like mad, worse than before.

'I could see what was in Freda's mind. She was thinking: Hello, this could be one of the Hollymount lot, probably not right in the head. She looked over at me. I could see he'd got the money in his hand so I told her: "If that's what the customer wants, then that's what you'd better give him." She started gathering up the papers and the moment she gave him the first one he grabbed it and began looking through it. She was picking them up and laying them down in front of him and he was snatching them up and looking through them.

'She said something like: "My, you are in a hurry." He looked up at her for a moment and said, "It's this case over at Foxwell Common where a woman was choked to death with a scarf." She pulled a face and said: "How horrible—was it somebody you knew?" He said, "No, not exactly, but I know the neighbourhood." He didn't say anything else. He paid for the papers and went.

'Later that morning, when we were having a cup of tea, Freda started reading the papers herself and there was a bit about the murder in some of them, nothing much, just a few lines, no details. All they said more or less was that the body of a woman had been found in a car at a cottage over at Foxwell Common. Freda said she couldn't find anything about her being choked to death with a scarf. I remember her saying: "I don't know where he got that from." I told her he'd probably heard it on the radio.'

Kelsey looked at him thoughtfully. No mention had been made of the scarf or the method of death in the early press and radio releases; the first time the police had mentioned either was during the first press conference, at nine-thirty on the Tuesday morning. Two and a half hours after Hynett had spoken to Freda.

'Did he say anything else, on any of the following mornings?' he asked.

'No, nothing else at all. He came in every day, Sunday included. Always the same thing, a copy of every paper. After the second morning, of course I didn't need to ask what he wanted. I just picked them all up and handed them over. The last time he came in was Monday, the day before yesterday.'

It turned out that the general practitioner who had been the Hynett family doctor had been retired for six months and had gone off to France, to live in his cottage in Gascony; the practice had been taken over by a woman. At half past eight on Thursday morning Sergeant Lambert drove the Chief over to Strettisham to get a word with her before surgery began. It was a single-handed practice. The new doctor wasn't a local woman; she had worked at a health centre in a London borough before deciding in middle age to seek less strenuous pastures in the provinces. Her only knowledge of Martin Hynett came from the practice records. These showed that he was still registered with the practice although there was no record of any contact with him during the last four years.

Kelsey asked her what Hynett's medical history had been. 'The usual childhood ailments,' she told him. 'Nothing of any consequence until he was ten years old.' She paused. 'I see there was a change of address shortly before that.' This was a change from the first to the second of the two addresses they had found in Hynett's papers.

Kelsey asked what trouble had developed when Hynett was ten.

'Psychological trouble of some kind.' She glanced up. 'You will appreciate that these notes are very brief. There's a referral to a special clinic and another to a speech therapist. One might guess school phobia, anxiety state, behavioural

125

difficulties of one kind or another. Probably a nervous, highly strung boy, they often develop a stammer. The change of address might indicate some difficulty at home, separation or divorce or bereavement.'

Kelsey asked if the trouble had persisted and she told him it would appear to have continued for the rest of his school life. 'He left school at sixteen,' she added, 'and very shortly afterwards there is an admission to Chelmwood Hospital as a voluntary patient. Severe personality disturbance, mood swings.' Hynett had spent some months in Chelmwood. After his discharge he reported back to the practice and was given repeat prescriptions of various drugs, mainly tranquillizers and anti-depressants. During this time a third address was entered for him in the records. A few months later he was again admitted to Chelmwood.

This pattern continued over the next few years. His admissions to Chelmwood were always voluntary, his difficulties always apparently the same. After each discharge a fresh change of address was noted. The last time he left Chelmwood, some four years ago, he hadn't reported to the practice and they had heard no more of him. She didn't know of any relatives and there were no other patients by the name of Hynett currently registered with the practice.

In reply to Kelsey's final question she told him that there was no record of any violence, any assault on a female, any attempt at suicide.

CHAPTER 13

The chapel Martin Hynett had attended as a boy was in a lower-middle-class district of Strettisham. There was no reply when Sergeant Lambert knocked at the minister's house a few yards away. As he knocked again a woman cleaner came out of the chapel. 'There's no one there,' she called out to them. She walked over. 'The minister's gone to London,' she told the Chief. 'His niece is getting married down there. He won't be back till tomorrow afternoon.'

Kelsey asked if she could direct him to Albany Street. No. 12 Albany Street was the address at which Hynett had lived between the ages of ten and seventeen.

Yes, she knew the street, only a few minutes' walk away. She gave him directions.

Albany Street consisted of a row of terraced houses facing the playing field. Lambert's ring at No. 12 went unanswered, as also did his ring at No. 10. At No. 14 a girl of seventeen or eighteen came to the door. Kelsey asked if she knew her neighbours at No. 12.

She couldn't tell him much about them, they were certainly not called Hynett. They were a childless, middle-aged couple, both out at work. Her own family had moved into No. 14 three years ago; the name Hynett meant nothing to her. 'There's an old woman in the end house who might be able to help you,' she added after a moment. 'I know she's lived here a long time.' She pointed up the street.

Lambert's ring at the end house was answered by a little, bent, smiling old lady with wispy white hair and ribbed, leathery skin. She peered expectantly out at them.

Kelsey asked if she had known the people who had lived at No. 12 seven or eight years ago. 'That's where the Dawsons lived,' she answered at once. 'Mr and Mrs Dawson. I can't say I knew them very well, they kept very much to themselves, but I was acquainted with them. I always wished them good morning if I met them in the street.'

'What kind of people were they?'

She looked shrewdly up at him. 'May I ask why you want to know?'

Kelsey disclosed his identity and told her he was making inquiries in connection with a case he was working on.

'But both the Dawsons are dead.' She frowned. 'How could they be connected with your case?'

'The case concerns someone who may have been connected with the Dawsons,' he answered patiently. 'We're trying to uncover the facts.'

She digested this for some moments, then she said with sudden decision, 'You'd better come inside.' They followed her into the little house, comfortably furnished a great many years ago. 'I was born in this house,' she declared with pride as she took them into a snug sitting-room where a canary sang in a cage. She waved them into seats. 'With any luck I'll die here.'

Kelsey asked her again what kind of people the Dawsons were.

'Very strict chapel folk,' she told him. 'Very solemn, serious folk, not the sort you'd think of cracking a joke with. Very upright and honest, wouldn't diddle anyone out of a farthing.' She jerked her head. 'Mr Dawson was a bit of a martinet. He was a floorwalker at that big draper's in the town. He'd be seventy, seventy-five, I suppose, when he died, nine or ten years ago. His wife didn't live long afterwards. She was dead inside a twelvemonth.'

'Can you remember exactly when she died?'

She stared up at the ceiling. 'Seven or eight years ago,' she said at last. 'That's the nearest I can come to it. You can ask the minister if you want to know exactly. He buried her. And her husband.'

'Did the Dawsons have any family?'

'They had a married daughter, she lived quite close.' She mentioned a nearby council estate. 'She died in a car crash, must be twelve or thirteen years ago now. Her husband was killed too, he was driving the car. And their daughter. A very pretty girl she was, lovely fair hair and blue eyes, she was only sixteen when she was killed.' She shook her head. 'It was a terrible thing. They'd been on holiday, they were driving home. The son was the only one of the family left alive. He hadn't gone with them on holiday, he'd stayed behind with his grandparents, the Dawsons.'

'Do you remember the boy's name?'

'Martin. Martin Hynett. He stopped on with his grandparents after that, they brought him up.'

'What kind of boy was he?'

'I never saw much of him. He was never allowed to play out in the street with the other children round here, the Dawsons were very strict with him. From anything I ever saw he always seemed a very quiet lad, very well behaved,

128

he never got up to mischief.' She paused. 'Is he the person you're interested in?'

'Yes, he is.'

'He's never gone and got into trouble?' she asked with astonishment. 'I'd never have credited it.' She paused again. 'Though they do say it's the quiet ones you should watch.'

'We're just making general inquiries,' Kelsey said. 'No more than that.'

She inclined her head in acknowledgment. 'Mr Dawson died quite suddenly in the end,' she told them. 'Pneumonia, it was, one winter, he'd been fit and well right up until then. Mrs Dawson went downhill very quickly after he died, it seemed to take all the heart out of her. She started to look very old and frail, then she got 'flu. She didn't make a fight of it, she just seemed to let herself go. I don't really know what happened to Martin, he'd not long left school. One day, soon after the funeral, he wasn't there any more. None of the neighbours knew where he'd gone, they weren't all that interested. They thought he'd probably gone to relatives somewhere.'

'Did you know of any relatives?'

She shook her head. 'I never heard of any. The Dawsons didn't come from these parts, they came from somewhere up north, I believe. They moved into this street a few years after they were married. They didn't own their house, it was rented, the same as mine is. A dealer came and cleared it out and a week or two later the new people moved in.'

At half past five Chief Inspector Kelsey sat at his desk contemplating the results of various inquiries over the last couple of days into any possible point of connection between Venetia Franklin and Martin Hynett: all entirely without result. None of Venetia's contacts knew Hynett's name, no one recognized his photograph. Nor had anyone been able to identify the embroidered handkerchief found in Hynett's wardrobe as belong to Venetia; certainly there was no similar handkerchief among her belongings at Foxwell Cottage.

Inspector Glover came into the office and sat down

opposite the Chief. 'We can draw a line under both cases at the same time,' he said with satisfaction. 'Not often that happens.' He linked his hands behind his head and tilted his chair back. 'Inquest on Hynett tomorrow morning, and then it's all over and done with.' Apart from the resumed inquest on Venetia, of course, but that shouldn't give them any headaches.

Kelsey regarded him in silence. Glover dropped his arms, banged down the legs of his chair. 'You surely haven't any doubts about it? He killed her without a shadow of doubt.' Still Kelsey said nothing.

Glover flung out a hand. 'It preyed on his mind. He got into a terrible state, put an end to his misery with a needle. Possibly by accident, probably by intent.'

'It's the motive that bothers me,' Kelsey said. 'Why did he kill her?'

'Why does a nutter do anything? He'd gone over to Foxwell Common, birdwatching. He chanced to sweep his glasses that way, caught sight of her, took a fancy to her, fantasized about her, got obsessed by her.'

'He doesn't seem to have been a genuine birdwatcher,' Kelsey objected. 'No books on birds in his room, no notebooks or records. And he only bought the binoculars a day or two before he went over to Foxwell. More as if he bought them in order to be able to watch her close up. And the newspaper cutting with the map of the cottage, that seems to me to imply a definite purpose in going over to Foxwell, not just an excursion to look at birds.'

'OK then,' Glover said, good-naturedly changing tack. 'He comes across the newspaper, sees her photograph, falls for her. He goes over to Foxwell to take a look at her, he starts hanging round the common. He buys the binoculars to be able to take a closer look, he invents the hobby of birdwatching in case anyone gets suspicious. On Friday afternoon he sees Franklin leave with the children, he realizes Venetia's alone. He goes down from the common and in through the gate. God knows what was in his mind, maybe he had no intention in the world of doing her any harm.

130

'She looks up and sees him as she's clearing the tea-things. A neat, clean, young man, nicely mannered, quietly spoken, nothing to alarm her. He apologizes for disturbing her, asks her something, anything—could she tell him where the farm is, where the little shop is. Maybe all he wants is to talk to her, hear her voice, see her at close quarters.

'She starts to walk with him to the gate to give him directions. He suddenly says something, makes some move, some approach, maybe amorous, maybe violent. Whatever it is, she takes fright. She starts to scream, tries to run away. He goes after her. Something sweeps over him. All of a sudden she's dead. He's appalled, terrified. He shoves her in the car.'

'He had sufficient control of himself to wipe his fingerprints from the doorhandle,' Kelsey pointed out.

Glover leaned forward. 'The shock of killing her brings him to his senses. He clears off, gets back to the hostel, shuts himself up in his room. A day goes by, two days, three days. Nothing happens, no one comes after him. The horror begins to recede. Maybe he imagined it, maybe it was a dream.

'Then the body is found. The obsession comes back again, full force. He buys all the papers, cuts out every reference to the case. He's excited, stimulated. The days are full now but the nights are something else. He can't sleep. If he does manage to doze off all the old nightmares of his childhood come back, a hundred times worse now. He doses himself with whatever pills he has, what he can buy at the chemist's, what he can beg, borrow or steal from the others. Still the nightmares come. He's forced to go to a doctor, to get something stronger. Still he can't shut out the visions, the memories. He falls into acute depression, he has the horrors, he can't live with what he's done. He mixes himself a brew, one that's going to work. He sticks the needle into his arm, he doesn't care whether it kills him or not, all he wants is peace.'

'Why go all the way to Cannonbridge to do it?' Kelsey asked. 'Why not do it in his bedroom?'

'Maybe he had some childhood memory of the hills, maybe he'd gone there in happier days. If you were going to put an end to it all, wouldn't you choose to do it in the open air, the birds singing, trees and grass, instead of locking yourself into a room in a lodging-house full of the rejects of society, with one of them likely to come knocking at your door just as you're setting about it?'

Kelsey made no reply and Glover got to his feet. 'I'm off home,' he said with finality. 'As far as I'm concerned it's all over bar the shouting.' He went off to his comfortable house, comfortable wife, his well-cooked supper and trouble-free digestion, his evening paper and television, easy chair and well-sprung bed.

Kelsey stayed at his desk for another half-hour, looking through files, staring at the wall, tapping his pen against his teeth. Then he went home, to his silent flat, his scratch supper and indigestion tablets, his spasmodic attempts to watch TV, his twitching calf muscles, intermittent pacing about the living-room.

At eleven o'clock he went to bed. For an hour or two he hovered on the borders of sleep, his brain refusing to switch off. Images passed and repassed behind his closed eyelids, brilliantly etched: Venetia with her knees drawn up, her sandalled feet sticking up in the air; Roy Franklin, talking too much; Jane Franklin pale and exhausted; Philip Colborn weeping and shuddering in the hallway of his magnificent house; Derek Wilesmith's eyes darting about, the medallion glinting against his sun-bronzed chest.

He moved his head restlessly on the pillow but still the images came: Hynett as a lad of sixteen alone and desolate in the little house in Albany Street after his grandmother's funeral; Hynett lying curled up like a baby in the womb, under the trees on the hill, with the morning breeze stirring his hair, the syringe and bottle in his pocket.

At last the images slowed and dimmed, he began to drift away, he felt the blessed relief of nothingness.

At ten minutes past four a blackbird uttered a chirrup from a branch of a tree in the garden of the flat. Kelsey's eyes flicked open, he came instantly and sharply awake. He shot up in bed, his mind clear and refreshed like a desert after rain. A thought flared in his brain: Hynett killed

Venetia all right, but at the behest of someone else, someone with a powerful motive for wishing her dead. Someone who cut Venetia's photograph out of the paper, inked a circle round her face, drew a little map for Hynett in the margin.

The same someone who ten days later, by way of thank-you for his pains, then in turn killed Hynett.

'It doesn't matter two tuppenny damns now where any of the original suspects was when Venetia was killed.' The Chief paced about his office, hands clasped behind his back, frowning down at the floor. 'What continues to matter, to matter even more, is the strength of everyone's motives for wanting her dead.' He came to a halt and threw a glance at Sergeant Lambert, sitting by the desk. 'And it matters a very great deal indeed where each one of them was last Monday evening when Hynett died on the hill.'

'Only if Hynett's death was murder,' Lambert pointed out. 'Even if you're right, and he killed her because he was talked into it by someone else, it doesn't alter the fact that he ended up in one hell of a state afterwards. He still could have killed himself—by accident or design—simply to get some peace.'

The Chief flung out a hand. 'His death was murder all right. I'll take my oath on that. The more I think of it, the more positive I am.'

'Hynett's prints were on the syringe,' Lambert said. 'And on the bottle.'

'Of course they were,' the Chief retorted. 'He injected himself with the stuff, there's no argument about that. But he hadn't the faintest notion it was going to kill him. Someone gave him the bottle and syringe, told him it was some stuff that would quieten his nerves, blot out the night-mares, let him get some sleep. He took it in good faith.'

He resumed his pacing. 'One person we can definitely rule out now, that's Derek Wilesmith. We'll check up on him of course, see where he was Monday evening, but I'm certain we can forget him. There's no way he gains by Venetia's death. The only conceivable reason he could have for killing her would be some weird kink of personality, and in that case he'd want to kill her himself, not get someone else to do it for him, that wouldn't make any kind of sense.'

'What earthly reason would Hynett have for letting himself be talked into killing Venetia?' Lambert asked. 'For money? There's no evidence of that.'

'Possibly money,' Kelsey said. 'Or the promise of it. I don't for one moment think he went up on the hill to listen to the birds and smell the grass, I believe he went there to meet someone by appointment, possibly to collect his fee. He was handed the cocktail as a preliminary, to steady his nerves.' He moved his shoulders. 'But it may not have been money. It could have been some other reward or favour, some consideration—or threat. What we're looking for now is some link between Hynett and one of the original suspects.'

Later in the morning the inquest on Martin Hynett was opened and adjourned, the body released for burial. The case had attracted little attention locally, the courtroom was almost empty. It was an unusual twelvemonth in Cannonbridge during which there were not two or three cases of this kind, patients or ex-patients of Chelmwood Hospital finding an end to their troubles in the river, on the railway line, in one of the quarries.

Old Ben Cresswell, totally sober for once, washed and shaved, smartened up in his decent black suit, gave evidence of finding the body. Jopling took the stand with a confident step and military bearing; he told of Hynett's stay at Hollymount crisply, without hesitation or digression.

Shortly before half past twelve Chief Inspector Kelsey walked down the courthouse steps beside Sergeant Lambert. Inspector Glover and Constable Rudge stood talking at the foot of the steps. Glover turned his head and gave the Chief a quizzical glance. 'Not changed your mind, then?' he asked as Kelsey reached them. 'Still pressing on?' Kelsey gave a single brisk nod. 'I think you're wrong,' Glover said amiably, 'but I wish you luck. I'm not sorry to be bowing out.' He went cheerfully off with Rudge beside him, back to his break-ins and brawls, his stolen cars and petty frauds.

Jopling came down the steps with one of his tenants, a tall, gaunt man with a stilled, ravaged, once-handsome face, dark hair strikingly silvered, dark bushy eyebrows. 'If we could have a word with you,' Jopling said to the Chief. 'Mr Fidoe here has something to tell you that might be of interest.' Fidoe said nothing. He stood with his hands hanging limply at his sides, looking fixedly ahead with an air of bleak neutrality. He wore an old dark suit, carefully sponged and pressed, left over from some other life.

'I'd be glad to hear anything you care to tell me,' Kelsey told him with hearty encouragement. Still Fidoe said nothing. He seemed locked inside some old memory, some old dream.

'You mustn't keep the Chief Inspector waiting,' Jopling said on a peremptory note. 'He's a busy man.'

The tone appeared to rouse Fidoe, like the voice of his master reaching through the slumbers of an old dog stretched out before the fire. He blinked, turned his head and looked at the Chief, his gaze filled with the remnants of old torments.

'It's about Hynett.' His voice held echoes of education and refinement. A clerk, perhaps, or a teacher, Sergeant Lambert thought, slid down to where he is now by heaven knew what painful and humiliating gradations. 'I don't know if it's of any importance, but I don't think he came to Hollymount direct from Devon.'

'That's of considerable importance,' Kelsey told him warmly.

Fidoe appeared on the ball now, temporarily directed and focused. The look in his eyes was intelligent and concentrated. 'It was the day he came to Hollymount,' he continued. 'It was a Sunday. He told us he'd come up from Exmoor that day, he said what time he'd left in the morning, he described the journey. Then later that night, when he was in his room unpacking, I looked in to see how he was settling in. We talked for a few minutes and he made a remark about a hostel here in Cannonbridge, where he'd spent the previous night. He said his room at Hollymount was a good deal better than the dormitory he'd slept in at

135

the hostel. I said: "I understood you'd come up today from Exmoor." His manner changed at once. He said yes, he had come up today. It was some time ago that he'd stayed at the Cannonbridge hostel, I'd misunderstood what he'd said. He didn't chat any more. He said he was tired, he wanted to get to bed, so I went. I never had any further talk with him, he always avoided me after that.'

'That's very useful indeed,' Kelsey told him. 'Did he mention the name of the Cannonbridge hostel?' Fidoe shook his head. 'That's all right,' Kelsey assured him. There were only a few places in Cannonbridge where a man like Hynett could walk in off the street in search of a night's cheap lodging. 'Is there anything else you've remembered?' the Chief asked. 'However trivial?'

'Just that he didn't expect to be in Hollymount long. He said so that first night in his room, before he clammed up. I asked him what he was going to do, if he intended looking for a job. He said he wasn't worried, he'd be OK, he knew someone who would help him, he'd soon be out of Hollymount.' Hynett had given no indication of who this person might be or where he was to be contacted.

When Jopling had taken Fidoe off Kelsey turned towards the car park. A few yards away he saw a couple of youngsters, lads of eleven or twelve, looking at him with a mixture of nervousness and bravado, pushing and nudging each other, talking in undertones. He walked over to them. They stood their ground, made no attempt to run off.

'Did you want to talk to me?' he asked in a friendly tone.

The smaller boy nodded vigorously. He gave his companion a sharp dig in the ribs, galvanizing him into speech.

'It's about what they said on the local radio yesterday morning,' the taller boy said in a rush. 'Asking if anyone saw him on the hill.' He jerked his head up at the courthouse. 'The man they found dead on Tuesday morning.'

'And did you see him?' Kelsey asked.

Again the smaller boy nodded vigorously. 'We both saw him. On Monday evening.'

'How do you know it was Martin Hynett?'

The boy stood with his head to one side, squinting up at

136

the Chief in the brilliant sunlight, frowning, pulling faces in his anxiety. 'It was what they said on the radio, the way he was dressed, the colour of his hair, and all that.'

'We're sure it was him,' the other lad put in.

'What was he doing when you saw him?'

'We were standing at the bottom of Bracken Hill, waiting for some mates. This guy came running up. I turned round to see if our mates were coming and he ran into me, he knocked me over, I went down with a wallop. He grabbed hold of me and pulled me up. He said he was sorry, he was in a hurry, he had an appointment. I said it was OK, I wasn't hurt, and he ran off again, up the hill.'

'You're sure he said that? That he had an appointment? He didn't just say he was meeting someone?'

'No, he definitely said he had an appointment, I remember that.'

'Did he seem anxious?'

'No, he seemed more excited,' the lad said after a moment's thought. 'He stammered when he talked.'

'Did he seem to be looking forward to this appointment?'

'Oh yes,' the lad said at once. 'He seemed as if he couldn't wait to get there.'

'What time was this?'

'Just going on half past seven. We'd arranged to meet our mates at half past and they came along a minute or two after he'd run off up the hill.'

A few minutes later Kelsey and Lambert were on their way back to the station. The Chief stared out through the windscreen in silence. Three or four people had already come forward in response to the radio appeal for any sighting of Hynett on Monday evening. All of them had noticed Hynett at various times when he was lying motionless under the trees; all had thought him asleep.

The earliest of these sightings was by an elderly woman, a cottager who lived close by. 'I saw the young man lying there as I was going back home after visiting a friend,' she told the Chief. 'It was about five past eight.' She was certain of the time, she had been hurrying back for a radio programme.

So Hynett was alive at seven-thirty, when the boys spoke to him at the foot of the hill, and by five minutes past eight he was lying comatose, if not already dead, under the rowans. A space of thirty-five minutes, the Chief pondered with relish; a precise, manageable, well-authenticated interval, something to get his teeth into. He leaned back and closed his eyes. Lambert glanced at him as he turned the car into the station forecourt and saw that he was smiling.

Early in the afternoon the Chief and Sergeant Lambert set out on a round of the Cannonbridge hostels and doss-houses. They struck lucky at their third try, a hostel run by a charitable trust. Hynett had stayed there on the night of Saturday, April 28th; the warden produced the register with his signature. In the space for home address Hynett had written: Westwater Farm, Longbarton, Exmoor, Devon. 'He told me he didn't have any home,' the warden explained, 'so I told him to put down wherever it was he'd just come from.' The space for a forwarding address had been left blank. 'I reminded him about filling it in when he was leaving,' the warden said. 'He told me he'd be sure to do it, but after he'd gone I saw that he hadn't.'

When Hynett arrived at the hostel he told the warden he'd just got off a coach coming up from Exmoor; he didn't know how long he would be staying at the hostel. There was someone local he was going to phone on the following day, someone he was sure would help him get a job. He would book in at the hostel for one night and see what happened next day.

'You're sure he said someone local?' Kelsey asked.

Yes, the warden was sure. He understood that that was the reason Hynett had returned to the area, because of this local contact. The following afternoon, Sunday, Hynett came into the office and said he would shortly be checking out. The warden asked if he'd had any luck with his contact. In contrast with his manner the evening before, Hynett was markedly uncommunicative; he had merely nodded. 'I saw that for some reason he didn't want to talk about it,' the warden added. 'So I left it at that.'

138

'Did he seem satisfied with the results of his contact?' Kelsey asked. 'Did he seem nervous or anxious?'

'He seemed guarded,' the warden answered after reflection. 'Guarded and purposeful.

At five o'clock Lambert drove the Chief over to Strettisham again, to see if the minister had got back from London. And he had; he was at work in his study when Lambert pressed the bell. A scholarly-looking man in his sixties with a quiet, contemplative face, an air of detached compassion.

He hadn't known of Hynett's death, he was shocked and grieved to hear of it. He at once assumed that the death was suicide. 'I can't say I'm altogether surprised,' he said. 'There was terrible tragedy in his life. I'm afraid he had to endure a great deal of suffering.' He had heard nothing of Martin for a year or two.

'It's the family background we'd like to know more about,' Kelsey said as the minister took them into the sitting-room. 'And Martin's medical history.'

'He was never an easy child,' the minister told him. 'The actual birth was very difficult, very long-drawn-out, and Mrs Hynett was unwell for some time afterwards. He was a fractious, crying infant, and she didn't have much patience with him, mainly because of her health. He was the second child. The first was a girl, Clara, a beautiful child with a sunny disposition, never any trouble from the day she was born.

'Of course that made the situation with Martin all the worse; the Hynetts had taken it for granted that their second child would be as beautiful and sweet-natured as the first. Martin was a very ordinary-looking little boy, on the plain side if anything. He became very jealous of Clara, hardly surprising. It always tended to be the three of them together, the parents and Clara, with Martin on his own, the outsider. Not that Clara was ever deliberately unkind to Martin, not from anything I was ever aware of, but she was six years older, so there wasn't much chance of their being close, even in the most favourable circumstances.'

'What did the father do?'

'He was a wages clerk for a small local firm. He was evacuated here as a child during the war, from the east end of London. He stayed on after the war, married and settled down. I thought both he and his wife—particularly the wife —very harsh with Martin, for no good reason. I tried to get them to understand the boy a bit more, to look at things from his point of view, but I didn't have much success. His mother clearly felt some guilt because she didn't love him as she loved Clara. She resented feeling guilty, and the way it came out was that she was very censorious of Martin, full of moral fervour for his so-called sins.

'You can imagine the result. Martin was perpetually see-sawing between doing everything he could think of to please her—an impossible task—and then being swamped with fury at the unfair way he was treated. He'd burst out into some peccadillo to express his fury.' The minister sighed deeply. 'It didn't add up to a very happy or stable childhood.' He lapsed into a brief silence. 'All that was bad enough, but when the accident happened—that was a truly appalling situation for him.'

'What happened?'

'The family were going to the seaside for a fortnight's holiday. They were never very flush with money and it was the first proper holiday they'd been able to afford. Mrs Hynett made Clara a couple of dresses for the holiday. She was a good needlewoman and she took a lot of trouble over them. She showed them to me one afternoon when I called, they were very pretty, very carefully made. When they were finished she hung them in a wardrobe. The day before they were leaving, Clara went to pack the dresses and found they'd both been slashed to ribbons.

'You can imagine the uproar. There was never any doubt about who'd done it. Martin didn't make any attempt to deny it—or to offer any explanation. Not that there was much mystery about that. There'd been nothing in the way of a new outfit for him for the holiday. He was ten years old, in the grip of a turmoil of emotions he couldn't understand, couldn't even begin to cope with. Slashing the dresses was the only way he could deal with the situation.

'There were the usual consequences, of course. He was treated as a criminal, a sinner, exposed to recriminations, vituperation. No attempt of any kind made to understand why he'd done it, what behaviour on the part of the others had driven him to it. As a punishment—I'm afraid his mother was a good deal stronger on punishment than she was on love or forgiveness—he was not to go on holiday with them, he would be left behind with the mother's parents, the Dawsons.

'For most of the fortnight, on his mother's instructions, he was barely spoken to, he was treated as a moral leper. It was the summer holidays, so he didn't even have school to escape to. He was forbidden to leave the house to play in the park, or go fishing with his schoolfriends. It was very hot weather and he spent the whole two weeks doing household chores or shut away upstairs in his bedroom, forced to learn appropriate passages of the Bible, made to recite them every evening—not a use of the Bible one cares to see.'

The minister stood up and crossed to the window, he stared out at the sunny garden. 'The Dawsons brought him along to me. They recited the list of his sins, they expected me to join in the condemnation.' He sighed again. 'I tried to make them see they were talking about a ten-year-old boy, not some hardened criminal. I tried to give them some insight into the child's mind.' He turned from the window and went back to his seat, dropped into it. 'I was wasting my time. Martin had become the family scapegoat by then. Once someone is allotted that position it's almost impossible for an outsider to do anything about it.'

Kelsey asked him how the accident had come about. 'The Hynetts were driving home at the end of the holiday,' the minister told him. 'It was raining hard. The car was old, it hadn't been properly maintained, the tyres were in a poor state. No other vehicle was involved. Hynett wasn't familiar with the road, he took a bend too fast. He went into a skid, hit the bank, the car turned over several times. The parents were killed outright, the girl died on the way to hospital.'

'How did Martin take it?'

'He became very quiet and withdrawn. He suffered from

141

bad nightmares for months afterwards. He developed a stammer, he wouldn't go to school. The social workers wanted to put him in a home, they reckoned the grandparents were too old to look after him properly. But old Dawson wasn't having any of that. He threatened to make an almighty row if they tried to take the boy away, he was now all the family they had left.

'Round about that time they were closing down the old-style orphanages and there was a shortage of foster-parents in this area. The social workers had been getting a lot of stick in the local press over the way they'd handled a couple of cases and they weren't at all anxious for any more bad publicity. Dawson was a very stubborn man. He threatened to appeal against any care order, take it right up to the House of Lords if necessary—so in the end they gave in and the Dawsons kept the boy.

'After a time Martin seemed to improve, to begin settling down. He attended various clinics, he went to school regularly, he appeared less withdrawn, his stammer improved. The grandparents were strict with him but there wasn't the emotional turmoil there'd been with his mother, and of course Clara was no longer there to be held up before him night and day as an example. There were none of the old outbursts of anger, he became quite amenable. He was very obedient to his grandparents, particularly to his grandmother.

'The grandfather died when Martin was about fifteen. After that Martin became very anxious about his grandmother, he scarcely wanted to let her out of his sight. Understandable enough. She was all he had left, he was terrified something might happen to her and he'd be on his own.' He jerked a hand. 'And of course that was exactly what did happen. She died less than twelve months after her husband. Martin was in his last term at school. He stayed at home to look after her, he nursed her with the most tremendous devotion, he was desperate for her to recover, but she just slipped away. It was a shattering blow.

'The landlord told him he'd have to look for somewhere else to live, he couldn't accept a lad of that age as a tenant,

142

and in any case Martin didn't want that, to live alone in a rented house. After the funeral he went completely to pieces. Within a day or two he was in Chelmwood Hospital as a voluntary patient. I went over there regularly to see him. He was never mentally ill in the sense of suffering from a recognizable illness such as schizophrenia. He was severely disturbed emotionally, and had been for most, if not all, of his life. He suffered from severe anxiety neurosis, agitated depression.

'He was in and out of Chelmwood over the next few years. He'd make some progress, he'd come out, I'd help him to find digs and a job of sorts. He'd get along fairly well for a month or two. Then it would all start to boil up again, fits of crying, moodiness, panic attacks. He'd become withdrawn again, he'd get worse, he'd be forced to give up the job, then it was back into Chelmwood. One of the greatest obstacles to his recovery was his conviction that he was responsible for the deaths of his parents and sister, that it was the strength of his hostile feelings that had somehow caused the accident. Sometimes he would see it as a terrible divine retribution for his disobedience to his mother.

'As he got older he could recognize logically that this was nonsense but he never managed to rid himself of the feeling of guilt. I spoke once or twice to the doctor who treated him in Chelmwood. He told me that if Martin could find some settled way of life, if he could form some stable relationships, find some work he liked that wasn't too demanding, then he might in time put the past behind him, he might achieve some kind of settled calm. But if none of those things happened, the outlook was very dark.

'The last time he came out of Chelmwood he seemed a good deal better. That was about four years ago. He said he'd decided to make a clean break, make a fresh start somewhere new. He had a small nestegg, the money left after his grandmother died, something under a thousand pounds, if my memory serves me. He'd put it into a building society. He was never a spendthrift, he'd been brought up to be very careful with money. He told me he intended to move round the country, getting casual work where he could. If he found a place he liked, if he saw some opening, he'd stay there.

'I told him he could always get in touch with me if he needed to. I'd be ready to help him at any time. I really thought things were beginning to look hopeful for him. He sent me a postcard now and then over the next year or two, just a few lines to say he was all right, keeping out of hospital, getting occasional work, managing reasonably well. He never mentioned making any friends or forming any relationships. He never gave me any address. Every card was from a different place, Scotland, Wales, East Anglia. About eighteen months ago the cards stopped coming and I heard nothing more from him.'

'It seems that he recently got in touch with someone in Cannonbridge,' Kelsey said. 'Someone he believed might help him find a job. Have you any idea who that person might have been?' The minister pondered but could offer no help.

When they got back to Cannonbridge Kelsey spent a few minutes looking through the snapshots from the plastic wallet inside Hynett's wardrobe. There were half a dozen of them, none of them recent, only one taken within the last year or two; it showed Hynett among a group of workers on a building site. He stood stripped to the waist in summer sunshine.

The rest were old family snapshots, taken in parks and gardens. Martin appeared in only one, a family group, taken when he was six or seven. An anxious-looking little boy standing apart from the other three, his face half turned from the camera. Clara stood between her parents, the three of them smiling, her father's arm round her shoulders. Mrs Hynett was still good-looking in early middle age. Her husband had a lively, energetic air. Clara was almost as tall as her mother, with the same delicate features. A very pretty girl, her long, curly, blonde hair drawn up in a pony tail.

As the Chief studied her smiling face a resemblance stirred in his brain. The photograph in the ornate silver frame on the Victorian whatnot in the corner of Mrs Stacey's sitting-room. Venetia as a schoolgirl, standing beside Megan

Brewster, smiling out at the camera with a cheerful, confident air.

CHAPTER 14

It was the weekend of the Spring Bank Holiday. Sergeant Lambert set off for Exmoor around noon on Saturday, well behind the main surge of holiday-makers. The day was fine and sunny, the traffic manageable. In the front gardens azaleas bloomed in bursts of crimson and scarlet. Between the towns the lanes were encrusted with snowy sprays of hawthorn, apple orchards flowered in pink and white, fields of yellow rape blossom patterned the landscape.

He found a bed for the night in a resort on the North Devon coast. After breakfast next morning he drove the twenty-five miles inland to Longbarton, across smoothly sculptured, rolling green downs. Longbarton was a hamlet of thatched cottages shaded by towering horse-chestnuts laden with pink and creamy florets, yellow laburnum and red may beside the garden gates.

He inquired for Westwater Farm and was told it lay two miles further on. He drove beside a clear brown stream rippling over grey stones, sparkling beneath alders and willows, through open downland dotted with sheep and goats, sturdy-looking ponies. The farm lay in a hollow of the downs. The farmhouse was a substantial old stone dwelling set among lilacs, purple and white; wistaria and clematis flowered along the walls.

A woman answered his knock at the door. In her middle forties, perhaps, comely enough, a placid, friendly air. She wore a print apron, she was drying her hands on a towel.

He apologized for disturbing her on a Sunday morning. He told her who he was, that he had called to ask what she could tell him about Martin Hynett. He outlined the facts of Hynett's death. She closed her eyes for a moment and stood with her head lowered, struggling against tears.

'The poor young man,' she said at last in her soft Devon

voice. 'Did something particular happen to make him do it?' She assumed at once that the death was suicide.

'We're still trying to uncover the facts,' Lambert said. 'We hope you'll be able to help us.'

'I'll tell you all I know,' she responded at once. 'I'm afraid it's not a great deal.' She stepped back. 'You'd better come inside. My husband's not here at the moment, he's gone over to his brother's on some family business.' She took him into a large, old-fashioned kitchen and invited him to sit down while she made coffee. He asked her how she had become acquainted with Hynett.

'He came here a few months ago, at the tail end of winter,' she told him as she took beakers from the dresser. 'He was looking for casual work. He gave us the names of some farms he'd worked at. We manage here without any regular help but we do sometimes take on casuals. He looked fit and strong, he seemed very willing. We were working flat out at the time, in the middle of lambing. My husband phoned the last place Martin had been at and they gave him a good reference. They said he'd worked there a few months, he'd been no trouble, very useful, they could thoroughly recommend him, so we took him on.'

She made the coffee, took milk from the fridge. 'He worked well while he was here. He picked things up quickly, he didn't have to be shown twice. He had his meals here in the kitchen and he slept in the room over the old stables. My sons had it as a rumpus room when they were teenagers, there's a sofa bed in there. My sons are both grown up now and working away, neither of them wanted to go into farming.' She poured the coffee and handed Lambert his beaker. 'Martin was very neat and tidy, he didn't smoke or drink.'

Lambert asked if he went out much while he was at the farm, if he had shown any interest in girls.

She shook her head. 'No, no interest at all.'

'Did he go birdwatching?'

Again she shook her head. 'I can't remember him being interested in birds. We get a lot of different birds here, particularly in the spring, but I never heard him pass any

146

remark about them, or show any interest. He spent his spare time over in his room, he read a lot. There's an old black-and-white television set over there, and a radio. Both of them needed attention when he came, they hadn't been used for long enough. He spoke to me about them, said he'd had a look at them and they didn't need much doing. Would it be all right if he repaired them and used them while he was here. I said he was very welcome.'

She sat down and began to drink her coffee. 'He made a first-class job of them, in no time at all. He borrowed one of the old bikes here and went off and got the spare parts that were needed for the sets, he never made any fuss about any of it. I was quite impressed. I told him he could earn a good living doing that kind of thing. He used the bike to go to chapel too, whenever we could spare him. The chapel's a good few miles from here but he never seemed to mind what the weather was.'

'Did he talk about himself at all?'

'Hardly at all. He was very quiet, though always pleasant and civil. Some days he'd be even more quiet, he'd scarcely speak a word and he'd look very down in the mouth, then a day or two later it would seem to pass and he'd be all right again. I did wonder if he suffered from depression. I've known one or two folk who suffered from it and you get to recognize the symptoms. But I didn't like to ask and he never said anything about it.'

'How did he come to move on from here?'

'When the work slackened off, towards the end of April, my husband told him he'd been very useful, we'd been glad of the extra pair of hands, but he wasn't really needed any more, he might think of moving on at the end of the week.'

'How did he take it?'

'He just nodded when my husband said that, but later the same day, when my husband was out, he came up to me and asked if there was any way he could possibly stay on here permanently. He said he didn't need a proper wage, he'd gladly work for his keep and a little pocket money.'

Tears came into her eyes. 'He begged and pleaded, he was stammering badly. He said he was happy here, he didn't

147

mind how hard he worked, he'd give anything to be part of a family, to belong somewhere.'

She looked up at Lambert. 'I was taken by surprise, him speaking out like that, when he was usually so quiet. But I had to tell him it was no good, there wasn't the work all the year round for three people. And in any case the sort of arrangement he was suggesting wouldn't do. It wouldn't be fair to him, it would be taking advantage of him, exploiting him. I knew my husband wouldn't hear of it. I told him it would be no kind of life for a single young man, he ought to go where there were more folk of his own age. He should mix more, try to make a more normal life for himself.'

'What did he say to that?'

'He said he didn't want any other kind of life, the life here was all he wanted. It was good for him, it suited him. Then he said something that's come back to me more than once since he left. He said, "You've been so kind and I've no one else at all." I said, "You must have some family, some relatives." He said, "No, I haven't. I have no one at all in the whole wide world."' She shook her head with a sigh. 'It seemed such a dreadfully lonely sort of thing to say, it's stuck in my mind. I could tell he wasn't just trying it on, looking for sympathy. His eyes when he said it, the tone of his voice, I knew it was true all right.' She shook her head again. 'But what could I do? I had to say: "I'm very sorry, but you see how it is. I'm afraid you'll have to move on."'

'Did he leave it at that?'

'Yes. He just said, "I quite understand." He went out of the kitchen, back to whatever job he was doing, he never said another word about it. He left at the end of the week, on the Saturday morning. He was very formal, very polite, when he was leaving. He thanked both of us for being kind to him, and off he went.'

'Did he say where he was going?'

'He didn't volunteer the information but I asked him, the night before he left. He said he'd thought about what I'd said, and I was quite right, it was time he stopped roaming about. He'd decided to go back to his own part of the country and try to settle down. He knew someone there who

148

might help him to get a more permanent job. He was quite calm when he was telling me all that, not intense and agitated like he'd been when he was asking if he could stay.'

Before he left Lambert showed her the embroidered handkerchief and asked if it belonged to her. She shook her head, she had never seen it before. Nor was she able to recognize the brown Paisley scarf. He saw that she was curious about why he was showing her these things but he offered no explanation and she didn't ask for one.

Next morning Lambert got to the police station in good time but, Bank Holiday Monday or not, the Chief was there ahead of him. He sat with his head lowered, listening intently to what Lambert had to tell him about his visit to Westwater Farm.

'Chelmwood Hospital,' Kelsey said when the Sergeant had finished. 'We'll get over there right away. They may have some idea who it was Hynett contacted here in Cannonbridge.' As they went out to the car he added, 'I'm definitely ruling out Derek Wilesmith.' An officer had been over to Ellenborough, delving into Wilesmith's background and past, as well as his movements last Monday evening. He had been unable to discover any kind of connection between Wilesmith and Martin Hynett.

And whoever it was that Hynett had bounded up the hill to meet, it assuredly couldn't have been Wilesmith. A party of Japanese businessmen had spent all day Monday visiting the factory where Wilesmith worked; in the evening the firm had laid on a lavish reception for them at the best hotel in Ellenborough. Wilesmith had been one of the young men detailed to dance attendance on the party during their tour of the works and afterwards at the reception. At seven-thirty on Monday evening Wilesmith was indubitably standing in the hotel foyer, forty-five miles from the hill path where Hynett ran with an eager, hopeful look, towards his quietus.

When they reached Chelmwood Hospital they found the medical superintendent was off duty. They were taken along to the office of his deputy, a young man who had been less than six months at Chelmwood; there wasn't much he could tell the Chief. 'But there's a retired charge nurse by the name of Grimshaw,' he added. 'There isn't much he doesn't know about any male patient here during the last twenty years. He left the hospital a couple of months ago, he's living in the village now. I suggest you speak to him.'

Ten minutes later Lambert drew up outside a stone-built cottage. When he pressed the bell the door was opened almost at once by a short, plump woman, sixty or so, smartly dressed in provincial fashion. She gave them a far from welcoming glance.

The Chief told her they were looking for a Mr Grimshaw. Her look became tinged with irritation. 'My husband,' she said aggressively. 'We're on our way out. What do you want with him?'

Kelsey had long and harsh experience of the martial qualities of well-dressed, short, plump ladies of a certain age. He assumed his most ingratiating smile and explained courteously who he was and the fact that he believed her husband might be able to give them some information about a case on which they were working.

A deep frown appeared between her brows. 'We're off to stay with friends for a few days,' she declared. 'We've over fifty miles to drive, in Bank Holiday traffic. We're none too early as it is.' She showed no sign of letting them in.

Kelsey promised to be as quick as humanly possible. 'Very well, then,' she agreed grudgingly. She flung back the door and stepped aside. She banged the door shut after them, then she went rapidly down the hall and levelled a powerful shout up the stairs. 'Edward!'

An answering cry came winging back from some remote region. 'Shan't be a tick.'

'Someone to see you,' she called up in even more strident tones.

'Right, I'm coming down.' A minute or two later Grimshaw appeared, shrugging on a tweed jacket. A stocky, jovial-looking man with an easy-going air.

'Police,' his wife said shortly, with a jerk of her head at Kelsey and Lambert. 'They think you can help them over some case.' She held up a hand with the fingers outspread.

'Five minutes. Not a second more.' She raked the three of them with a challenging gaze. 'We'll be stuck in the traffic if we don't get off.' She vanished towards the kitchen quarters.

Grimshaw took them into a sitting-room. Yes, he remembered Martin Hynett. The Chief gave him the unadorned facts of Hynett's death and saw once again that the death was immediately assumed to be suicide. He explained briefly about the person Hynett was believed to have contacted in Cannonbridge and asked Grimshaw if he had any idea who that person might have been.

'Someone does come instantly to mind,' Grimshaw answered at once. 'He always took an interest in Martin and he certainly offered more than once to help him about a job, particularly the last time Martin left Chelmwood—but Martin didn't take him up on that, he'd made up his mind to strike out afresh, somewhere new.'

'Can you give me the name of this person?' Kelsey asked.

'Yes, of course. It's Colborn, Mr Colborn from Springfield House.'

CHAPTER 15

Kelsey sat for a moment with his eyes closed. 'Mr Colborn was a hospital visitor at Chelmwood for several years,' Grimshaw explained. 'A colleague of his, another bank clerk, came into the hospital after a nervous breakdown, and Mr Colborn used to come over to see him. He got talking to some of the other patients, those that had no families to visit them. He started taking an interest in some of the younger ones, those with a bit more intelligence, that he thought might make something of their lives. He took up regular visiting after his colleague left.' He moved his head. 'Very nice man, Mr Colborn, very understanding. He told me once he'd gone through a bad time himself after his mother died, he knew what it was to be depressed. He gave up the visiting after they started the run-down at Chelmwood, and it was mainly old people left in the hospital.

And he'd been made manager at his bank by then, he had a lot more demands on his time.'

'Was he particularly interested in Hynett?' Kelsey asked.

'Actually, it was the other way round,' Grimshaw told him. 'Martin was particularly interested in Mr Colborn. He thought the world of him, used to follow him round, I think he looked on him as a father.' He went over to a bureau and opened a drawer. 'I've got some photographs here, I came across them again the other day. I believe there's one of Mr Colborn with Martin among them.' He opened a folder of snapshots and glanced through them. 'They were taken at a sports day at the hospital five or six years ago.'

The sitting-room door suddenly jerked open and Mrs Grimshaw's face appeared. 'If we don't get off now we might just as well not go at all,' she announced in tones of simmering anger.

Grimshaw smiled at her without rancour. 'Two minutes, my dear,' he said mildly. She reluctantly withdrew.

Grimshaw picked out a snapshot and showed it to the Chief. Neither Colborn nor Hynett appeared aware of the camera. Colborn was talking, gesturing into the distance, where the figures of runners could be descried. Hynett, looking very young, his hair cropped short, was looking up at him with an intense, serious gaze. Nearby, Ruth Colborn, in a summer dress and flowery hat, stood listening with an earnest, attentive expression, to two women who, judging by their appearance, were patients of the hospital.

The door flew open again and Mrs Grimshaw stood on the threshold, menacing and implacable. 'We've just finished,' Grimshaw told her cheerfully. 'I'm on my way.'

The gates of Springfield House stood open when Sergeant Lambert turned the car in shortly after midday. As he drove past the entrance to the rose-garden he glanced in and saw Mrs Colborn, in shirt and slacks, busy spraying the roses; she looked up as they went by. Lambert stopped the car. They got out and walked back.

The soft warm air in the rose-garden was filled with an exquisite blend of fragrances. Mrs Colborn was directing the spray at a pale lavender shrub rose coming into full bloom. 'This is a magnificent show you've got here,' the Chief said as he approached.

She continued her task. 'With luck they'll be at their very best on Saturday.'

The Chief apologized for disturbing her on a public holiday but she waved his apology aside. 'I'm not going anywhere,' she said lightly. 'As long as you don't mind my carrying on with this. It's got to be done.'

No, he didn't mind at all. 'But it's your husband we really want a word with,' he told her.

'He's out playing golf at the moment, but he should be back soon, if you don't mind waiting.'

No, he didn't mind in the least. 'Perhaps we might have a chat while we're waiting,' he added. 'One or two details you might be able to help us with.'

'Go right ahead. I'm always glad to help.' She turned her attention to another rose, a beautiful deep pink, festooned with half-open flowerheads.

'If you could cast your mind back to last Monday evening,' the Chief said. 'A week ago today.'

She gave a nod. 'Yes, I remember it. That was my Benevolent Fund evening.' She mentioned a charity that made grants to the elderly infirm and handicapped living in their own homes. 'I'm the local representative, I do my visits on the third Monday in the month.'

'Can you tell me how your husband spent that evening?'

She glanced up at him as if about to ask why he wanted to know. But she didn't ask. 'He came in from work as usual,' she told him. 'After we'd eaten I gave him a lift to his club, on my way to do my visits. His own car was in dock.'

'What time was this?'

'My first visit was for seven-thirty, so we left here just after seven, that gave me time to drive him to the club and then get over to the other side of town, to Pump Street. I got back here a little after nine. Philip came in around ten-fifteen. We were in bed by eleven.'

'Can you substantiate the time you both left here?'

'I can, as it happens. I stopped the car on the way out, to speak to a girl who was coming in to see me. I wasn't expecting her, she called on the off-chance. She's a school-girl, she does voluntary work at Lyndale. She asked if I'd give her a reference for a preliminary nursing course she's applying for, for after she leaves school. I told her I'd be happy to give her the reference if she'd call round the following evening—which she did.' She gave Kelsey the girl's name and address.

She moved on among the roses and the Chief moved after her. 'Do you know a young man by the name of Hynett?' he asked.

'The young man who killed himself on the hill? Philip read about it in the paper, he showed it to me. He told me Hynett was one of the young men he tried to help when he used to go over to Chelmwood Hospital. I sometimes went over to open days or sports days with Philip. He says he introduced me to Hynett once, but I can't place him.'

'Hynett never came to the house?'

'No. Philip never brought any of the patients here.'

'Had your husband been in touch with Hynett recently?'

'No. He told me he hadn't heard from him for a year or two.'

There was the sound of a car turning in through the gates. 'That'll be Philip now,' she said. A few moments later the blue Orion drove past; Colborn didn't glance their way. Kelsey turned to go. Ruth drew off her gardening gloves and made to accompany him towards the house. Kelsey halted. 'We'd appreciate it if we might have a word with your husband on his own,' he told her.

'Yes, of course.' She drew on her gloves again.

'We won't keep him long,' Kelsey promised. 'I realize it's almost lunch-time.'

'Don't worry about that,' she said easily as she turned back towards her shrub roses. 'It's a cold lunch, there's nothing to spoil.'

Lambert followed the Chief out of the rose-garden. The Orion was drawn up outside the front door which stood open. As they approached they could see Colborn standing

154

in the hall, talking to a middle-aged woman in a nylon overall. He turned his head. 'There you are, Chief Inspector. I saw your car, I was wondering where you'd got to.' His tone was easy and friendly. 'Mrs Drake thought you must have come across my wife in the garden.' He glanced at the woman. 'That's all right then, Mrs Drake.' She gave a nod and took herself off, back to her duties.

Once again the Chief apologized for calling on a public holiday. Colborn waved a dismissive hand. 'No matter,' he said amiably. 'I don't imagine Bank Holidays mean very much when you're busy on a case.'

'If we might come inside,' the Chief suggested.

'Yes, of course.' He took them along to his study. His manner was relaxed, he didn't appear at all nervous, but there were dark rings round his eyes, his face was thinner, haggard, as if he no longer ate or slept properly; in spite of his round of golf his skin looked pale. He had a hunched, pinched look as if an interior chill struck through his being.

'A few days ago,' Kelsey said, 'one of my men called on you here. He showed you a photograph of a young man, Martin Hynett. You didn't tell the officer that you were acquainted with Hynett.'

'He didn't ask if I knew him,' Colborn rejoined on a note of protest. 'He asked if Mrs Franklin had ever mentioned Hynett to me. I told him she hadn't.'

'What was your last contact with Hynett—however brief or trivial?'

'I had a postcard from him now and then after he left the area. The last one was about eighteen months ago.'

'Did he phone you recently?'

Colborn frowned. 'No, he did not.'

'Were you surprised when you read of his death?'

'Not altogether. It was always a possibility with someone like Martin.'

'Were you surprised when the officer called asking if Mrs Franklin had known Hynett?'

'Not altogether,' Colborn said again. 'I'd always thought —and I still think—that Venetia was murdered by someone deranged. I imagine the police are of the same opinion.

When Hynett committed suicide shortly after her death I would expect them to consider if he might have killed her.' His tone grew ragged and hesitant, he looked even more haggard.

'Do you think it's possible he did kill her?'

'I've thought about it, of course, since the detective was here. I don't know if you have any evidence to suggest he did it, but my own opinion, for what it's worth, is no, I would be very surprised indeed if he had anything to do with it.' He looked paler than ever, he pressed his hands together.

'Why are you so certain?'

'It wouldn't fit in with anything I knew of Martin—though it's four years since I saw him, he could have changed a good deal in that time. But I can't think of any conceivable reason why he should have done such an appalling thing. He never struck me as the type who might be a danger to women.'

'What makes you believe Hynett took his own life?'

Colborn looked startled. 'Surely that's what I read—or heard? That he died of a drug overdose?' He paused. 'I took it for granted that meant suicide.'

'It didn't strike you that it might have been an accident?'

He stared down at the carpet. 'No, it didn't.'

'Did you tell your wife that an officer had called here with Hynett's photograph? That you thought the police might be wondering if Hynett killed Mrs Franklin?'

He shook his head, he showed signs of increasing agitation.

'Why didn't you mention it to your wife?'

Colborn glanced briefly up at him. His eyes looked tormented. 'Ruth had been very distressed by all that business about Venetia. It would have been lunacy to stir it up again.'

Kelsey dipped a hand into his pocket and produced a plastic envelope displaying the newspaper cutting taken from the first page of Hynett's scrapbook. He held it out. 'Did you see this photograph of Mrs Franklin in the local paper?'

Colborn stared down at Venetia's face smiling up at him, carefree and light-hearted, at the little map in the margin, the inked cross with the letters F.C. beside it. 'Yes, I believe I did see it. A few weeks back.'

'Did you cut the photograph out of the paper?'

Colborn glanced sharply up at him. 'No, I did not.'

'Did you give the cutting to anyone?' the Chief persisted, as if Colborn had answered yes instead of no.

Colborn shook his head in silence.

'Did you draw that map? Showing the location of Foxwell Cottage?'

Again Colborn shook his head. He appeared to be struggling for self-control.

Kelsey still held the cutting out in front of Colborn who stared down at it again with a bewildered, hypnotized air. Kelsey said nothing. The silence lengthened. Colborn suddenly burst out, 'Where did you get that cutting?'

Kelsey didn't answer.

'Did Martin have it?' Colborn asked with the same explosive air, as if forced to speak against his better judgment.

Still Kelsey said nothing.

Colborn grew deathly pale. A tremor started in his limbs, in his head and neck. 'Did Martin kill her? Do you know for certain that he killed her?' His teeth chattered so that he could scarcely get the words out.

Kelsey still said nothing but continued to hold out the cutting. Colborn looked up at him with a ravaged face. 'My God! You do know it! He did kill her!' He dropped his head in his hands and broke into terrible, convulsive weeping.

Kelsey lowered his hand and sat regarding Colborn until his shoulders stopped shaking and the sound of his weeping died away. Colborn took out a handkerchief and dabbed at his face.

'Last Monday evening,' Kelsey said. 'A week ago today. How did you spend that evening?'

Colborn looked vaguely up at him as if he had forgotten the Chief was in the room.

'Monday?' After a few moments he gave an account of the evening that tallied with what his wife had told them.

He managed to take a hold on himself, his tone grew steadier, stronger.

'Did you leave your club at any time during the evening?' Kelsey asked.

'No, I didn't. There was a meeting of the entertainments committee, to arrange the autumn programme.' His manner was concentrated now, alert and wary. 'I'm on the committee. I had a drink in the bar when I arrived, I stood talking there until the meeting began. It started on time, at eight o'clock.' The meeting had lasted a good hour. Afterwards he had chatted to various friends, had a couple of drinks, had been given a lift home by one of the members.

'You told us a couple of weeks ago,' Kelsey reminded him, 'that when you decided to break off your association with Mrs Franklin there were no scenes, no rancour, you remained on friendly terms.' Colborn gave a nod. His eyes never left Kelsey's face, his gaze was sharp and focused.

'I put to you now,' Kelsey went on in an easy, conversational tone, 'another view of events at that time.' Colborn sat rigid and motionless, his eyes fixed on the Chief. 'You did indeed attempt to break off with Mrs Franklin, but she wasn't in the least compliant. She understood your reasons very well, she saw how fearful you were of the consequences for your career and your marriage, if the affair should become known.' Colborn began to struggle up from his chair but the Chief waved him down again. 'Mrs Franklin appears to have been a lady with a liking for money she could lay her hands on without overmuch tedious effort on her own part. I put it to you that she made it clear she would be happy to fade from the picture—for a price, a regularly recurring price. You attempted to resist her demands but she wouldn't be budged.'

Colborn clenched his fists. His face looked gaunt and worn. 'Not one single word of that is true,' he said in a low, shaking voice. 'She would never have behaved like that.'

Kelsey continued as if Colborn hadn't spoken. 'At just about that time, when you were at your wits' end over how to deal with her, Martin Hynett returned to the area. He

158

picked up the phone one Sunday morning and asked if you were still willing to help him.

'In a flash you saw your solution. Here was a young man, alone and friendless, a young man over whom you had always been able to wield a strong influence, a highly disturbed, unstable, young man of powerful, primitive, religious views, to whom you could easily depict Mrs Franklin as an evil, unprincipled woman, a temptress who was endangering your marriage, your career, your whole way of life. A young man you could persuade, bribe, even force, to dispose of Mrs Franklin for you, who would almost feel it a religious crusade to destroy her.'

'This is madness,' Colborn said on a note of horror.

Kelsey stabbed the air. 'You worked on Hynett, wrought him up, promised him whatever it was necessary to promise him. You gave him the photograph of Mrs Franklin taken from the paper, you explained the location of the cottage. I've no doubt you instructed him most particularly to destroy the cutting afterwards, but he kept it—as a souvenir, maybe, or as a trophy. You left it to him how he dealt with Mrs Franklin, you didn't want to know the ugly details in advance, time enough afterwards, when they were common knowledge.'

Colborn shook his head slowly and rhythmically, like a mechanical toy.

'I've no doubt also,' Kelsey said, 'that you told Hynett not to get in touch with you afterwards for some considerable time but he very soon got into a terrible state. He was driven to phone you, ask for your help. I dare say it was always your intention to get rid of him after he'd served his purpose. He was unpredictable, liable to talk, always a danger. Now you had to get rid of him earlier than you had planned. You arranged to meet him in a secluded part of the hills, gave him the bottle and the syringe, told him it was something to quieten his nerves. Before you reached the foot of the hill he had plunged in the needle, obligingly disposed of himself. You had been able to eliminate first Mrs Franklin and then Martin Hynett without so much as soiling your hands.'

There was a brief silence. The Chief sat back in his chair.

'I believe that that, near enough, is what happened.'

Colborn appeared on the point of collapse. 'I wouldn't have harmed a hair of her head,' he said in a weary monotone. 'I worshipped her.'

'You were tired of her,' Kelsey threw back at him. 'You wanted to be rid of her.'

Colborn suddenly pushed back his chair and got to his feet. He stood like a baited bear among snapping dogs. He looked down at the Chief, his face contorted. 'I loved her more than anything on God's earth,' he declared with passion. 'I loved her from the moment I laid eyes on her, when she was seventeen years old. I couldn't do anything about it then, I had my mother to look after, exams to study for. I had to stand by and watch her marry someone else.'

He struck his fists together. 'Then one day she walked into the bank. Divorced, free. I couldn't believe it, I had another chance.' He closed his eyes for an instant. 'I'd have married her like a shot if she'd have had me. I wouldn't have given a damn about my career or my marriage.' He halted abruptly. 'Ruth has been a wonderful wife to me but she was never Venetia. Ruth is strong, she'd have got over it.'

He stared fiercely down at the Chief. 'It was always my intention to tell Ruth the moment it was settled, I always hated deceiving her.'

The tremors started up again in his head and neck. 'A couple of months ago Venetia told me she'd reached a decision. She wasn't going to marry me. She didn't want to be tied down again, she must be free, able to please herself, she would never again be accountable to anyone.' He put a hand up to his face. 'I couldn't believe it, I was totally shattered. I tried to argue with her, to get her to change her mind, but she wouldn't listen, she said it was absolutely final. I kept away from her, didn't phone or write. I tried to put her out of my mind. But it was no use, I couldn't forget her. I couldn't sleep, couldn't eat, couldn't work properly.

'Last Thursday afternoon when I rang her about the shares, I couldn't help myself, I started pleading with her, begged her to see me. She refused. She told me she was going away next day for the weekend, she was meeting some man.' He gave a convulsive shudder. 'I had to go off to Danehill with that thought in my mind. I had a terrible weekend. I couldn't concentrate, couldn't get her out of my head, I kept seeing her with another man.' He closed his eyes. 'Then on Tuesday morning when I went into the bank I heard she was dead, murdered.' Tears ran down his face. He made no attempt to wipe them away.

Kelsey looked up at him dispassionately. 'This isn't what you told us before.'

'It's what I'm telling you now,' he declared with force. Tears still coursed down his face. 'It's the truth.'

Kelsey regarded him in silence. 'Last Monday,' he said at last, 'I put it to you that it was not around seven-fifteen when your wife dropped you at your club, but some time later.'

Colborn shook his head. 'It was definitely not later.' He made a visible attempt to take a grip on himself. 'Ruth had an appointment at seven-thirty, she'd never be late.'

Again Kelsey regarded him. 'Your wife is devoted to you, deeply concerned to protect your interests. I believe she would say anything to shield you.'

Colborn gave him back a defiant stare. 'She has no need to shield me. I had nothing to do with Martin's death, nothing to do with Venetia's death.'

Kelsey sat looking at him in silence, then he got to his feet. 'We'll need the names of the men you spoke to at the club. And the names of the other committee members.'

Colborn gave him the details. 'Check what you like,' he said in a voice full of despair and defiance. 'Do what you like. I don't care any more.'

By the end of Tuesday afternoon the checks had been carried out. There was no doubt about it: Colborn's alibi for Monday evening held firm. He had left Springfield House just after seven, sitting beside Ruth in her car. Ruth had halted the car by the gate to speak to the schoolgirl. She had dropped him at his club at seven-fifteen. He had chatted in the bar until the meeting began at eight, he had been present throughout the meeting. Afterwards he had remained active and visible in the club until given a lift home shortly after ten.

Martin Hynett's funeral took place at three o'clock on Wednesday afternoon. He was laid to rest in the Strettisham cemetery, not far from the graves of his grandparents, close to his sister, his father and mother, united at last with the family who had driven off on holiday that sunny Saturday morning long ago.

The service was conducted by the minister who had known all the Hynett family. The ceremony aroused no interest among the townsfolk; not a single reporter was present. Neither Inspector Glover nor Constable Rudge was there; there was no one from Chelmwood Hospital. And yet, the Chief reflected as he surveyed the little congregation— which, apart from himself and Sergeant Lambert, consisted entirely of Mr Jopling and his men—he was aware of a sense of grief as genuine as at many a funeral attended by larger and more fashionable gatherings.

Every last man of the Hollymount tenants had accompanied Jopling, all of them scrupulously washed and shaved, dressed in their soberest clothing. There had been no need for them to dip into their thinly-lined pockets to help pay for the funeral, so they had splashed out on a magnificent cross of white roses, lilies and stephanotis, richly fragrant. Throughout the service they gazed at it with visible pride. During the hymns they sang with fervour, loudly and raggedly. Later, as the coffin was lowered into the earth under a pale blue sky, Lambert saw tears run down more than one of the faces watching it descend.

On the way back to Cannonbridge Kelsey sat in brooding silence, finally breaking it as the car ran on to the forecourt. 'The maintenance side of Franklin's business,' he said. 'The repair and servicing. He seems to do a lot of contract work. He might have a contract with Chelmwood Hospital. Get on to them, find out.'

Ten minutes later Lambert came into the Chief's office. Yes, Franklin had held a contract with the hospital for a number of years, until some months ago. No contracts had been issued or renewed during the last twelve months; any necessary work was now dealt with on an *ad hoc* basis.

At five-fifteen Sergeant Lambert drove the Chief over to Northwick Road. It was half-closing day and Franklin was busy in his workshop when they arrived. He took the two men up to the flat. He offered them tea, which Kelsey declined. Franklin didn't sit down but stood over by the window, leaning against the wall.

'One of my men called here recently with a photograph of a young man named Martin Hynett,' Kelsey began as soon as he was seated.

'Yes, I remember,' Franklin said. 'The young man who was buried today. I knew him slightly. It's some years ago now, when he was a patient at Chelmwood. I used to go over there regularly at one time, in the way of business.'

'You didn't tell the officer that you knew Hynett.'

'Didn't I? I suppose I answered what he asked me. I was in a hurry, I usually am. He wanted to know if Hynett knew Venetia at all. I told him that to the best of my knowledge, he didn't.'

'How well did you know Hynett?'

'Not very well. He was in and out of hospital. I got to know a good many of them in a casual fashion.'

The Chief produced the cutting and held it out. Franklin was obliged to take a few steps into the room to look at it. Kelsey asked if he had seen the photograph in the local paper.

'I may have done,' Franklin said. 'I can't recall.' He drifted back to the window and took up his stance again.

'Did you cut the photograph out of the paper and later give it to Hynett?' Kelsey demanded. 'Did you draw Hynett a map, showing the position of the cottage?'

Franklin's body gave a convulsive jerk as if an electric current had passed through him. 'I did nothing of the sort,' he retorted fiercely. 'What are you suggesting?'

'Did you ever bring Hynett home?'

'No, of course not. I never brought any of them home.'

'Maybe Hynett called at the shop one day when you were

out, he could have spoken to Venetia then.'

'She was never much in the shop,' Franklin answered. 'She certainly never mentioned such a thing to me. I'm sure she'd have told me if he'd called. And in any case why would he have called?'

'To ask you for a job. Did you ever employ him? Even for a very short time?'

'No, never. He did drop a hint once or twice about me taking him on as an apprentice. He used to hang about while I was working in the hospital, he picked up quite a bit that way. But I would never have dreamed of taking on someone like that. Dealing with the public, going into people's homes, far too big a risk. And you can't have someone with a speech impediment working in a shop, it would be hopeless.' He spread a hand. 'Of course I didn't go into all that with Martin, I didn't want to cast the lad down. I just told him I was sorry, I didn't have an opening.'

There was a brief silence, then Kelsey said, 'A week ago last Monday, May 21st. Where were you between seven and seven-thirty in the evening?'

Franklin's brows came sharply together. 'Why do you want to know?' he demanded.

'If you would just answer the question,' Kelsey said calmly.

There was another brief silence, then Franklin said, 'As far as I remember, I was out on a couple of jobs. I'd have to look in the book to give you details.'

'Then by all means look in the book.'

Franklin went downstairs and came back a few minutes later with an open ledger and a clip of papers. 'There you are.' He jabbed a finger at a page in the ledger. 'The addresses of both calls.' He took the jobsheets from the clip and laid them down on the table in front of the Chief.

Kelsey regarded the entries. Neither address anywhere near Bracken Hill. He scanned the jobsheets. The first call was entered for six thirty-five, the second for seven twenty-five. He asked if both householders were in when Franklin called.

'There was no one in at the first address,' Franklin told him. 'The woman left a key in the shed, she's done that before.'

'And the second call?'

'The son was in, he was there all the time I was in the house. That's his signature on the jobsheet. Michael Plimmer.'

'Did Martin Hynett phone you one Sunday morning a few weeks back?' Kelsey asked casually. 'To ask if you'd help him to find a job?'

'He did not,' Franklin replied with emphasis. 'I've had no contact of any kind with Hynett since the last time he left Chelmwood. Must be over four years now.'

'I put it to you once again,' the Chief said in a tone markedly less casual, 'that your attitude to Venetia in recent ti nes was a good deal less friendly and easy-going than you make out. The truth of the matter is that you bitterly resented the drain on your finances.'

Franklin uttered a sound of exasperation. 'OK,' he said angrily. 'I did resent Venetia. I resented what she was doing to the business, to Jane, to my marriage. But that doesn't mean I wanted her dead.' He fell abruptly silent.

Kelsey glanced at the clock. 'What time are you expecting your wife? We'd like a word with her.'

'Any time now,' Franklin answered. 'She's on a terminal case, sometimes she's a little late.'

Kelsey froze on a sudden thought. 'How long has your wife worked for the agency?'

'About eighteen months.'

'Where did she work before that?'

'At Chelmwood Hospital. That's where I met her.'

CHAPTER 16

Downstairs there was the sound of the street door opening and closing. 'That'll be Jane now,' Franklin said. Footsteps ascended the stairs, slow, dragging steps. The door opened.

Jane halted on the threshold. She stood surveying them all, in silence. She looked pale and listless.

'The Chief Inspector's called to ask a few questions,' Franklin told her across the room. 'He'd like a word with you.'

She roused herself but didn't look at Franklin. She glanced round the room. 'You didn't give them any tea,' she said flatly.

'Your husband very kindly offered us tea,' Kelsey told her, 'but we'd already had some back at the station.'

'I'm making some for myself,' she said brusquely. 'I've got a splitting headache, I've had a very tiring day.' She moved wearily towards the kitchen. 'If anyone wants a cup, better speak up now.' No one wanted any.

She went into the kitchen, leaving the door open. After a minute or two she returned to stand in the doorway. 'What do you want to ask me?' she said to Kelsey. She glanced pointedly at the clock. 'I'd like to get my feet up for ten minutes before Sharon brings the children in.'

'We'll be as quick as possible,' Kelsey assured her. 'Did you know a young man by the name of Martin Hynett?'

'The young man who committed suicide? Yes, I knew him. He was a patient at Chelmwood when I worked there.'

'Did you know him well?'

'Not particularly. Just in the way one knows any patient.'

'He came from Strettisham. You come from Strettisham.'

'What of it? In my day half the patients at Chelmwood came from Strettisham. It's the nearest town.'

'Maybe you knew Hynett at home, before he went into hospital?'

'No, I didn't. I'd never come across him in Strettisham, he was years younger than me.'

'Perhaps you knew his family?'

She shook her head without speaking.

'Did you make a point of befriending him in hospital, seeing you both came from the same place?'

She shook her head again with an air of irritation. She turned back into the kitchen without any word of apology. After a minute or two she came out again, carrying a cup of tea. She sat down at the table and began to drink it.

'Did Hynett phone you here one Sunday morning a few weeks ago?' Kelsey asked. She shook her head again, continued to drink her tea.

'Did he call in at the shop? Asking for your husband?'

She gave the Chief a hard, direct stare. 'No, he did not.'

'Maybe it was you he came to see? To ask you to help him get a job—some kind of hotel or domestic work, perhaps, through the agency?'

'He never called here at all,' she answered flatly. Throughout the exchange she hadn't once glanced at her husband but Sergeant Lambert had again the sense of the two of them being strongly united, against the outsider. Is it possible they were in it together? he wondered. That they planned it carefully between them, right from the start?

Kelsey held out the newspaper cutting. She flicked it a glance. 'Did you see this photograph in the local paper?' he asked.

'Yes, I believe I did.'

'Did you cut it out?'

She flashed him a look. 'No, I did not.'

'Did you give the photograph to Hynett?'

'No, I did not. He never came here. I was never in touch with him. It's years since I last saw him.'

'Where were you a week ago last Monday, May 21st? Between seven and eight in the evening?'

She raised both hands and pressed her fingers against her temples. She sat with her head lowered, her elbows resting on the table. 'I was up at Lyndale. I do relief work there. I was there from six till eleven, then I came back here and went to bed.'

Kelsey stood up. 'We'll be checking that, of course.'

She picked up her cup and saucer and went towards the kitchen. 'Check what you like,' she retorted without looking round. 'It makes no difference to me.'

Kelsey followed her across the room. He halted in the kitchen doorway. She turned from the sink and gave him a hostile glance. He produced from his pocket the plastic envelope holding the embroidered handkerchief. He asked if she had ever seen it before. She glanced down at the handkerchief and shook her head.

'Does it belong to you?' he persisted.

She uttered an angry sound. 'I've just told you I've never seen it before.' She turned on the tap and dealt with her cup and saucer with noisy, energetic movements.

When the two policemen left a few minutes later neither Franklin nor Jane went down with them to the street door. 'That lad Plimmer,' Sergeant Lambert said as they got into the car. 'Michael Plimmer. The second call Franklin made that Monday evening.'

'Do you know the lad?' Kelsey asked.

'I've come across him once or twice.' Lambert set the car in motion. 'Unemployed, mother dead, father a building labourer—when he's at work. Hopeless type, no control over the lad, lets him have his head ever since the mother died. The lad's not an out-and-out tearaway, but he'll bear watching. He's on the fringes of things, knocks about with some dubious types. Only a matter of time before he's up in front of a court.' He slowed for a junction. 'He'd shop his grandma for a fiver. If Franklin slipped him ten or twenty, I'm pretty certain he'd forget or remember whatever Franklin wanted him to forget or remember about that Monday evening.'

Shortly after nine next morning Lambert drove the Chief to the two addresses Franklin had given them. At the first, a small semi in a respectable working-class neighbourhood not far from Franklin's shop, the door was opened by a middle-aged woman dressed in outdoor clothes. Kelsey told her who he was and began a spiel about investigating a number of break-ins and attempted break-ins in the area over recent weeks.

She interrupted him before he had got fairly started. 'No one's tried to break in here. If you'll excuse me, I've got a bus to catch.' She made to close the door.

Kelsey raised a hand. 'Just a couple of questions, then we'll let you get off. Monday evening last week, May 21st, about seven o'clock. Notice anyone hanging round?'

'I was out,' she said at once. 'I always am in the evenings. I work in the kitchen at the Crown Hotel, four till ten.'

'So there was no one at home here all evening?'

She pondered. 'That was the evening the TV man came. Someone from Franklin's. I left the key for him. I couldn't tell you what time he came or left.'

The second address was a small dilapidated terrace house some distance away, in a seedy area of Cannonbridge. Lambert rang the bell several times without any response. 'But I'm positive he's in,' he said, pressing his finger down yet again on the bell, this time keeping it there. 'He's never got up and gone out by this time in the morning. I'll bet my bottom dollar he's upstairs in bed.'

At last there was a sound from the upper regions. The lower sash of a window was thrust up, a head was stuck out. Kelsey looked up at the scowling young face, flushed with sleep. The scowl vanished as the lad recognized Sergeant Lambert and was instantly replaced by a look of keen anxiety overlaid with wariness.

The two policemen stood gazing up at him in silence. 'I'll be down in a moment,' he told them. He slammed the window shut and vanished. A minute or two later the front door was flung open.

'Michael Plimmer?' the Chief asked.

'That's right.' He glanced from one to the other of them. He was very thin, dressed in a grubby T-shirt and faded jeans; his feet were bare and very far from clean.

'We'll come inside,' Kelsey told him.

The lad gave a vast uninhibited yawn. He closed the door behind them but stayed where he was, he made no move to take them further into the house. Kelsey walked along the passage and in through an open door on the right, into a room in an appalling state of disorder and neglect. An overpowering smell of stale alcohol, old tobacco fumes, ancient sweat, accumulations of dirt, the remains of meals long gone.

'If you've nothing to do all day,' Kelsey said with unconcealed disgust, 'you could try cleaning this place up.'

The lad followed after them. 'Yes, right,' he said in tones

169

of facile compliance. He seemed wholly unabashed.

Kelsey didn't venture to sit down but remained standing in the midst of the chaos. This time he didn't bother to trot out any disarming spiel. 'A week ago last Monday,' he said abruptly. 'May 21st. Seven, eight o'clock in the evening. Where were you?'

A succession of thoughts flickered over the youngster's face. He held his head very still but his eyes darted about the room.

'Got it!' he cried suddenly. He grinned in triumph. 'I was here, in the house. I had to stop in for the TV man. The set was on the blink.'

'I want the exact time,' Kelsey told him on a menacing note. 'The time the TV man called, the time he left.'

'Just before half past seven,' the lad said at once. 'That's the time he got here. I know that because there was a film on at eight o'clock that I wanted to watch, I told him that as soon as he came. He looked at the set and said not to worry, he'd have it going inside half an hour. And he very nearly did. He had it going by five past eight, the film had just started.' He stared defiantly up at them. 'I never moved from here the rest of the evening. My dad came in when the pubs shut. You can't pin anything on me.'

Kelsey eyed him sourly. 'Suppose I told you we know for a fact that Mr Franklin didn't get here till well after eight?'

The lad shook his head with vigour. 'You're wrong there. He was definitely here before half past seven.'

'You'd stand up in court and take your oath on that?'

'Yes, of course I would,' he answered without hesitation. 'It's the truth.'

'Are you always such a stickler for the truth?'

The lad looked up at him in bold-eyed silence.

'If someone slipped you a few notes you'd swear the moon was made of green cheese.'

He moved his shoulders, opened his mouth in another gigantic yawn. 'I don't know what you're on about.'

Kelsey said no more but turned to go. The moment they left the room the lad bounded back up the stairs. They went along the passage and Lambert opened the front door. I'll bet he's back under the bedclothes by now, he thought, dead to the world.

Lyndale was a Victorian mansion in a residential suburb on the edge of Cannonbridge. A domestic opened the door to the two policemen. Kelsey asked if he might speak to Matron.

'She's in the common room, talking to the residents,' the woman told him. She glanced up at the hall clock. 'They'll be finished any minute now.' She made a face. 'It's about the arrangements for Saturday, who can go to the carnival and who can go to the garden afternoon at Springfield House. It's always the same when the two things fall on the same day, everyone wants to go to both of them, and of course they can't, far too tiring—and it would take too much arranging.' She grinned. 'The old Matron never bothered with all this discussion. She just drew up two lists and that was that. I can't ever remember anyone complaining.'

Kelsey didn't know the present Matron. He had had some slight acquaintance with her predecessor, a formidable Scotswoman of unbending principles, tall and raw-boned.

A few minutes later a door opened along the hall and Matron came towards them, followed by a straggle of residents, male and female, some in wheelchairs, others walking with the aid of sticks or frames, one or two bent forward almost at right angles. Palsied limbs, knobbed hands, hearing aids, dark glasses. A few appeared perfectly normal. They drifted into the hall and congregated in twos and threes, in animated discussion.

Matron was a fluffy, pretty little woman, not much over forty, still with something kittenish about her. She wasn't in uniform but wore a softly tailored suit. She gave the two men a friendly smile as she approached; her manner was pleasant and helpful.

Kelsey fell back again on his spiel about break-ins and attempted break-ins. Matron cast her mind back to the evening of Monday, May 21st, but couldn't recall hearing anything out of the ordinary. Nor had any of the staff mentioned anything unusual. Kelsey asked who—apart from resident staff—had been on duty that evening. She reflected, and then mentioned the name of a young widow who lived nearby; she had been on duty from four until ten. 'And Mrs Franklin,' she added, 'from the agency. She was here two nights that week, one of them was Monday. She was here from six till eleven.'

Kelsey asked about the duties of the two women, what chance they might have had of noticing anything unusual. He was soon forced to the conclusion that it would have been impossible for Jane Franklin to slip away unnoticed from Lyndale for as much as ten minutes, let alone for the time it would need to keep a rendezvous with Hynett on the hill.

'While we're on the subject of break-ins,' Matron said when the Chief indicated that he had finished, 'I wonder if you'd mind taking a look at our ground-floor windows while you're here. I'd like your opinion about the locks.'

'Certainly,' Kelsey said. He indicated by a glance that there was no need for Sergeant Lambert to follow them.

'It's particularly the windows in my office,' Matron said as she led the Chief away, 'and the room with the drug cupboard.' This was a small room at the rear of the house, originally a butler's pantry. It was presided over by a male resident, busy now cleaning the paintwork.

'This is our Mr Booth,' Matron told the Chief. 'He keeps all this in apple-pie order.' Booth was an undersized little man of fifty or so, with an anxious, humble face. He had lived in institutions of one kind or another since the day he was born. The by-blow of a female vagrant, he had a number of congenital defects of varying degrees of severity. His mother had absconded from the hospital where she had gone for her lying-in and had never returned to claim him. He was of average intelligence, industrious and compliant.

Ruth Colborn had come across him some years ago in the geriatric ward of a county hospital where he had somehow landed up. She had taken pity on him, had persuaded the Lyndale committee to admit him as a resident. He had settled in well, had always done his best to justify Mrs

Colborn's confidence in him, was never the slightest trouble to anyone.

While Matron and the Chief discussed window locks, Booth continued to rub diligently at the paintwork, accustomed all his life to conversations between persons in authority taking place with no more regard for his presence than if he had been a block of stone.

Back in the hall Sergeant Lambert conversed casually with one of the female residents, a Miss Wragg, a woman in late middle age, confined to a wheelchair. She had some secretarial skills and helped with the Lyndale office work. She told Sergeant Lambert about the residents' meeting that had just taken place. It seemed the meeting had been full of complaints from those who couldn't or wouldn't understand why there might not be an exception, just for them, why they couldn't, just this once, go to both the carnival and Springfield House.

'Things are a lot slacker here these days,' Miss Wragg said with strong disapproval. 'It's all very well talking about a more relaxed, informal atmosphere, but in my opinion that very soon turns into a general disregard for rules of any sort.' She jerked her shoulders. 'Even Mrs Colborn doesn't always stick to the rules these days, not even when it's a rule she's made herself.'

Lambert glanced idly out of the window at the serene lawns, the residents wandering along the gravel paths. 'Take this new rule,' Miss Wragg said. 'No one to be admitted here under the age of twenty-one. That was Mrs Colborn's idea in the first place. She spent a lot of time trying to talk the old Matron into it but she couldn't budge her, and if the old Matron was against something, the committee wouldn't even consider it. As soon as the old Matron retired Mrs Colborn got going again on this new woman and in the end she talked her into it, she couldn't stand out against someone like Mrs Colborn. After that of course it was easy to get the committee to adopt it.'

Lambert studied a coloured lithograph on the nearby wall: a woman in a summer dress and straw hat walking through a field of poppies. 'Only three weeks ago,' Miss

Wragg continued with animation, 'the committee turned down an application from a girl of seventeen, under the new rule. A very nice, quiet, well-behaved girl, able to do a good deal for herself, the kind of person who could contribute a lot to the life here. Mrs Colborn was adamant, the new rule must stand.' She flung out a hand. 'And then she goes and pushes the rule aside, persuades them to admit Terry Pickard—and that took a bit of persuading, I can tell you, he's not in the least suitable for Lyndale. When his sister first applied here, Mrs Colborn was dead against admitting him.'

The Chief came back into the hall and Lambert followed him out to the car. 'Terry Pickard,' Lambert said as he switched on the ignition. 'I gather he's being admitted to Lyndale. That'll be a load off Dorothy's mind.'

'Surely Lyndale turned him down flat?' Kelsey said. 'I'm sure that's what Dorothy said.'

'It seems they changed their minds.' Lambert gave him the gist of what Miss Wragg had told him.

Kelsey listened with a frown. 'Was any reason given for this change of mind?' Lambert knew of none.

Kelsey chewed the inside of his lip. He never liked unexplained details, however trivial, however insignificant-seeming, on the fringes of a murder case. They left him uneasy till they'd been looked into, sorted out.

He glanced at his watch. 'We've time to nip along to Dorothy's,' he said. 'See if we can get a word with her.'

But when they reached the council estate where Dorothy lived there was no one at home in the little semi-detached dwelling. Lambert went next door and asked the woman if she had any idea when Miss Pickard would be back.

'Not till tomorrow evening,' the woman told him. 'She's taken Terry over to Ellenborough, to see her cousin and his wife, a sort of farewell visit before Terry goes into Lyndale. It'll be late when she gets back. Her cousin did ask them to stop over Friday night as well, but Dorothy wants to be back for the carnival on Saturday. She never misses that, Terry always enjoys it so much.'

Ah well, the Chief thought as they went back to the car,

nothing for it but the office desk and the avalanche of paperwork. 'I used to live round here when I was first married,' he observed idly to Lambert. Not on the council estate but in the ground-floor flat of a converted Edwardian house in a nearby road.

He sighed, remembering the early years of his marriage, the good times, before the rot set in. 'We had some very nice neighbours then,' he added. 'I hardly ever see any of them these days.' His brain suddenly flung up a memory of the Beales, who'd lived a few doors away. 'Winifred Beale,' he said on a sharper note. 'I'd forgotten her. She worked at the Allied Bank, she was there over forty years.'

The last time he'd spoken to Winifred was over twelve months ago. He'd seen her in the street, had stopped for a moment. She told him she was retired now, still living in the same house, on her own these days. She had never married. Her mother had died a few years back, her father had lived on till a couple of years ago.

Kelsey rubbed his chin. Winifred had always liked a gossip in the old days, no reason to suppose she was any different now. 'She's Cannonbridge born and bred,' he told Lambert. 'Not much she doesn't know about local folk. We'll get round there now, see if she's in.'

CHAPTER 17

Winifred wasn't precisely in when they arrived, she was out in the front garden, hard at work. As Lambert drew up beside the gate the Chief spotted her, kneeling with her back to them, bedding out plants in a border. At the sound of the car doors she turned her head. Kelsey opened the gate and walked over to her.

Her face broke into a broad smile. 'What a surprise! It's lovely to see you!' She struggled to her feet, grimacing as her muscles registered their protest. 'We don't get any younger,' she added with a laugh. She had a good-natured face, a friendly, open look.

'We were out this way,' Kelsey told her. 'We thought we'd look in, see if you still make a good cup of tea.'

She took them into the kitchen and set the kettle on to boil, chatting about the old days, her parents, neighbours they had both known. 'It was a sad blow when Dad died,' she said with a little shake of her head. 'However long you've been expecting it, it's a terrible loss when they go. And then you're all on your own, time on your hands. Dad being an invalid so long, I'd fallen out of the habit of going out in the evenings, being sociable. I was dreading retirement. I'd got very low, I couldn't think how I was going to pass the days when I didn't have the bank to go to.' She took cups and saucers from a cupboard. 'Mrs Colborn was very good to me, she made me snap out of it. She got me to join some of her charitable groups. She drew me into things, wouldn't take no for an answer. I owe her a lot.'

The kettle came to the boil and she made the tea. 'I think she felt some sympathy with me, being on my own, I don't think she has any of her own family left. Not that she talks about her family, but from one or two remarks she's passed, I get the impression that's how it is. I fancy that may have been the reason she got herself transferred to the Cannonbridge branch of the bank. She may have been left on her own, thought she'd make a complete break, a fresh start.'

Kelsey began to drink his tea. 'Which branch did she work at before?' he asked.

'The Martleigh branch. She comes from a little village near Martleigh, she told me that when she first came to Cannonbridge. Brockheath, that's the name of the village. It stuck in my head—brock's an old name for a badger. Ruth Emerson she was then, of course. She worked at the Cannonbridge branch for about a year before she and Philip Colborn were married. He was in a pretty low state himself when Ruth came to the branch, his mother had died not long before.'

She stared into her cup. 'I remember his mother from when I first started work at the bank, just after I left school.

She was a very quiet, delicate-looking woman, very pretty in those days. She used to come into the bank sometimes with Philip, when he was a small boy—the Colborns always banked at the Allied.' She sighed. 'I can understand a lot better now how Philip must have felt when his mother died, leaving him all by himself in that big old house. Ruth taking him under her wing was the best thing that could have happened to him, it improved him out of all recognition.' She gave the Chief a knowing look. 'And he'll go a lot further before he's done, you mark my words.'

'Something in the wind then?' Kelsey said.

'Between you and me, yes, I believe there is. And before much longer, too. He's made a very good job of managing the local branch, he's well liked in the town. What would suit Ruth would be a step up for him that wouldn't mean they'd have to leave Cannonbridge. I gather that's on the cards. He could go to the local head office, or a larger branch not too far away, then they needn't move. Neither of them wants to leave Springfield House.'

She hesitated, and then said, 'I know what case you're working on, I read about it in the papers. I know you can't talk about it, but I must just say what a terrible shock it was to us all, what a dreadful business. Poor Venetia, I cried when I heard about it. She was such a lovely, happy girl. I often had a chat with her when she used to come into the bank for change, when she worked at Youngjohn's.' Tears sparkled in her eyes. 'And then to end up like that, at the hands of some maniac.' She glanced up at him. 'That's what they say in the town.'

Kelsey gave a noncommittal grunt.

She poured more tea. 'When Venetia married Roy Franklin I didn't come across her for a long time, but after they were divorced she walked into the bank one day and opened an account.' She hesitated again and then said in a rush, 'You wouldn't credit what spiteful tongues some folk have. Someone at the bank, one of the women clerks—she's not there now, she got married a few months back, she's living in Bristol now. She was always a bit of a troublemaker, always liked stirring things up. She never really liked Ruth, though she was always as nice as pie to her face.' She gave the Chief a confidential glance. 'I always thought she had her eye on Philip Colborn herself, but he wasn't the sort to notice anything like that.

'When he got engaged to Ruth, this woman went out of her way to say to Ruth one day that it was Venetia Philip had always wanted to marry, that he'd always been potty about her.' She made a dismissive gesture. 'Of course Ruth was far too sensible to pay any attention to such nonsense. That's all it was, of course, pure nonsense, not a word of truth in it. Philip never had a girlfriend before he met Ruth, I'd take my Bible oath on that.'

She gave an angry little jerk of her head. 'And then, as if that wasn't enough, do you know what else this woman did? I met her in the street at the tail end of last year, after I'd retired from the bank, not long before she got married and took herself off to Bristol. She told me that she'd been at some charity do and got talking to Ruth. She told Ruth that Philip was seeing Venetia, seeing her on a personal level, that is, away from the bank.' Her cheeks flushed with indignation. 'I let her know in no uncertain terms what I thought of her mischief-making, peddling wicked lies like that. But you can't shame some folk, their hide's too thick. I'm sure Ruth gave her very short shrift. Nothing but envy and malice, that's all it was.'

'Tomorrow afternoon,' Kelsey said to Lambert a few minutes later when they were in the car, headed back to the station. 'Take half an hour, get over to Brockheath. Have a ferret round, see if there's anything there.'

Brockheath was a hamlet of fewer than three hundred souls, seven miles from Martleigh. The afternoon was well advanced as Sergeant Lambert drove through narrow lanes bright with yellow hawkweed and wild parsley, under a sky of lucent blue. He halted his car in the centre of the village.

Brockheath would have been a very long way down anyone's list of the prettiest or best-kept villages. A small, seedy-looking pub, a huddle of old but far from picturesque cottages around the green, itself little more than a neglected stretch of tussocky grass beside a stagnant pond half choked with gigantic flowering weeds.

The village lay drowsing in the sunshine; there was no one about. Lambert walked across to the pub and lifted the knocker. After a minute or two the landlord came to the door, a slovenly, grey-haired man in shirtsleeves. Lambert explained that he was trying to trace any members of a family by the name of Emerson.

'There's no one of that name in Brockheath now,' the landlord told him. 'There were some Emersons years ago, when I first took over this pub. Quarryman, he was, wife and one child—a girl. I can't remember her name. Sparrowhall Cottages, the first one you come to, that's where they lived.' He gestured up the road. 'Straight through the village, a couple of hundred yards ahead on your right. It's a young couple living there now, but you won't find them at home. They both work up at the farm, and anyway, they wouldn't have known the Emersons. But there's Mrs Prebble, at the cottage next door. You have a word with her, she knew the Emersons, she was their neighbour for years.'

He gave his chest a good scratch. 'Emerson's dead now, of course, died years ago. His missus left the village not long afterwards, she wasn't a Brockheath woman. The daughter had left home before that. I couldn't tell you where either of them is now.'

Lambert drove through the village, past a Norman church with mossy tombstones rising drunkenly out of long grass strewn with litter ancient and modern. Sparrowhall Cottages were four pairs of semi-detached dwellings set in a small close.

The door of the second cottage was propped open and a woman reclined in a deck chair in the little porch. As Lambert walked up the path he saw that she was asleep, her head slipped to one side. A pair of spectacles perched on her nose, a newspaper lay open on her ample lap. He stood looking down at her. A short, shapeless woman, late fifties perhaps. Sparse ginger hair tightly crimped, skin a deep brick-red, thickly sprinkled with dark brown freckles. Her cotton dress had risen above her fat knees.

He went quietly back to the gate, clanged it loudly open and shut. The woman sat up with a start, she uttered a sound of consternation. By the time Lambert had made his way discreetly up the path a second time she was fully awake, her dress decently arranged, in command of herself.

'Mrs Prebble?' Lambert asked. She gave a nod. Her small grey eyes held a look of shrewd common sense. He apologized for disturbing her and explained his errand.

'Yes, I knew the Emersons,' she said at once in a tone of lively interest. 'Are you a relative?'

He shook his head. 'It's a bit of legal business.'

'The Emersons were living next door when I moved in here with my husband, not long after we were married,' she told him. 'We came here from a village the other side of Martleigh.'

The sun beat down on Lambert's head, he felt a powerful thirst rise in his throat. 'The Emersons only had the one child, Ruth,' Mrs Prebble went on. 'She was eight or nine when we came here. A very sharp, knowing sort of child, small and dainty, always kept herself very neat and clean.'

'Did you know the family well?'

She grimaced. 'Depends what you mean by well. I never had much to do with them, for all they lived next door. I tried to be neighbourly when we first came but they made it pretty clear they wanted to keep to themselves. They never had anything to do with the other folk here at Sparrowhall— or anywhere else in the village, for that matter—not any more than they could help. They never asked a soul across the doorstep.'

'Were they local people?'

'Emerson worked in the local quarry but he came from a village a few miles away. Mrs Emerson came from the other side of the county. She was a well-spoken woman, very good manners, very quiet and reserved. Always nicely dressed. Nothing showy of course, she wasn't the type for that. I did hear she'd been in service in some big house before she was married.'

She looked up at Lambert with a grim little smile. 'Emerson used to knock her about.' She saw the surprised move-

180

ment of his head. 'Oh yes, he did, for all he was so quiet. He never drank, or anything like that. He'd go along perfectly all right for weeks, months even, then all at once it would be like a pan coming to the boil.' She threw her hands out in a dramatic gesture. 'I used to wonder if he was one hundred per cent right in the head, there certainly didn't seem to be any other sort of reason for it. I'm sure Mrs Emerson never did anything to provoke him. She always struck me as a woman who would go out of her way to avoid trouble.'

She pursed her lips. 'She never let on there was anything wrong, never a word or a look. But I'm not stone deaf or blind now, and I certainly wasn't then. You can't keep that sort of thing secret from your next-door neighbour, not in properties like these.'

She fanned herself with the newspaper. 'My, it's hot today. I've got some lemonade inside. Would you like a glass?'

'I'd be very glad of it,' Lambert said with fervour.

She levered herself up on to her feet and he followed her into the little kitchen. She took a jug from the fridge and poured the lemonade. Lambert, who had been resigned to some gassy commercial concoction, was delighted to discover, as soon as he swallowed the first delicious mouthful, that it was homemade, like nectar.

'Did Emerson also ill-treat his daughter?' he asked when they were both seated, facing each other across the table.

She shook her head vigorously. 'Not from anything I ever saw or heard. I'm sure he knew better than to try. Ruth was made of different stuff from her mother.' She swirled the lemonade in her glass. 'I saw the way she looked at her parents sometimes, not like a child at all. I always felt she despised her mother for putting up with it.'

She drank her lemonade. 'She won a place in the girls' grammar school at Martleigh. I had a niece there myself, from my own village, she was there at the same time as Ruth Emerson. Ruth used to stay on after school in the evening, to do her homework. She never once brought a schoolfriend home—I don't even know if she made any friends at school. My niece told me she kept very much

181

to herself, never bothered with clubs or societies, wasn't interested in sports. She was a very hard worker, determined to get on, to make something of herself. She got a job in a bank in Martleigh, as soon as she left school. She went into digs in Martleigh right away, though she could have gone in every day on the bus, the same as she'd done all the years she was at school. I've no idea where she is now.'

She was silent for a moment. 'Do you know, she never came back here, after she left to go into digs. Not once, ever.' She stared at that ancient fact, still with some measure of disbelief. 'Her father died a year or two after she left.' She lowered her voice. 'Cancer, it was, very rapid. He went into hospital in Martleigh, he died there a bare month after he went in. Of course I couldn't say if Ruth went to see him in hospital or if she went to his funeral, she may have done, for all I know. Her father was cremated, and after the way the Emersons had behaved, I didn't go to the funeral. And I don't know anyone else from the village who went either.'

'What happened to Mrs Emerson?' Lambert asked.

'She left here soon after the funeral. She didn't tell me where she was going but I heard afterwards that she was working as a housekeeper on a farm over in her own part of the county.' She turned down the corners of her mouth. 'I did hear a few years later that she'd died, but I couldn't say if that's true or not.'

At half past nine next morning Chief Inspector Kelsey and Sergeant Lambert again walked up the path leading to Dorothy Pickard's front door. But they were still out of luck; Dorothy had already gone out. 'I didn't see her to talk to, after she got back,' the neighbour told Kelsey. As she'd stood at her bedroom window shaking out a duster, shortly before nine this morning, she had seen Dorothy coming out of her garden gate. She had called down good morning to her and Dorothy had smiled and waved, had called back that she was taking Terry over to Britannia Park, to watch the men getting the floats ready for the carnival procession.

Britannia Park lay half a mile from the town centre. It took Sergeant Lambert a good fifteen minutes to negotiate the traffic; the usual Saturday-morning bustle had been greatly increased by the streams of cars and lorries making for the park.

The strains of a Dixieland jazz band drifted towards them as they left the car and made their way towards the large central stretch of grass. Sunlight glittered the leaves, the sky was a pearly blue, the air warm and caressing, full of the scents of wallflowers and lilacs.

A throng of bystanders watched the men assemble the floats in a lively holiday atmosphere. Dogs yelped and barked among the milling mass of excited children. Nursery rhyme characters, spacemen, grenadiers, shepherdesses, helped with the decoration.

It didn't take the two policemen long to spot Terry Pickard in his wheelchair. He wore a gilded cardboard crown, he clutched a coloured paper windmill, he had a red balloon tied to his wheelchair. He was watching with a show of interest and pleasure a band of pirates erecting a wheelhouse and deck structure on board a truck.

Kelsey slowed his pace to a saunter. 'Hello, there,' he called amiably to Dorothy as they approached. Terry turned his head and gave them a vast, slack grin. 'He seems to be enjoying himself,' Kelsey observed.

Dorothy smiled broadly. 'He loves it all, the music, the crowds, the colours.' She glanced at her watch. 'But I mustn't forget the time. I'm going along to Springfield House, to give a hand for this afternoon.' She flashed the Chief a look full of joy and radiance. 'I don't know if you've heard my news—I'm getting married.' Her voice overflowed with delight. 'Terry's going into Lyndale on Monday, it's all settled, he can stay there permanently.' She closed her eyes for a moment in an access of happiness.

'That's wonderful news,' Kelsey said warmly. 'I was under the impression Lyndale had turned Terry down.'

'That's right,' she said with feeling. 'They did turn him down. But Mrs Colborn fixed it for me in the end. I always knew she would.'

'How did she manage it?'

'I had a letter from the committee on the Monday morning.' She was eager to pour out her tale. 'Saying they couldn't admit Terry, the decision was final. I was that upset, I can't tell you. I cried my eyes out. Then that evening I was out walking with Terry, I'd been delivering my leaflets. I'd finished for the day but I didn't want to go back home, I felt too fed up and restless.

'I chanced to see Mrs Colborn's car turning into Springfield. I didn't stop to think, I went straight in after her. She was getting out of the car by the front door and she saw me coming in. She stood there, waiting for me. I told her about the letter. I begged and pleaded with her to see if there was anything she could do to get them to change their minds.' She grimaced. 'She was pretty short with me. I know it was a piece of cheek on my part, bothering her at that time of the evening—'

'Getting late, was it?' Kelsey asked.

'A quarter past seven, I heard the church clock strike as I went in through the gates. She told me I had to accept the committee's decision, there was no chance at all that they'd change their minds. But I couldn't just leave it at that, I seemed to be driven on.'

She gave the Chief a deprecatory grin. 'I'm afraid I did go on a bit, I was really wound up. Mrs Colborn said she had to get off out again, she had two appointments, it was the evening for her charity visits. She couldn't keep Mr Hodges waiting, he was expecting her at half past seven, he'd be upset if she was late. Of course I know old Mr Hodges, in Pump Street. He's one of my bedridden folk that I pop in and see when I'm on my rounds.'

She put a hand up to her mouth. 'When I look back on it, I'm astounded at myself. I said to her, as bold as brass, "Mr Hodges doesn't know what day of the week it is, half the time, let alone noticing if you're twenty minutes late." And off I went again, nineteen to the dozen, about getting Terry into Lyndale.'

'How did she take it?' Kelsey asked on an amused note. Around them the children laughed and shouted, the adults worked and joked, chatted and flirted.

Dorothy moved her shoulders. 'She got very abrupt, very

stiff. She said, "This isn't doing any good. I'll have to ask you to excuse me." And she went into the house. I stood there, feeling terrible. For two pins I'd have burst into tears. After a minute or two I pushed off. I couldn't go back home, I knew I wouldn't be able to settle, so I walked about for a bit, to calm myself down. It was a lovely evening, very warm. Then Terry let me know he wanted to go to the toilet.'

She laughed. 'You don't hang about when that happens, it's full speed ahead, and pray you're in time. The nearest public toilet I could get the wheelchair into was the one by the car park at the bottom of Bracken Hill, so I shot over there as fast as I could. There were only half a dozen cars parked there and I saw that the first one was Mrs Colborn's.'

She spread a hand. 'I thought: That's funny, she was in a tearing hurry to get over to see Mr Hodges, and of course Pump Street's right over in the opposite direction. Anyway I didn't stop to think about it, I rushed Terry into the toilet. We were quite some time in there, he takes a bit of managing. When we came out again I stopped in the entrance to see he was properly settled in his chair. I looked over at the hill path and I saw a woman coming down the path, very fast, almost running. She had a raincoat on, with the collar turned up, she had her head down. She had dark glasses on and a scarf tied under her chin, pulled forward over her forehead, you could hardly see her face.

'I stood watching her, it was such a warm evening to be dressed like that. She even had a pair of gloves on, I saw her pull them off and shove them in her pocket. Then she suddenly looked across and saw me. She stopped dead, she stood there, looking at me. Then she smiled and waved, she started on down again, and across the car park.' She paused. 'I suddenly realized who it was. It was Mrs Colborn. I hadn't recognized her, dressed like that.'

CHAPTER 18

Dorothy gazed earnestly up at the Chief. 'I was dreadfully embarrassed. I was sure she thought I'd been lying in wait for her, ready to start ranting on again about Lyndale. But when she came up she was very nice. She smiled and said, "I'm so glad I've run into you again. I'm afraid I was very sharp with you just now." She said she couldn't stop, but all the things I'd said had made an impression on her and she was going to have one last try to see if she could do something about Terry. She couldn't promise anything but she'd go round to see Matron first thing in the morning, and she'd look in on me at lunch-time to tell me how it went. Then she went off in her car and I went back home with Terry. I was that excited, I never closed an eye all night. Next day she popped in as she'd said. As soon as I opened the door and saw her face I knew it was going to be all right.'

She drew a long breath, reliving that exquisite moment. 'She told me she'd put all the points I'd made to Matron, and Matron had agreed there was a lot in them. The two of them decided to raise the matter again at the next meeting, on the Friday. She'd let me know the result as soon as the meeting was over.'

She clasped her hands. 'I told her I'd hate for her to think I'd been trying to waylay her by the car park, it was just that I had to take Terry to the toilet, that was why I was there. She said, "To tell you the truth, I'd like you to forget you saw me there. I'll tell you this in confidence—" Dorothy suddenly stopped and clapped a hand to her mouth, then she shrugged. 'Oh, I don't suppose it matters, me telling you, it was her husband she didn't want to know about it.'

Kelsey gave her an inquiring look.

'No, I'm sure she wouldn't mind,' Dorothy said on a decisive note. 'You're certainly not going to go running round to tell Mr Colborn about it. And anyway, I've told you this much, I might as well finish it.' She took up her tale again with relish. 'She said she'd gone up on the hill to meet a relative of hers, a cousin, a young woman. A bit of a scapegrace, she called her, she'd been in and out of trouble ever since she left school. Mrs Colborn had always done her best to help her but in the end Mr Colborn had got fed up with it and said it was a complete waste of time, the young woman would never be any different, she was just taking advantage of Mrs Colborn's good nature. He really put his foot down, made it plain he didn't want her to have anything more to do with the cousin.

'And Mrs Colborn promised him she wouldn't. But she said to me, "I felt I couldn't just write her off, without a penny, heaven knows how she'd end up—and she is family, I can't get away from that." She said she knew I'd understand, the way I'd always coped with my own family responsibilities told her that. So she'd decided to help the young woman one last time and that would be the end of it. Of course Mr Colborn wasn't to know anything about it. In the circumstances she couldn't have her coming to the house, so she arranged to meet her on the hill.'

Dorothy smiled with reminiscent pleasure. 'Mrs Colborn called round straight after the committee meeting and told me it was all settled, they'd agreed to admit Terry.' She looked proudly up at the Chief. 'And I'm getting married three weeks today.'

The crowd was even denser as the two policemen struggled back to the car. Kelsey got in and sat for some time without speaking, his head lowered, one hand shielding his eyes. Sergeant Lambert sat looking out at the shifting, changing scene, the brilliant kaleidoscope of colours. A rousing cheer went up at the arrival of the carnival queen and her attendants on a dray skilfully decorated with massed flowerheads in an intricate pattern of whorls and scrolls. Lambert gazed with keen appreciation at the radiant, glowing faces of the girls as they were borne past. Beside him the Chief sat wrapped in thought, oblivious of the cheers, the bevy of beauty floating by.

Kelsey suddenly sat up. 'Lyndale,' he said abruptly. He sank back in his seat.

Lambert set about the tricky task of negotiating the traffic that by now congested the centre of town, forcing him to weave in and out of side streets. The journey was long and tedious, subject to frequent halts and interruptions. During the entire ride the Chief uttered not one syllable. When at last they reached the leafy suburb where Lyndale stood, they didn't drive in, but left the car parked round the corner.

The Chief walked casually in through the gates, Lambert a pace or two behind him. Kelsey didn't approach the front door but went with the same easy gait round to the rear entrance. He didn't knock or press the bell; he turned the handle, which yielded. He went silently inside and a few yards along a corridor to the room where the drugs were kept.

Booth was in the room, assiduously rubbing at surfaces already immaculate and gleaming. He glanced briefly up as they came in but didn't speak or pause in his task.

'My word, you keep this place looking spotless,' the Chief said with the impersonal, magisterially benevolent air of an official visitor on a routine tour of inspection.

Booth gave a little inclination of his head in acknowledgement and continued to work.

Kelsey strolled over to the drug cupboard and tried the door; it was locked.

'You have a key to this cupboard?' he asked Booth in the same tone of patriarchal interest, the general inspecting the troops.

'No, sir.' Booth continued his rubbing, conditioned since childhood to exchanges in which officialdom asked all the questions and he supplied all the answers, never—not once in fifty years—the other way round.

'Who keeps the key?' Kelsey asked.

'Matron.'

'Does anyone else have a key?'

'No, sir.'

Still in the same easy tone, Kelsey asked him how the

various medicines were distributed. Booth abandoned his task and stood with his hands at his sides, looking up at the Chief. He seemed pleased to answer. He spoke with an air of pride in the way he discharged his duties, the responsibilities involved.

He told the Chief that at various set times he went along to Matron's office and collected the key to the cupboard. He set everything out on a large tray which he carried to the common room where the residents awaited his arrival, supervised by a member of staff. Afterwards he gathered everything up again and carried the tray back. When he had locked the cupboard again he returned the key to Matron's office.

Kelsey suddenly became aware of footsteps in the corridor. He stood silent. A woman glanced in as she passed, one of the domestic staff, carrying a bucket and mop. She halted for a moment and gave the three of them an appraising look. She said nothing but turned and went rapidly back the way she had come.

'Does anyone ever help you to set the medicines out on the tray?' Kelsey asked Booth, restraining himself with an effort from quickening the pace of his questioning. Booth shook his head.

'Do you mean to say,' Kelsey asked on an amused, rallying note, 'that no one has ever helped you take the bottles out or put them away again? Some visitor, perhaps?'

'Oh yes,' Booth answered. 'I didn't think you meant that. Mrs Colborn sometimes does that, if she's in here, having a chat.'

Again there came the sound of approaching footsteps, this time brisker and more purposeful. A minute or two later Matron appeared in the doorway. There was nothing kittenish about her now. She stood surveying them, her eyes cold and displeased.

'I had no idea you were here, Chief Inspector,' she said in an icy voice. She sent a rapid glance over the three of them.

'We just looked in for a moment,' the Chief told her blandly.

She was in no way mollified. 'I expect to know of any callers.'

'We were only talking about the medicines,' Booth explained with an anxious look. 'I was just saying how Mrs Colborn likes to help me sometimes with the tray.'

Matron's eyes narrowed. 'I believed you knew better than to discuss the actions of committee members with outsiders—whoever the outsider may be.' Booth hung his head, wilting visibly under her tone of sharp reproof.

'You mustn't blame Mr Booth,' Kelsey put in soothingly. 'It was entirely my fault. We'll get along now, out of your way.'

He said not a word till they reached the car. 'Springfield House,' he instructed Lambert as they got in. He sank back into his seat in brooding silence.

This time the drive back across town took even longer; it was now impossible to escape from the main stream of traffic and make a detour through side streets. The carnival procession had left Britannia Park and was winding its course through the town, following a circular route designed to lead it back to the park for the presentation of prizes. At the central intersection the line of cars was held up for several minutes while the procession made its way across. A brass band played spirited music; clowns and pierrots rattled collecting-boxes. The air was full of laughter, clapping, cheering. Kelsey sat with his eyes closed, locked away from it all.

Sergeant Lambert gazed out at the passing floats: a Red Indian tepee, Keystone Cops, Young Farmers in a Victorian hayfield. A girl of eight or nine, dressed as a ballerina, thrust her tin in at the car window and Lambert found a coin for her. As she went off to the next car he had a sudden memory of the photographs in the local paper: Ruth Colborn at Polesworth, guiding the children forward to present the purses. He turned his head and glanced across at the handsome frontage of the Allied Bank, at the gift shop, a few doors further along, where Venetia had worked, slipping out to the bank, on days like this perhaps, cloudless and sparkling, stepping light-heartedly over the threshold, smiling, chatting, asking for change.

The line of cars began to move. The Chief Inspector opened his eyes and stared out at the crowded pavements with an expressionless gaze.

The gravelled area before the front door of Springfield House was the scene of lively activity as Lambert drove in. A lorry was drawn up and men were busy unloading trestle tables, chairs, wooden stalls, carrying them down to the lower lawn. The front door stood open and a trickle of female helpers went in and out with a variety of burdens. Nearby, Terry Pickard sat in his wheelchair, watching the unloading; at his side Dorothy exchanged cheerful badinage with the men.

As Lambert halted the car Mrs Drake, the Springfield daily woman, came out of the house. She paused to speak to the workmen and was about to set off again for the lower lawn when she caught sight of the two policemen. She walked swiftly over to them. 'If you're looking for Mr Colborn,' she told them with a friendly, authoritative air, 'I'm afraid he's not here. He's at the bank all morning.'

'Perhaps we could speak to Mrs Colborn, then?' Kelsey suggested. She began to shake her head. 'We won't keep her long,' he assured her.

She shook her head again, with finality. 'I'm afraid there's no question of speaking to her now. She's one of the judges for the floats this year.' She waved a hand. 'In addition to all this.' She glanced at her watch. 'She's due at Britannia Park at twenty to—with all that traffic to get through, she'll have her work cut out to make it. She only went upstairs five minutes ago, to shower and change.'

'We'll wait till she comes down again,' the Chief said easily. 'She may be able to spare us a moment on her way out.'

She moved her shoulders, turned and went rapidly off. Kelsey strolled over to where Dorothy Pickard and Terry watched the men unload the heavy canvas sections of the marquee. Terry looked absorbed and happy, still clutching his paper windmill.

Dorothy gave the two men a good-natured smile as they approached. 'If I didn't have a clear conscience,' she said with a laugh, 'I'd begin to think you were following me.' She flung out a hand. 'Talking of consciences, I had it on my conscience that I'd gone and told you about what I'd promised Mrs Colborn I'd forget. I know it was her husband she didn't want to know about it, but, look at it how you will, I did break my word, and that's something I never like doing. So the moment I got here I went and told her about it.' She grinned. 'Of course it was perfectly all right, I needn't have worried. She was ever so nice, she said she quite understood, I wasn't to give it another thought.'

Mrs Drake came hurrying up from the lower lawn and went into the house. The men unloaded the last sections of the marquee. Terry began to bounce up and down in his wheelchair. He stared beseechingly up at his sister, emitting little grunting sounds. 'Oh, all right then,' Dorothy said. 'I'll take you along there in a minute.' He subsided, satisfied. 'He wants to watch the men putting up the marquee,' she explained to Kelsey. 'He remembers it from last year,' she added with fond pride. She laid hold of the wheelchair and set off for the lower lawn.

A baker's van came round from the rear of the house. The driver waved and smiled at Terry as he drove past on his way to the gate. Kelsey strolled in through the front door. The spacious hall was deserted and he stood glancing round.

A phone rang suddenly from a table along the hall and Mrs Drake came through from the kitchen quarters to answer it. Kelsey stood watching as she dealt with the caller. She spoke briefly and crisply, jotting down a message. When she had replaced the receiver he went over to her and asked if she could recall answering the phone some little time back to a young man named Hynett. He saw the name meant nothing to her. 'Martin Hynett,' he added. 'He may have spoken with a stutter.'

'Oh—him! She smiled. 'M . . . M . . . Martin. Yes, I remember him. I took two calls from him. The first time he rang he could hardly speak for stuttering. He never did get as far as telling me his surname, it was all he could do to get his first name out.'

Kelsey asked if she could recall precisely when Martin had first phoned but she shook her head, she could only say that it was a few weeks back. 'He asked to speak to Mr Colborn.' She paused. 'I remember it was a Sunday morning, I come in on Sundays if I'm needed—I'm a widow, I've no ties, I'd just as soon be here as on my own at home. I told him Mr Colborn was out playing golf but Mrs Colborn was in the garden, I could fetch her for him if he liked. He said OK.'

Kelsey asked about Martin's second call. 'That was a week ago last Monday,' she said after some moments' thought. 'It was in the morning, just after I'd got here. I hadn't even taken off my coat when the phone rang and Mrs Colborn called out to me to answer it, she was busy with her mail. As soon as I heard his voice, stammering fit to beat the band, I knew who it was. He asked to speak to Mrs Colborn.'

'Mrs Colborn?' Kelsey echoed. 'Not Mr Colborn?'

She shook her head with certainty. 'No, it was definitely Mrs Colborn. I went and told her and she took the call.'

A woman in an apron came hurrying along from the kitchen quarters with a query about sandwich fillings and Mrs Drake went off with her to sort it out. A moment later footsteps sounded along the corridor and Winifred Beale came into view. She was carrying a suitcase and a large brown-paper parcel.

'Hello there!' she called out at the sight of the Chief. 'Come to keep an eye on us all?' She came up to them and set down her suitcase. She dropped the parcel on a table and began to undo the twine.

'If you've got a moment,' she said to Kelsey, 'I'd be glad of your opinion about this stuff I've made for the needlework stall. I spent I don't know how long yesterday pricing it but I'm not at all sure I've got it right. It's so difficult to know what to charge. I've got cold feet now, I think I've probably priced it all far too high. It's the first year I've made anything for the stall and it would be frightful if it was a total fiasco, everything left unsold. If you could just take a look at one or two things, see what you think they're worth. No need to pull any punches. If you think I've gone over the top, come straight out with it and say so.' All the time she was rattling on she was opening up the parcel, kneeling to unfasten the suitcase, taking out cushion covers, table mats, fancy aprons, lacy pillowcases. 'All my own designs,' she declared with pride.

The Chief glanced at half a dozen items and gave it as his opinion that it all seemed very reasonably priced. He didn't bother to add that his opinion in such matters was entirely valueless. He had never in his life bought a table mat or a fancy apron, he hadn't the remotest idea what such articles might be expected to fetch on the open market.

Winifred began to look a good deal more cheerful. She took out a white traycloth, delicately embroidered with clusters of pale blue flowers. 'This is one of my favourites,' she told him. Kelsey became very still, staring down at it. She saw his intent look. 'You like that?' she said, pleased at his interest.

'It's beautifully done,' he told her. 'That kind of work would look well on a lady's handkerchief.'

'Yes, it does,' she agreed. 'I haven't made any handkerchiefs for the stall but I did make a dozen as a present not long ago, they came out very well.' She began to pack the articles away again. 'They were a birthday present for Mrs Colborn.'

Kelsey remained silent and motionless. The tick of the long-case clock sounded loudly in the hall. 'Her birthday's in March,' Winifred said as she refolded the parcel. 'I took very special care over the handkerchiefs, Mrs Colborn's been so good to me. I wanted them to be very personal, so I designed the flowers to suit her name.' She saw his questioning glance. 'I put sprays of lily of the valley in the corners,' she explained. 'For Mrs Colborn's second name, Lilian. Ruth Lilian Colborn. I thought they looked very pretty.'

She knelt to close the suitcase. 'I had such a nice little chat with her this morning, busy as she was. That's one of the things I most admire about her, she always has time to listen to you.' She got to her feet and smoothed down her skirt. 'I told her I'd seen you the other day, that we'd had a nice little gossip about the old days.' She smiled cheerfully up at him. 'She was really interested. And then Mrs Drake came along to tell her Matron was on the phone from Lyndale. Matron was upset about something, she wanted to speak to Mrs Colborn personally, she wouldn't leave a message.' She glanced up at the clock. 'But I mustn't stand here chattering. I must get off, help to set out the stall.'

Kelsey raised a hand. 'Just a moment. We're trying to get a word with Mrs Colborn ourselves. I know she's in a bit of a rush but if she knew we were here I'm sure she'd manage to find us a moment. Do you think you could slip upstairs and tell her we're here?'

'Oh, that won't be necessary,' she told him with a wave of her hand. 'She'll be down any moment. She already knows you're here.'

'Are you certain of that?' he asked sharply.

'Quite certain, I told her myself. The baker came with the order and there was a query about the bridge rolls. Mrs Colborn had just gone upstairs, she went up straight after she spoke to Matron on the phone. I knew she wouldn't have had time to go into the shower so I popped up to ask her about the rolls. As I was coming downstairs again I glanced out of the landing window and I saw you and Sergeant Lambert drive up. I went back to the bedroom and told Mrs Colborn. She said: "I've no time now to bother with them, Mrs Drake can deal with them, whatever it is they want." She said I'd better get down and see to the baker, not keep him waiting.'

Winifred took herself off, out through the front door. Kelsey went swiftly up the staircase with Lambert at his heels. At the head of the stairs he halted and glanced round. Five doors opened off the wide landing. All five were closed; there was no sound from behind any of them.

The two main bedrooms overlooked the front garden. He rapped on the door of the first, calling out, 'Mrs Colborn!' in tones of urgency. There was no reply. He opened the door and sent a raking glance round the room. A man's bedroom, no one there. He went to the second door and gave a couple of loud, peremptory knocks, again calling out her name. Still no reply. He turned the handle and went in.

The room was full of green-gold light, flickering and shimmering, the air heavy with the scent of roses and lilacs, drifting up from the garden. On the bed a light, silky dress and jacket had been carefully laid out beside a wide-brimmed hat of fine, pale straw.

Kelsey turned his head and saw two envelopes, large white rectangles, lying side by side on a table near a side window. A tall wing chair stood with its back to him, near the window. He crossed the room in rapid strides.

Ruth Colborn was reclining in the wing chair, her head resting against a cushion, her eyes closed, her face stilled and peaceful. She was dressed in slacks and a casual shirt; her left sleeve was rolled up above the elbow. Beside her, on the seat of the chair, lay an empty syringe, where it had fallen from her fingers.

He laid a hand on her forehead, turned back an eyelid, felt for her pulse. There was no sign of life. Nevertheless, as he straightened himself up, he directed a glance at Lambert, who at once began a methodical—even though clearly useless—attempt at resuscitation.

Kelsey looked down at the envelopes, addressed in a bold, feminine hand, one to Philip Colborn, the other to himself. He didn't touch either of them, he left them where they lay.

He crossed to the phone on the bedside table and lifted the receiver. As he dialled he heard in the distance the approaching sounds of the carnival procession. Waves of clapping and cheering, the brazen clamour of the music, and underneath, the insistent, deep-toned pulsing of the drums, like the uneasy, stuttering rhythms of a disordered heart.